ALL SUMMER LONG

ALSO BY HOPE LARSON

Madeleine L'Engle's
A Wrinkle in Time: The Graphic Novel

Compass South (Four Points Book 1)
Illustrations by Rebecca Mock

Knife's Edge (Four Points Book 2)
Illustrations by Rebecca Mock

ALL
SUMMER
LONG

HOPE LARSON

Farrar Straus Giroux
New York

For the weirdos and the part-time punks

Farrar Straus Giroux Books for Young Readers
An imprint of Macmillan Publishing Group, LLC
175 Fifth Avenue, New York, NY 10010

Copyright © 2018 by Hope Larson
All rights reserved
Printed in China by Toppan Leefung Printing Ltd.,
Dongguan City, Guangdong Province
Designed by Hope Larson and Andrew Arnold
First edition, 2018
Colored by MJ Robinson

Paperback: 10 9 8 7 6 5 4 3 2 1
Hardcover: 10 9 8 7 6 5 4 3 2 1

mackids.com

Library of Congress Control Number: 2017956974
Paperback ISBN: 978-0-374-31071-4
Hardcover ISBN: 978-0-374-30485-0

Our books may be purchased in bulk for promotional, educational,
or business use. Please contact your local bookseller or the Macmillan
Corporate and Premium Sales Department at (800) 221-7945 ext. 5442
or by e-mail at MacmillanSpecialMarkets@macmillan.com.

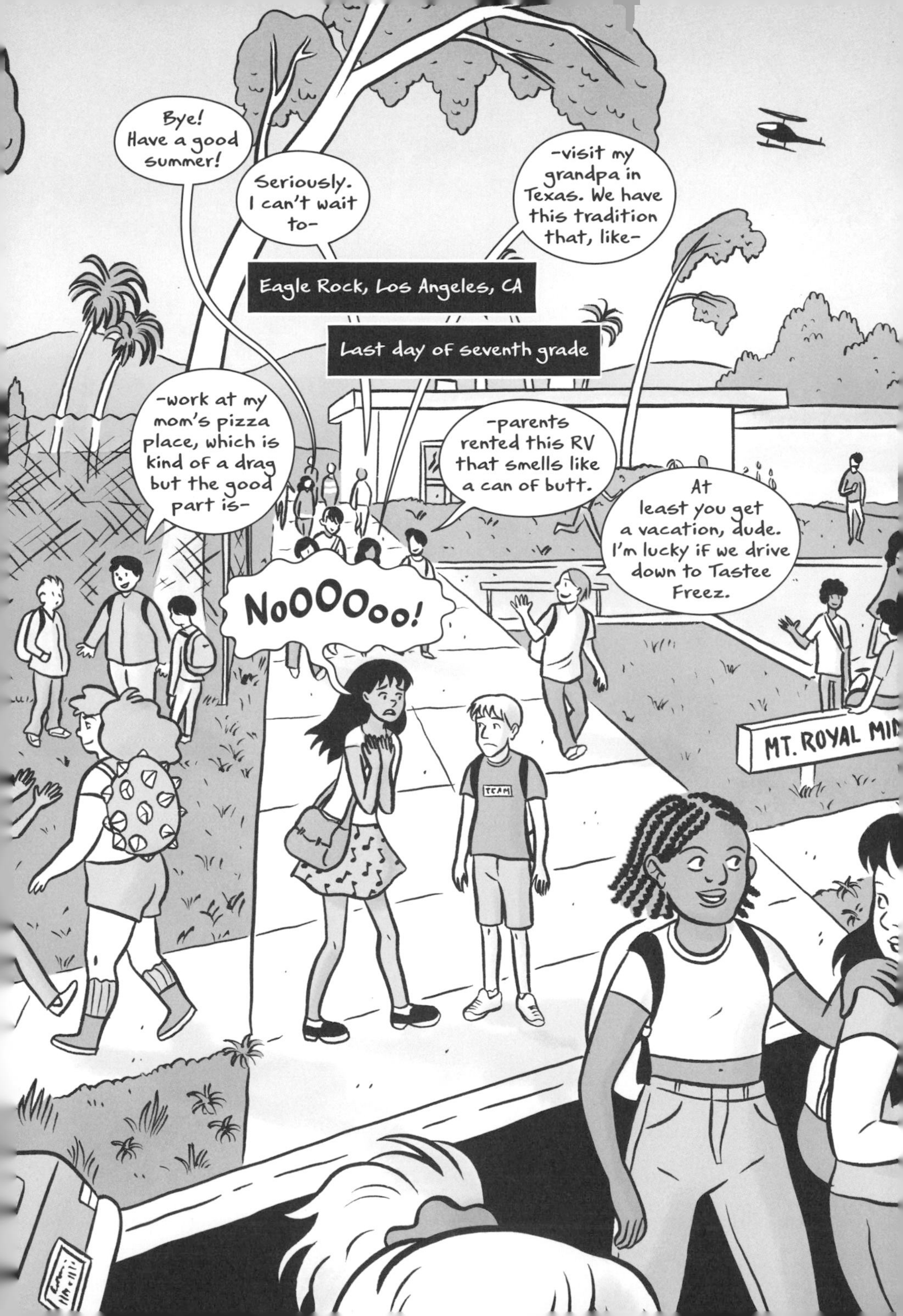
Bye! Have a good summer!
Seriously. I can't wait to-
-visit my grandpa in Texas. We have this tradition that, like-
Eagle Rock, Los Angeles, CA
Last day of seventh grade
-work at my mom's pizza place, which is kind of a drag but the good part is-
-parents rented this RV that smells like a can of butt.
At least you get a vacation, dude. I'm lucky if we drive down to Tastee Freez.
NoOOOoo!
TEAM
MT. ROYAL MI

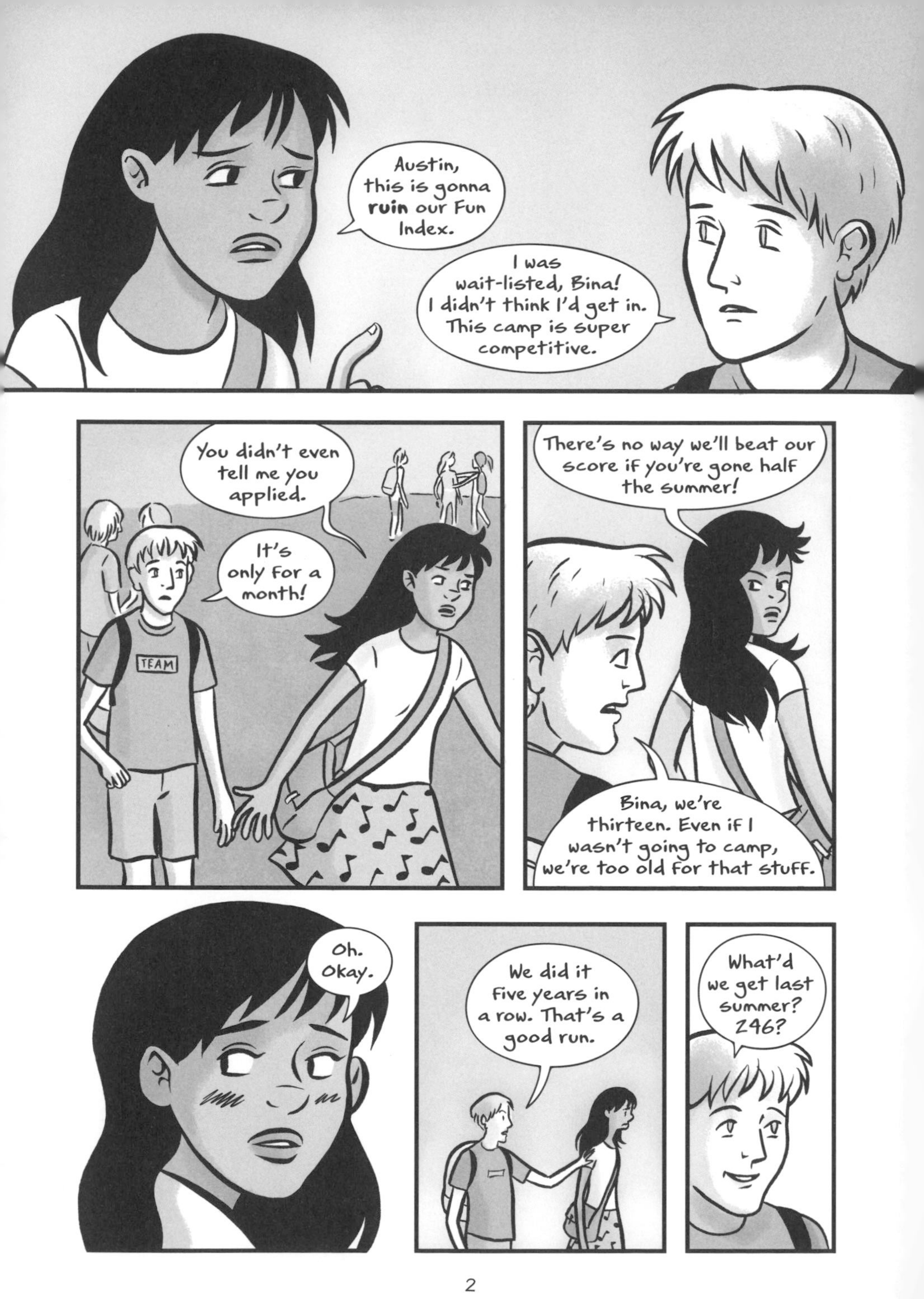
Austin, this is gonna **ruin** our Fun Index.
I was wait-listed, Bina! I didn't think I'd get in. This camp is super competitive.
You didn't even tell me you applied.
It's only for a month!
TEAM
There's no way we'll beat our score if you're gone half the summer!
Bina, we're thirteen. Even if I wasn't going to camp, we're too old for that stuff.
Oh. Okay.
We did it five years in a row. That's a good run.
What'd we get last summer? 246?

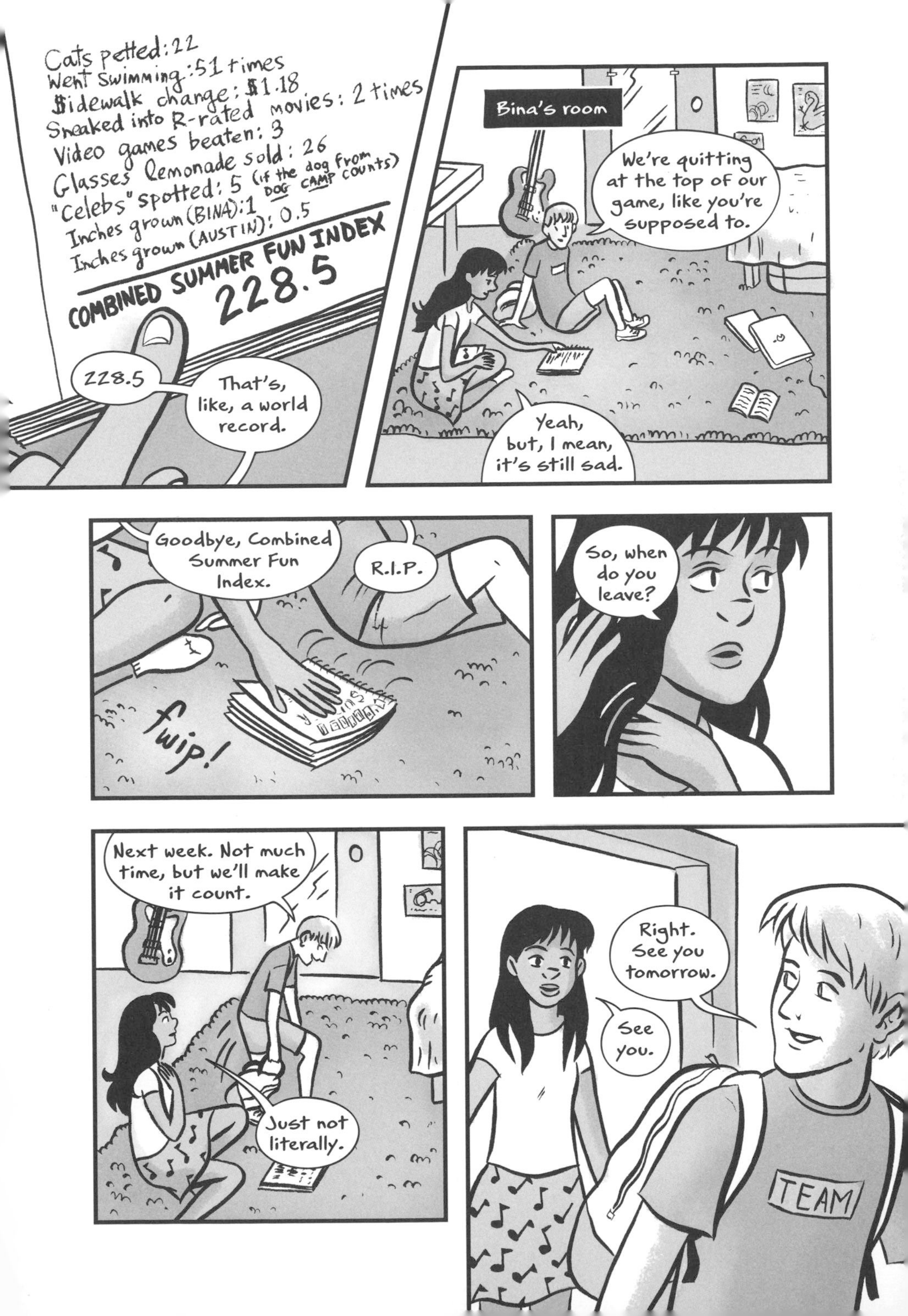

Cats petted: 22
Went swimming: 51 times
$idewalk change: $1.18
Sneaked into R-rated movies: 2 times
Video games beaten: 3
Glasses lemonade sold: 26
"Celebs" spotted: 5 (if the dog from DOG CAMP counts)
Inches grown (BINA): 1
Inches grown (AUSTIN): 0.5
COMBINED SUMMER FUN INDEX
228.5
228.5
That's, like, a world record.
Bina's room
We're quitting at the top of our game, like you're supposed to.
Yeah, but, I mean, it's still sad.
Goodbye, Combined Summer Fun Index.
R.I.P.
fwip!
So, when do you leave?
Next week. Not much time, but we'll make it count.
Just not literally.
Right. See you tomorrow.
See you.
TEAM

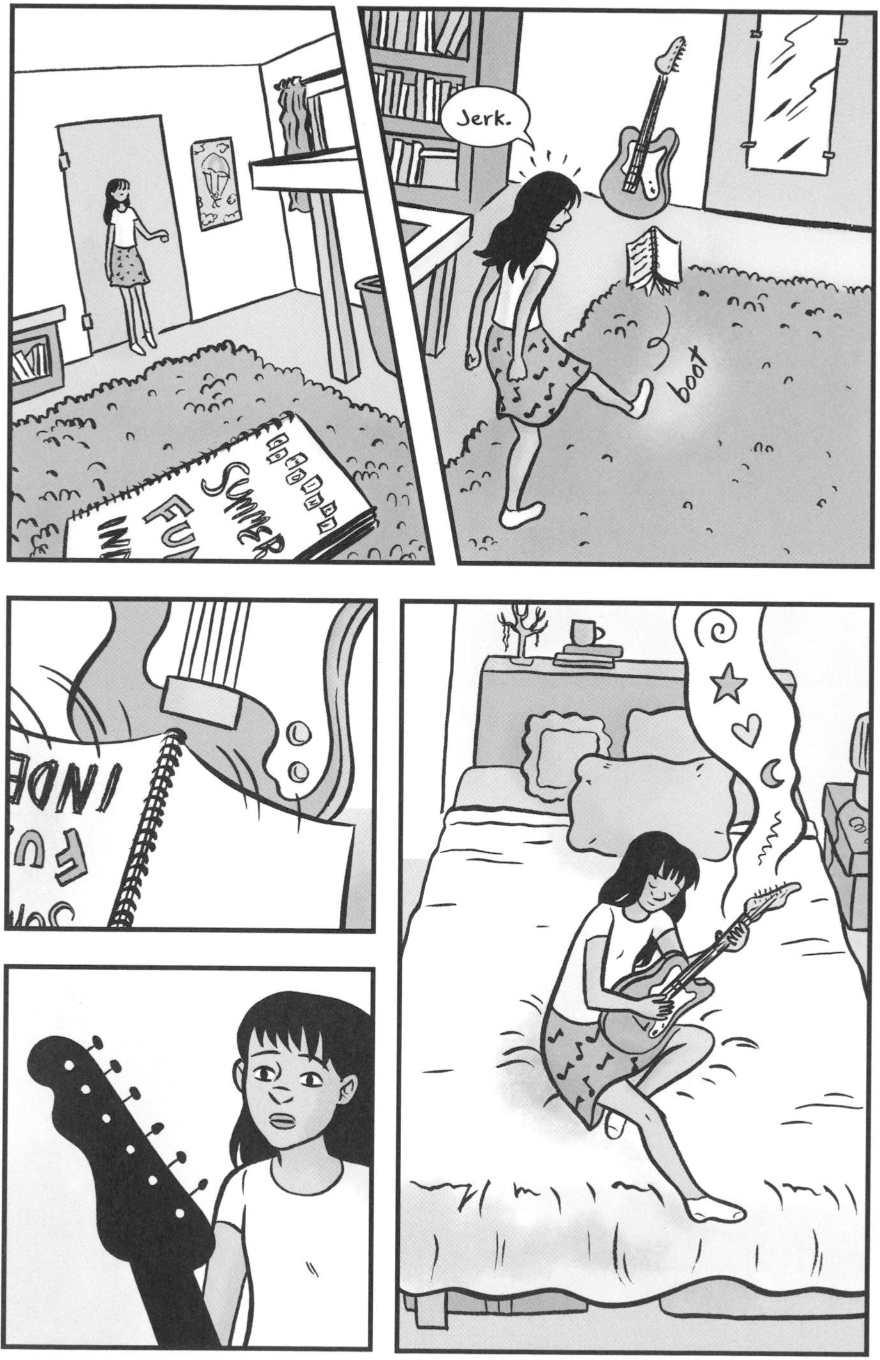
SUMMER
Jerk.
boot

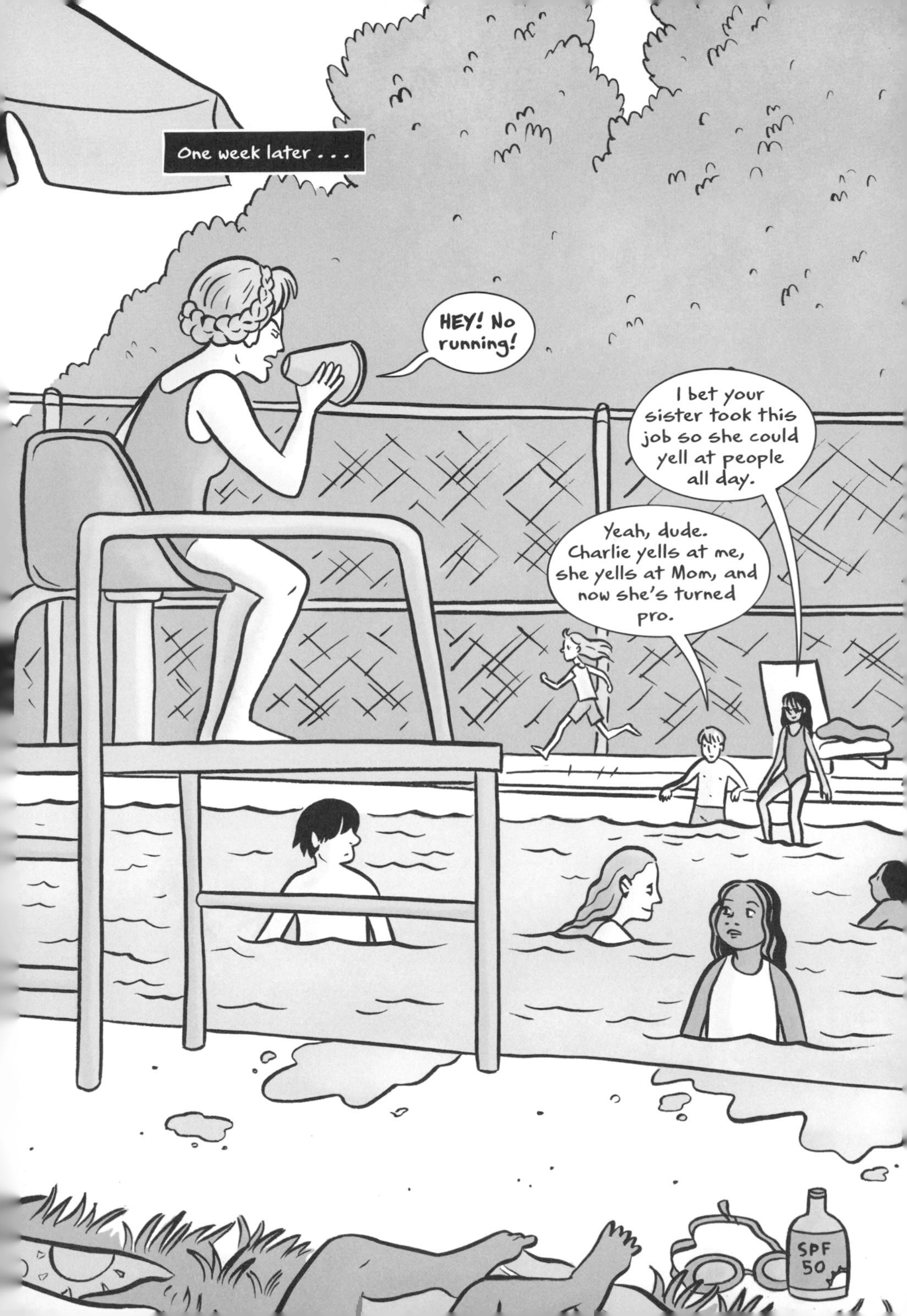
One week later . . .
HEY! No running!
I bet your sister took this job so she could yell at people all day.
Yeah, dude. Charlie yells at me, she yells at Mom, and now she's turned pro.
SPF 50

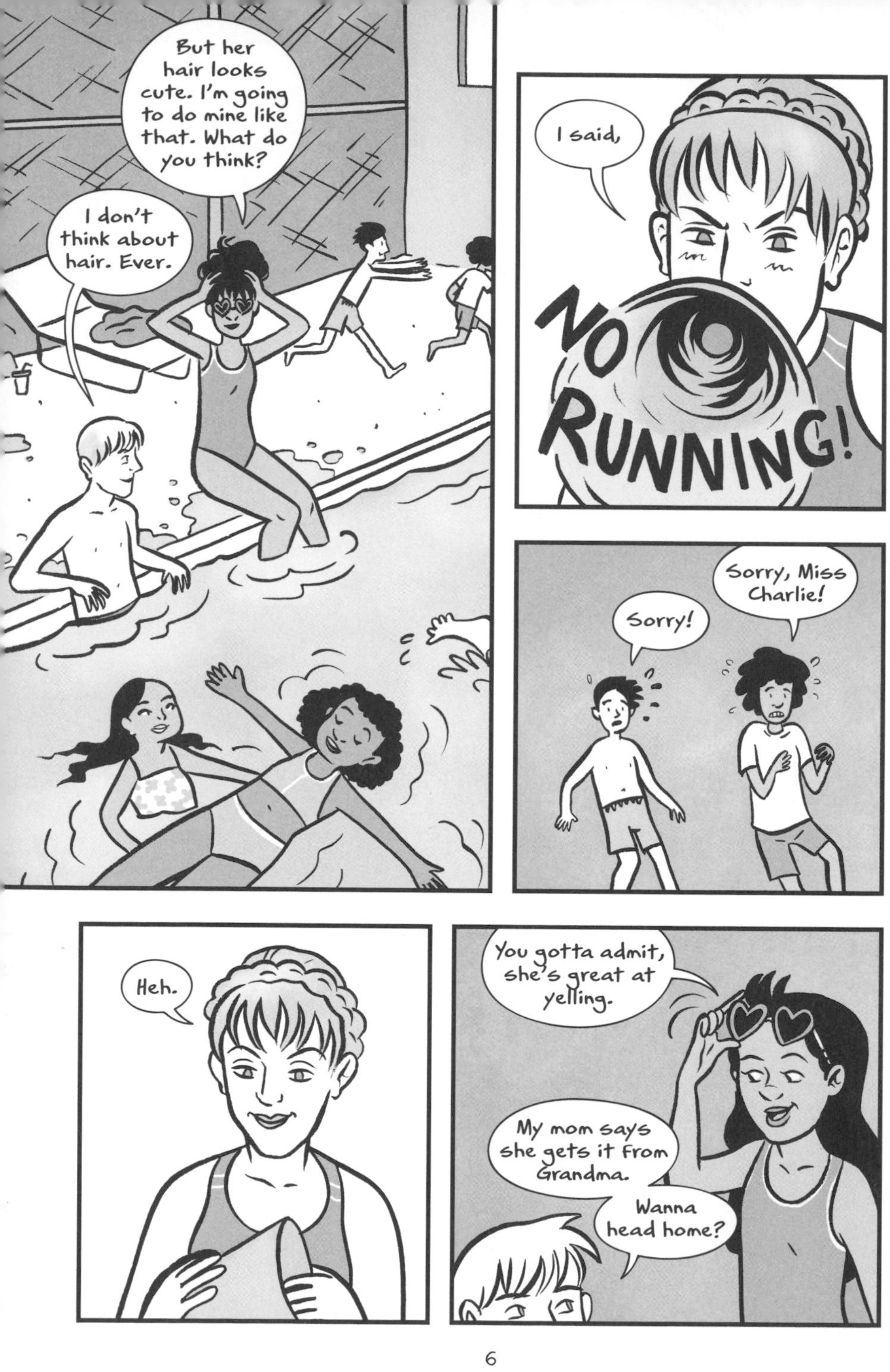

But her hair looks cute. I'm going to do mine like that. What do you think?
I don't think about hair. Ever.
I said,
NO RUNNING!
Sorry!
Sorry, Miss Charlie!
Heh.
You gotta admit, she's great at yelling.
My mom says she gets it from Grandma.
Wanna head home?

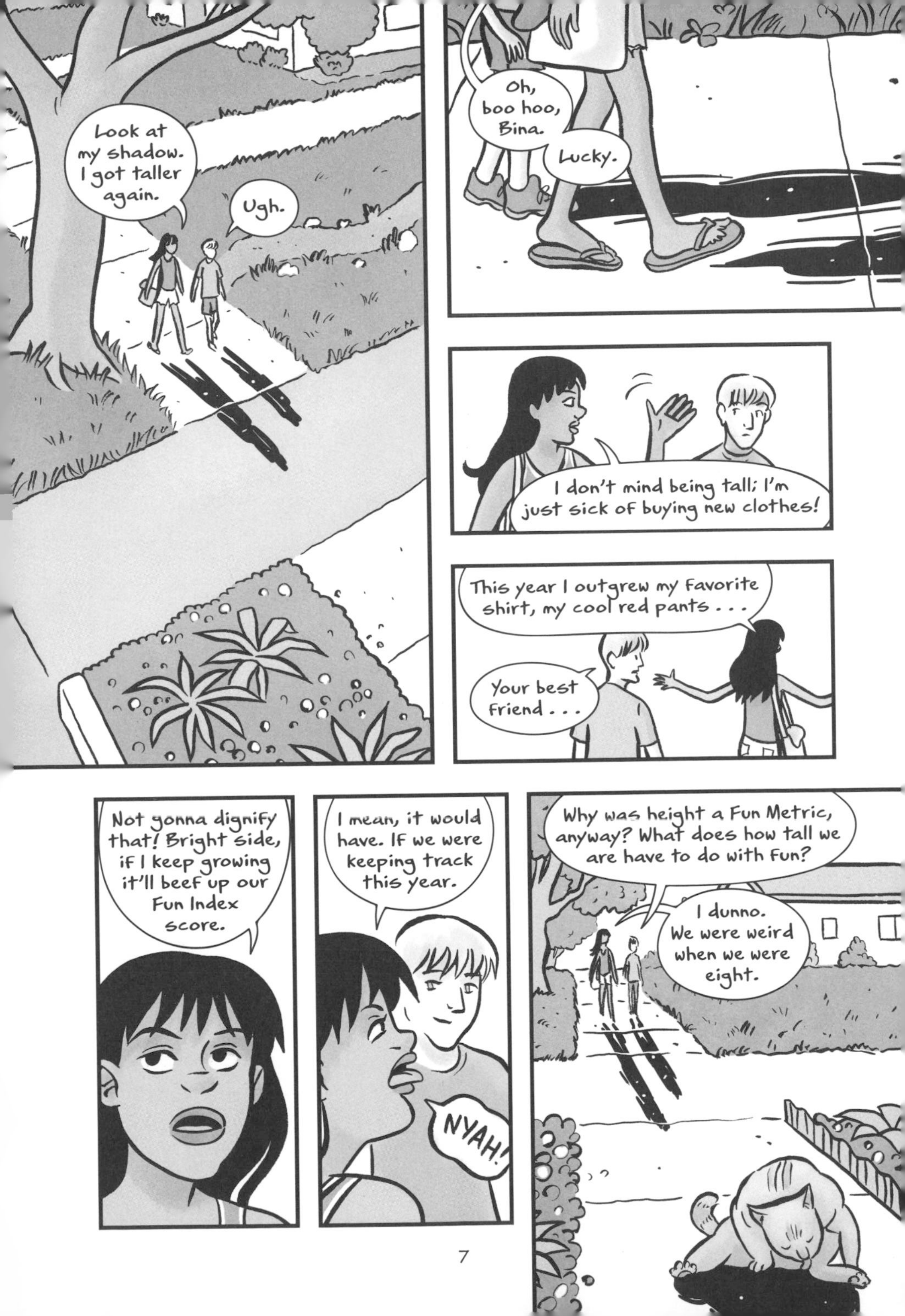
Look at my shadow. I got taller again.
Ugh.
Oh, boo hoo, Bina.
Lucky.
I don't mind being tall; I'm just sick of buying new clothes!
This year I outgrew my favorite shirt, my cool red pants . . .
Your best friend . . .
Not gonna dignify that! Bright side, if I keep growing it'll beef up our Fun Index score.
I mean, it would have. If we were keeping track this year.
NYAH!
Why was height a Fun Metric, anyway? What does how tall we are have to do with fun?
I dunno. We were weird when we were eight.

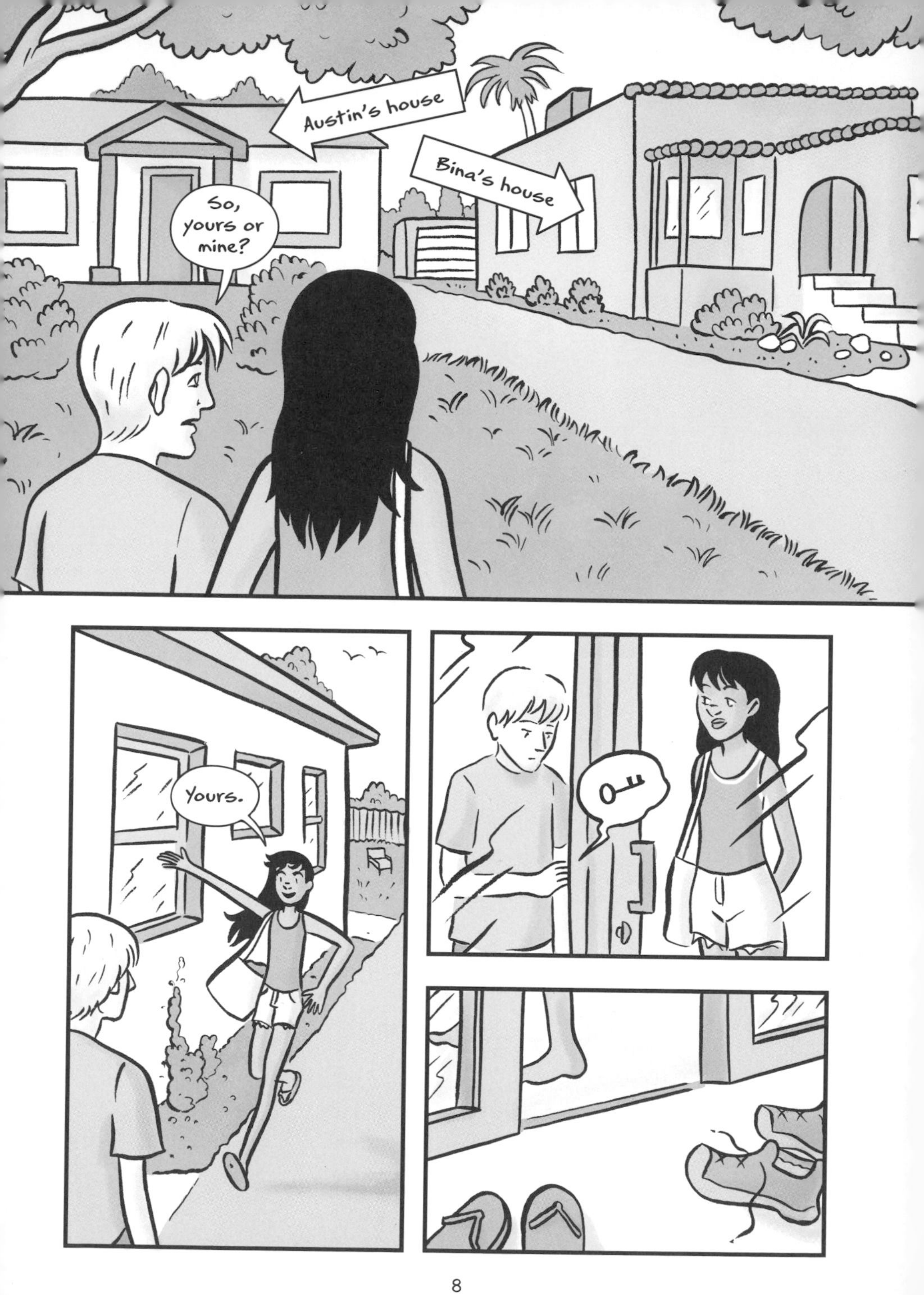
Austin's house
Bina's house
So, yours or mine?
Yours.

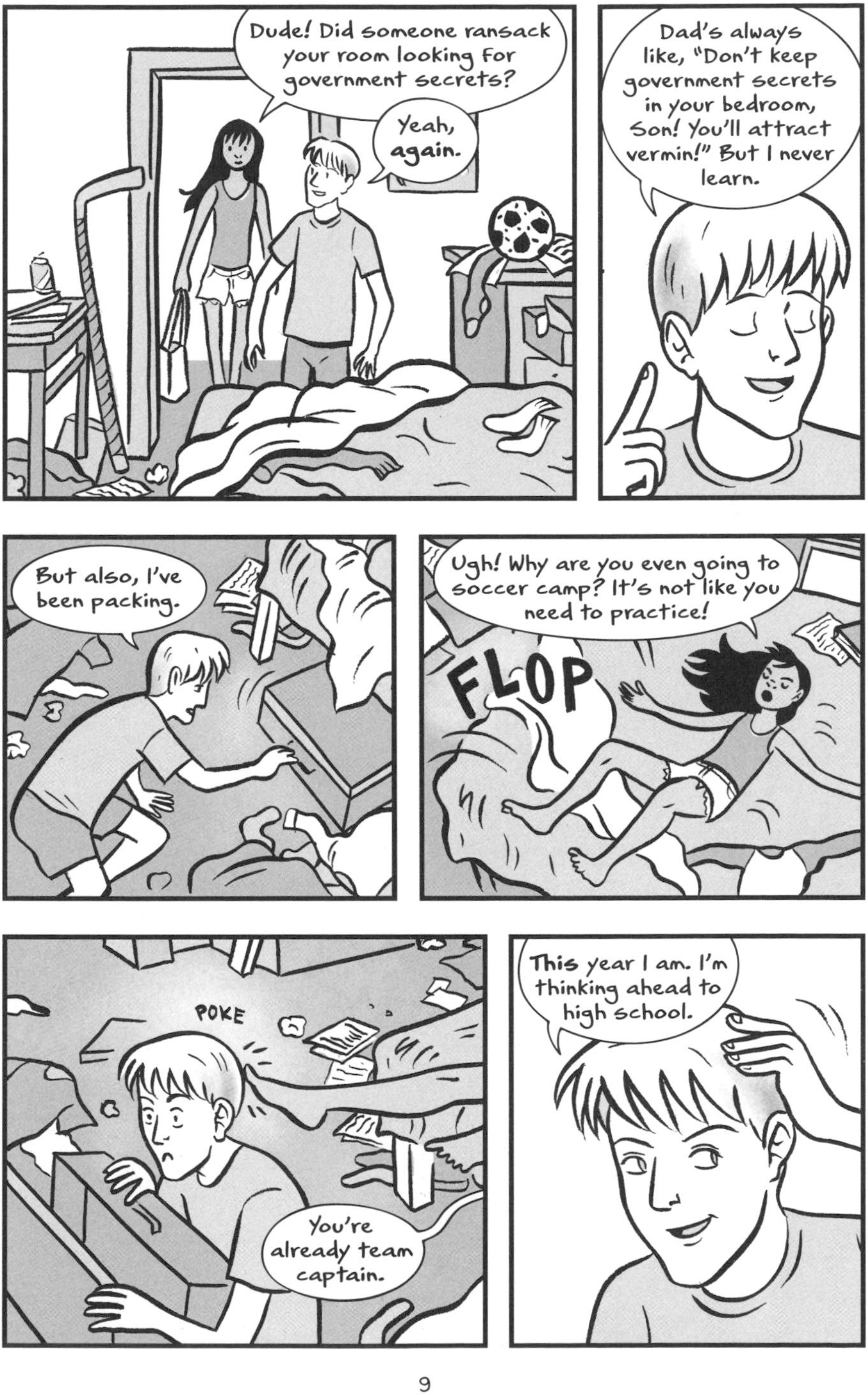
Dude! Did someone ransack your room looking for government secrets?
Yeah, again.
Dad's always like, "Don't keep government secrets in your bedroom, Son! You'll attract vermin!" But I never learn.
But also, I've been packing.
Ugh! Why are you even going to soccer camp? It's not like you need to practice!
FLOP
POKE
You're already team captain.
This year I am. I'm thinking ahead to high school.

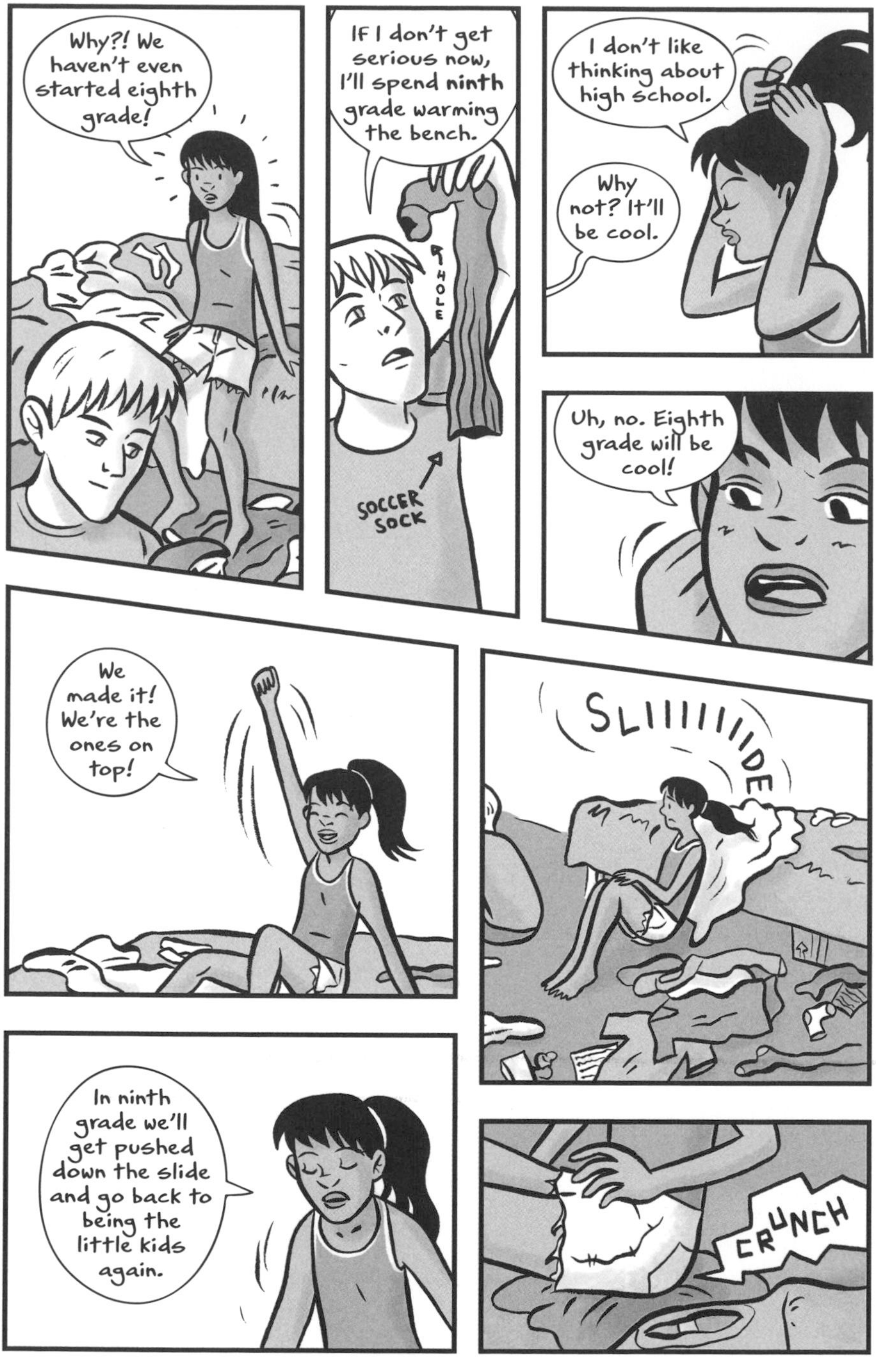
Why?! We haven't even started eighth grade!
If I don't get serious now, I'll spend **ninth** grade warming the bench.
HOLE
SOCCER SOCK
I don't like thinking about high school.
Why not? It'll be cool.
Uh, no. Eighth grade will be cool!
We made it! We're the ones on top!
SLIIIIIIIDE
In ninth grade we'll get pushed down the slide and go back to being the little kids again.
CRUNCH

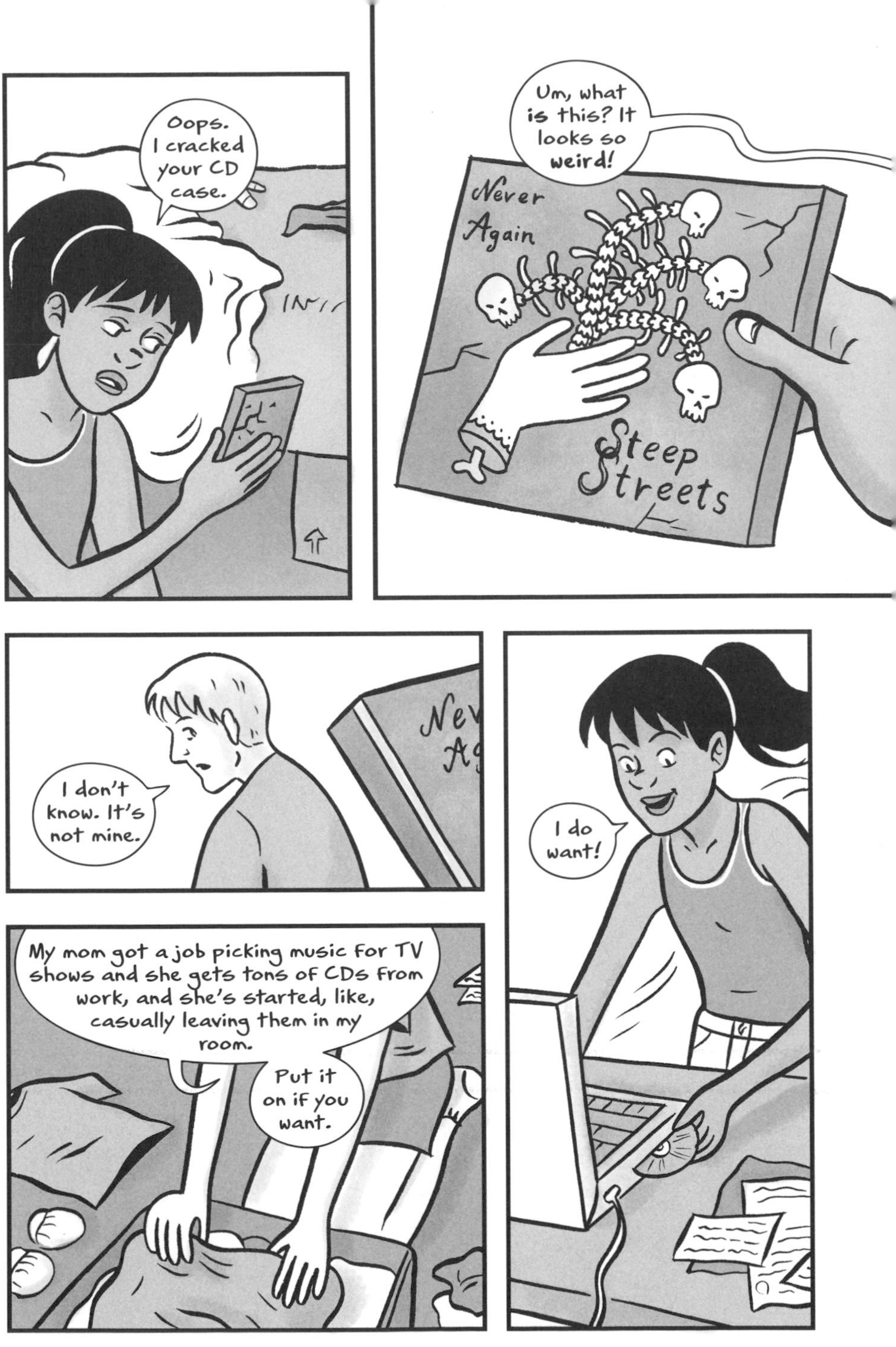
Oops. I cracked your CD case.
Um, what is this? It looks so weird!
Never Again
Steep Streets
I don't know. It's not mine.
Never Ag
My mom got a job picking music for TV shows and she gets tons of CDs from work, and she's started, like, casually leaving them in my room.
Put it on if you want.
I do want!

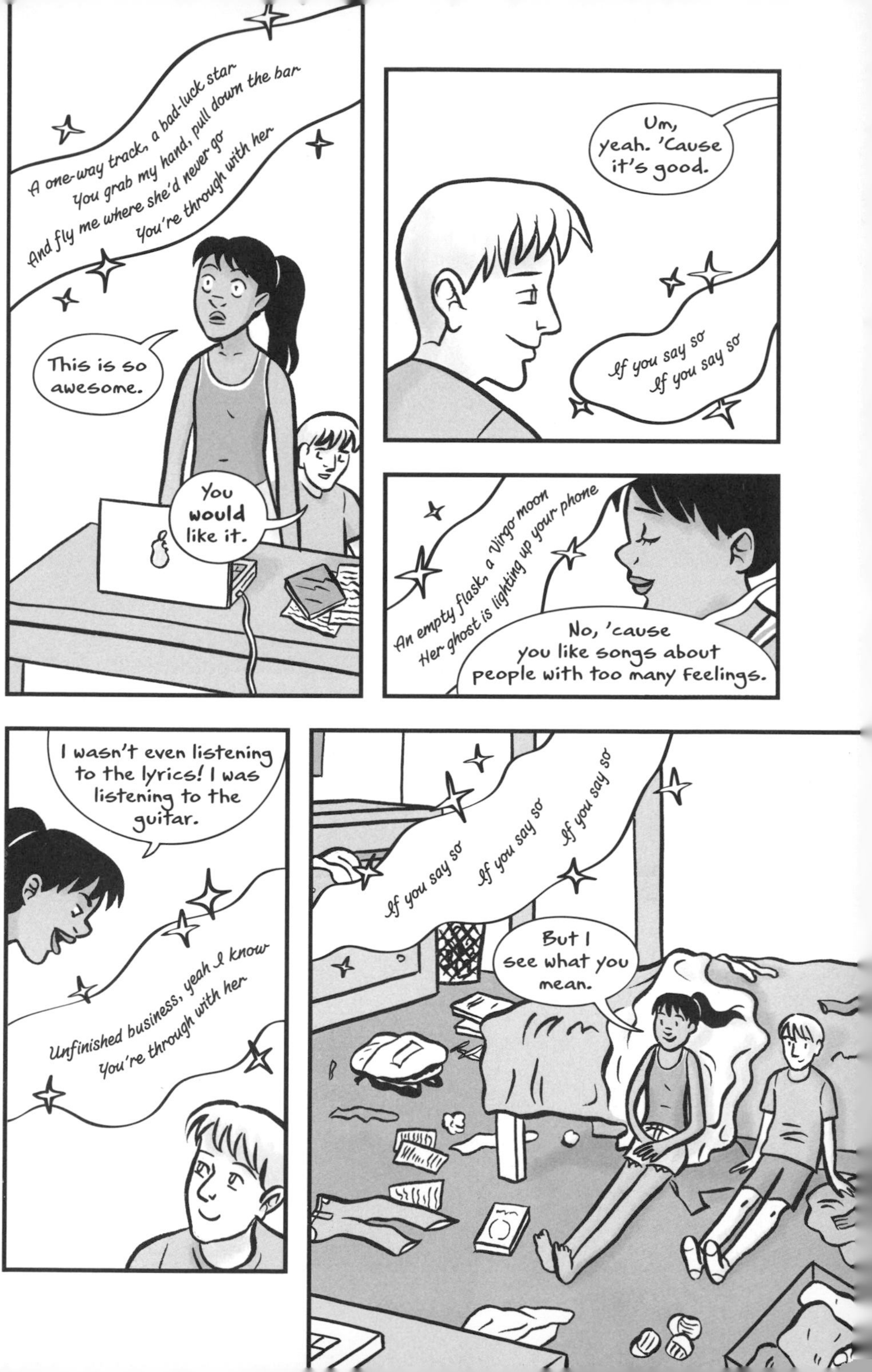
A one-way track, a bad-luck star
You grab my hand, pull down the bar
And fly me where she'd never go
You're through with her
This is so awesome.
You would like it.
Um, yeah. 'Cause it's good.
If you say so
If you say so
An empty flask, a Virgo moon
Her ghost is lighting up your phone
No, 'cause you like songs about people with too many feelings.
I wasn't even listening to the lyrics! I was listening to the guitar.
Unfinished business, yeah I know
You're through with her
If you say so
If you say so
If you say so
But I see what you mean.

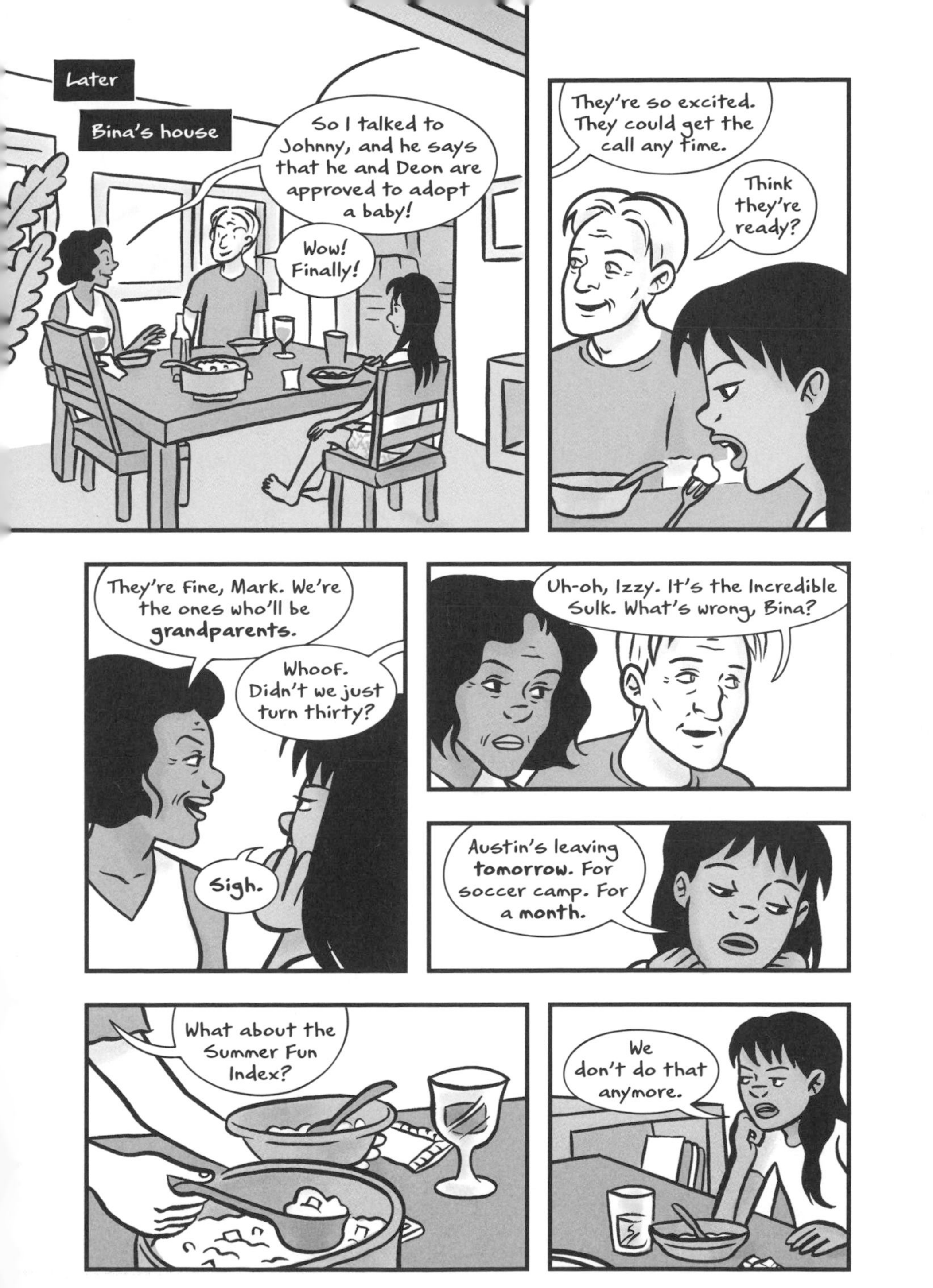
Later
Bina's house
So I talked to Johnny, and he says that he and Deon are approved to adopt a baby!
Wow! Finally!
They're so excited. They could get the call any time.
Think they're ready?
They're fine, Mark. We're the ones who'll be **grandparents.**
Whoof. Didn't we just turn thirty?
Sigh.
Uh-oh, Izzy. It's the Incredible Sulk. What's wrong, Bina?
Austin's leaving **tomorrow.** For soccer camp. For a **month.**
What about the Summer Fun Index?
We don't do that anymore.

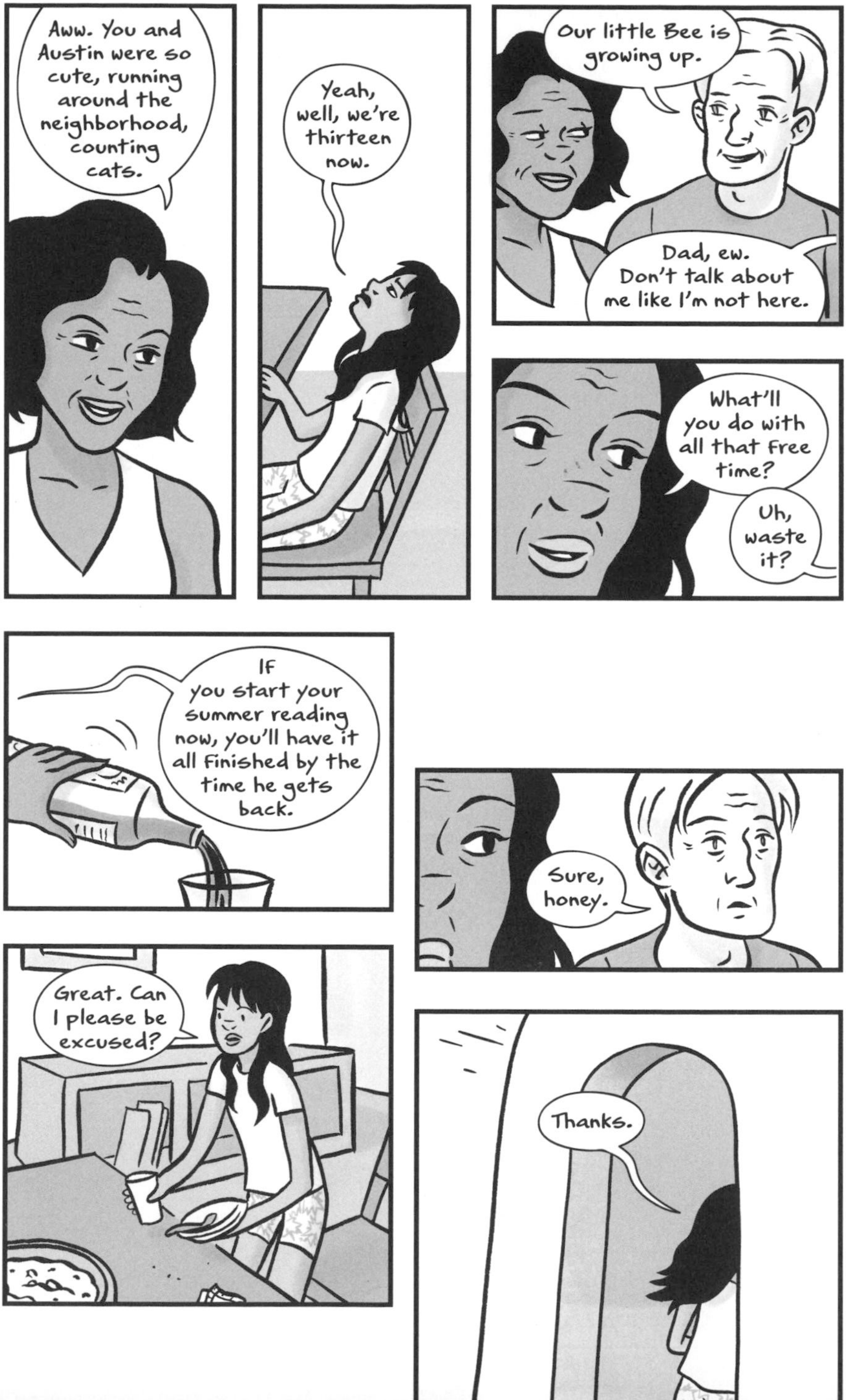
Aww. You and Austin were so cute, running around the neighborhood, counting cats.
Yeah, well, we're thirteen now.
Our little Bee is growing up.
Dad, ew. Don't talk about me like I'm not here.
What'll you do with all that free time?
Uh, waste it?
If you start your summer reading now, you'll have it all finished by the time he gets back.
Sure, honey.
Great. Can I please be excused?
Thanks.

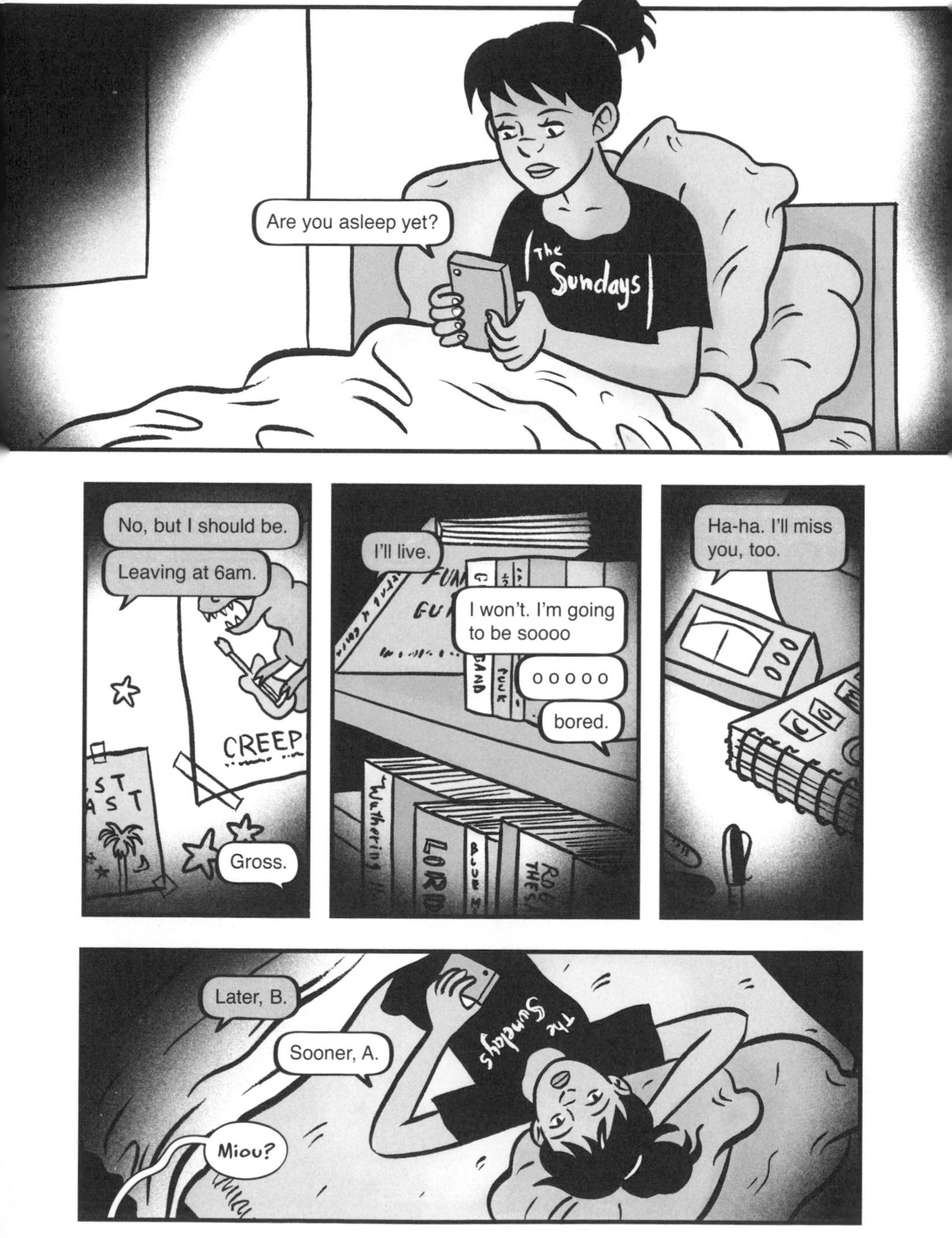
Are you asleep yet?
The Sundays
No, but I should be.
Leaving at 6am.
CREEP
Gross.
I'll live.
I won't. I'm going to be soooo
ooooo
bored.
Ha-ha. I'll miss you, too.
Later, B.
Sooner, A.
The Sundays
Miou?

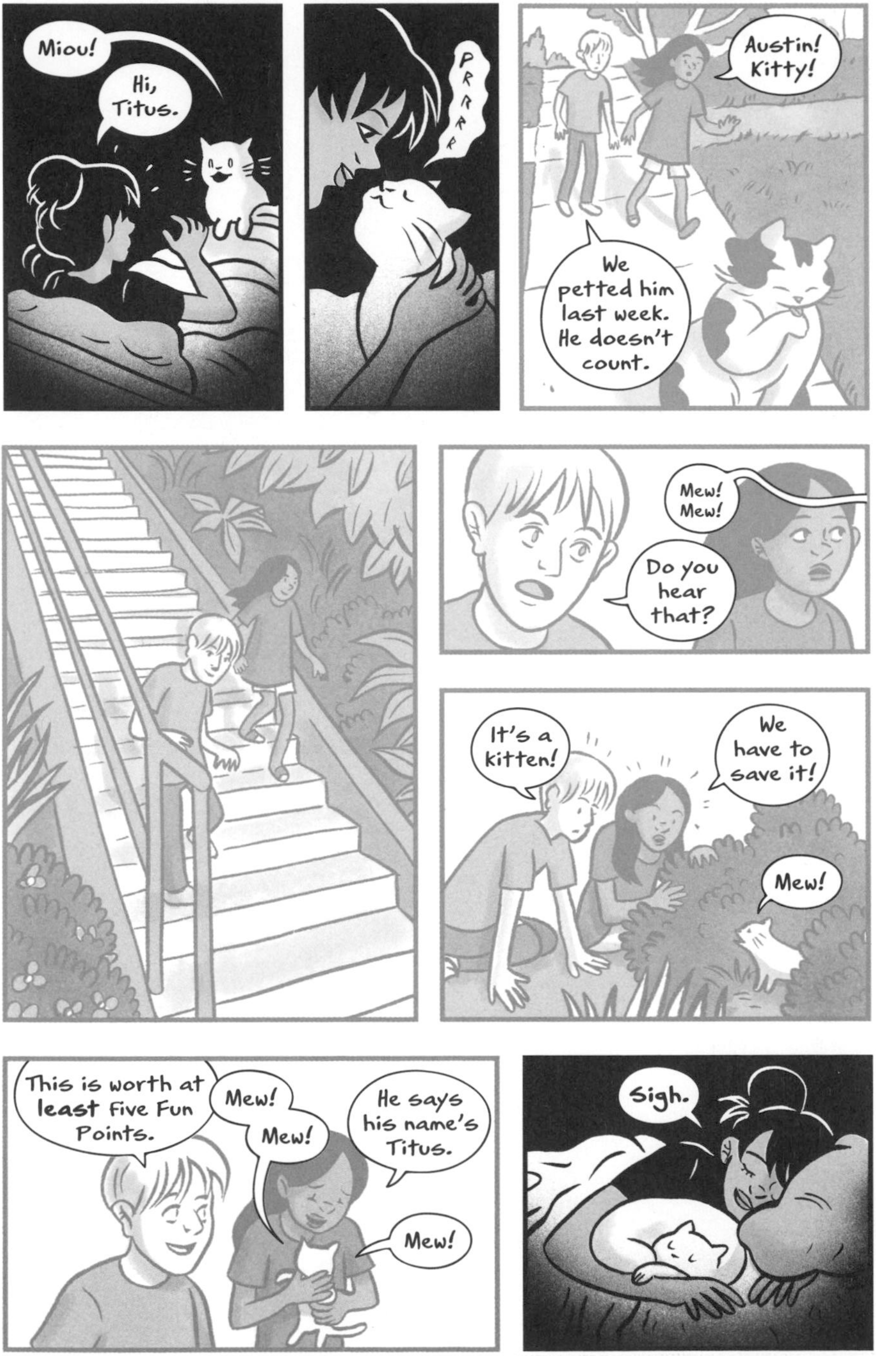
Miou!
Hi, Titus.
PRRRRR
Austin! Kitty!
We petted him last week. He doesn't count.
Mew! Mew!
Do you hear that?
It's a kitten!
We have to save it!
Mew!
This is worth at **least** Five Fun Points.
Mew!
Mew!
He says his name's Titus.
Mew!
Sigh.

Week One

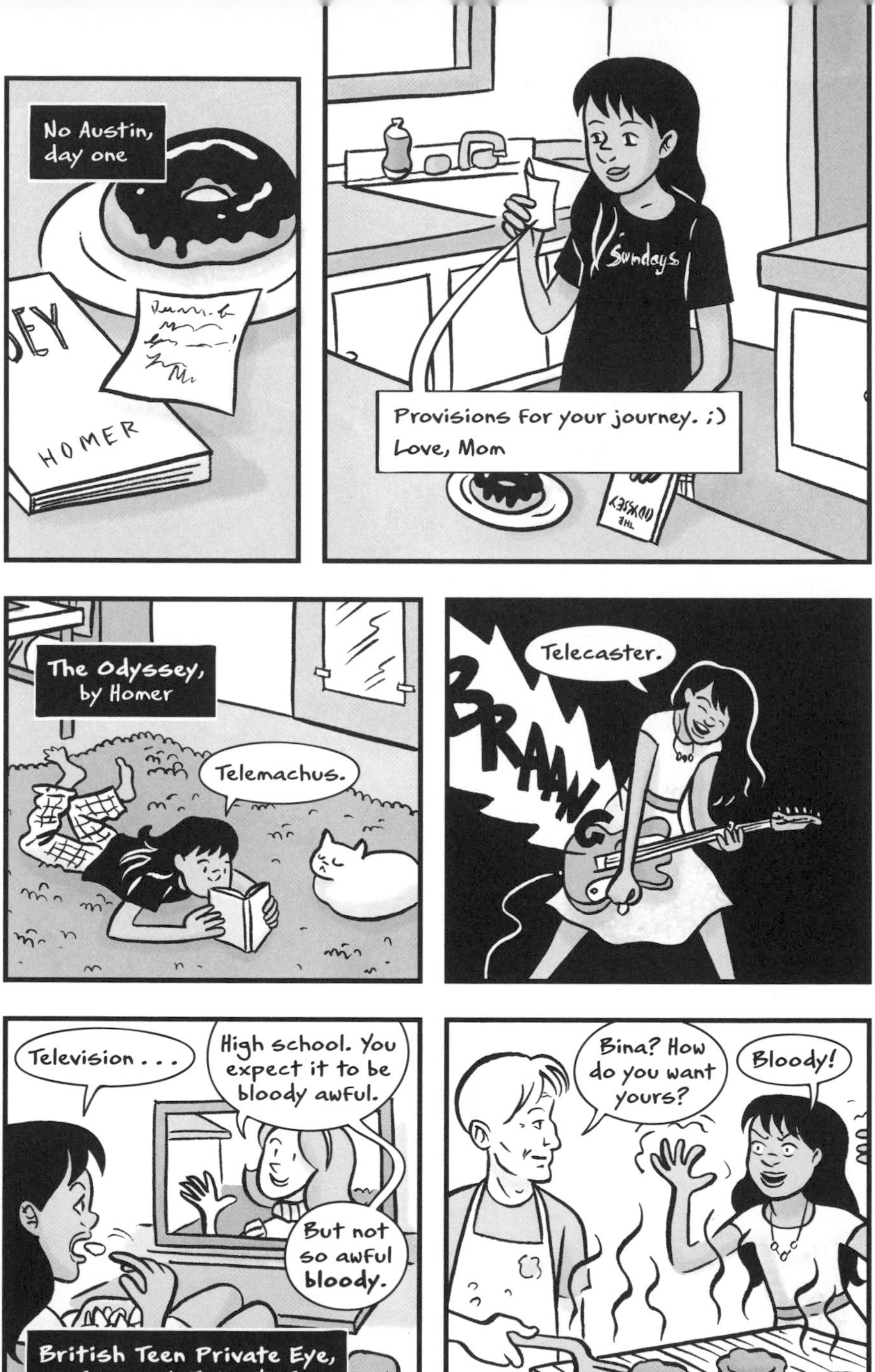
No Austin, day one
DEY
HOMER
Sundays
Provisions for your journey. ;) Love, Mom
THE ODYSSEY
The Odyssey, by Homer
Telemachus.
Telecaster.
BRAAANG
Television . . .
High school. You expect it to be bloody awful.
But not so awful bloody.
British Teen Private Eye, Season 1, Episode 2
Bina? How do you want yours?
Bloody!

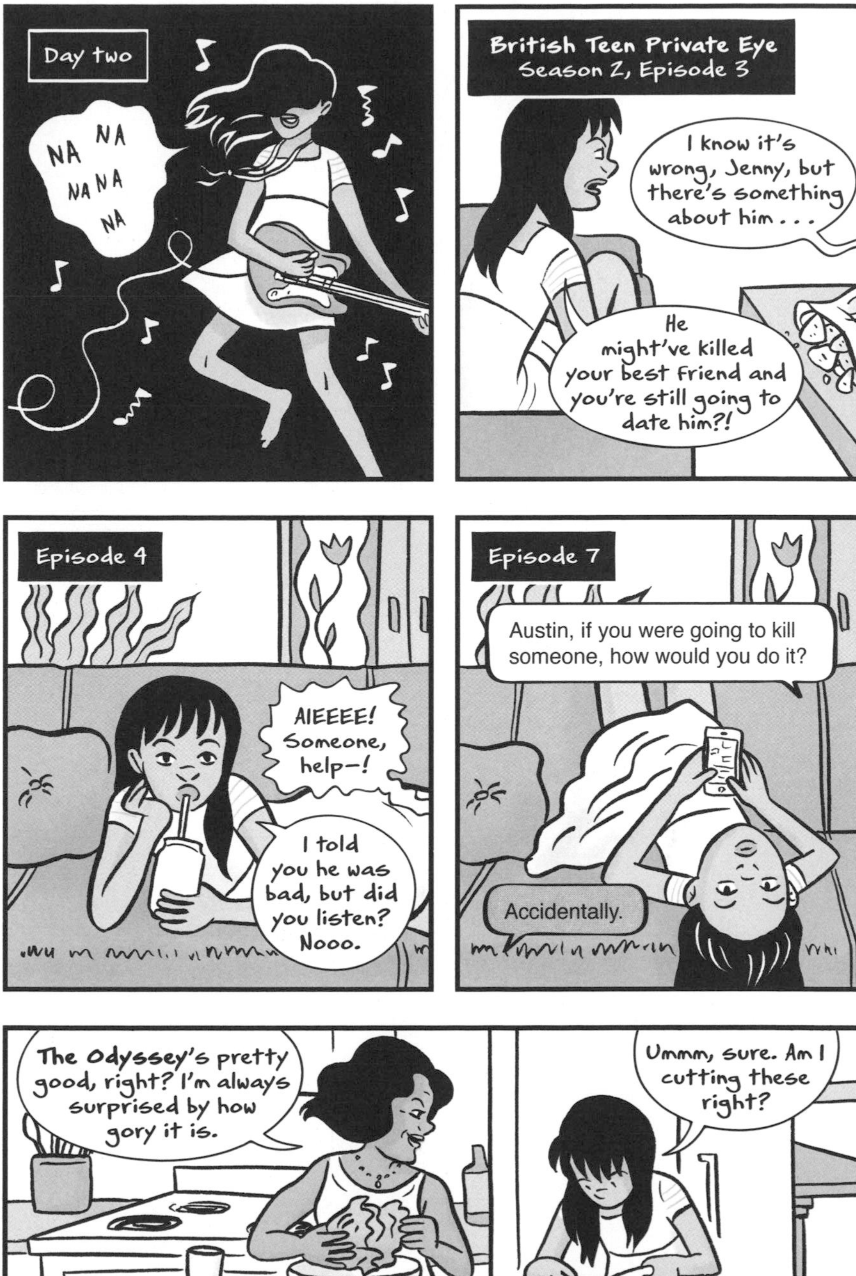
Day two
NA NA NA NA NA
British Teen Private Eye
Season 2, Episode 3
I know it's wrong, Jenny, but there's something about him . . .
He might've killed your best friend and you're still going to date him?!
Episode 4
AIEEEE! Someone, help—!
I told you he was bad, but did you listen? Nooo.
Episode 7
Austin, if you were going to kill someone, how would you do it?
Accidentally.
The Odyssey's pretty good, right? I'm always surprised by how gory it is.
Ummm, sure. Am I cutting these right?

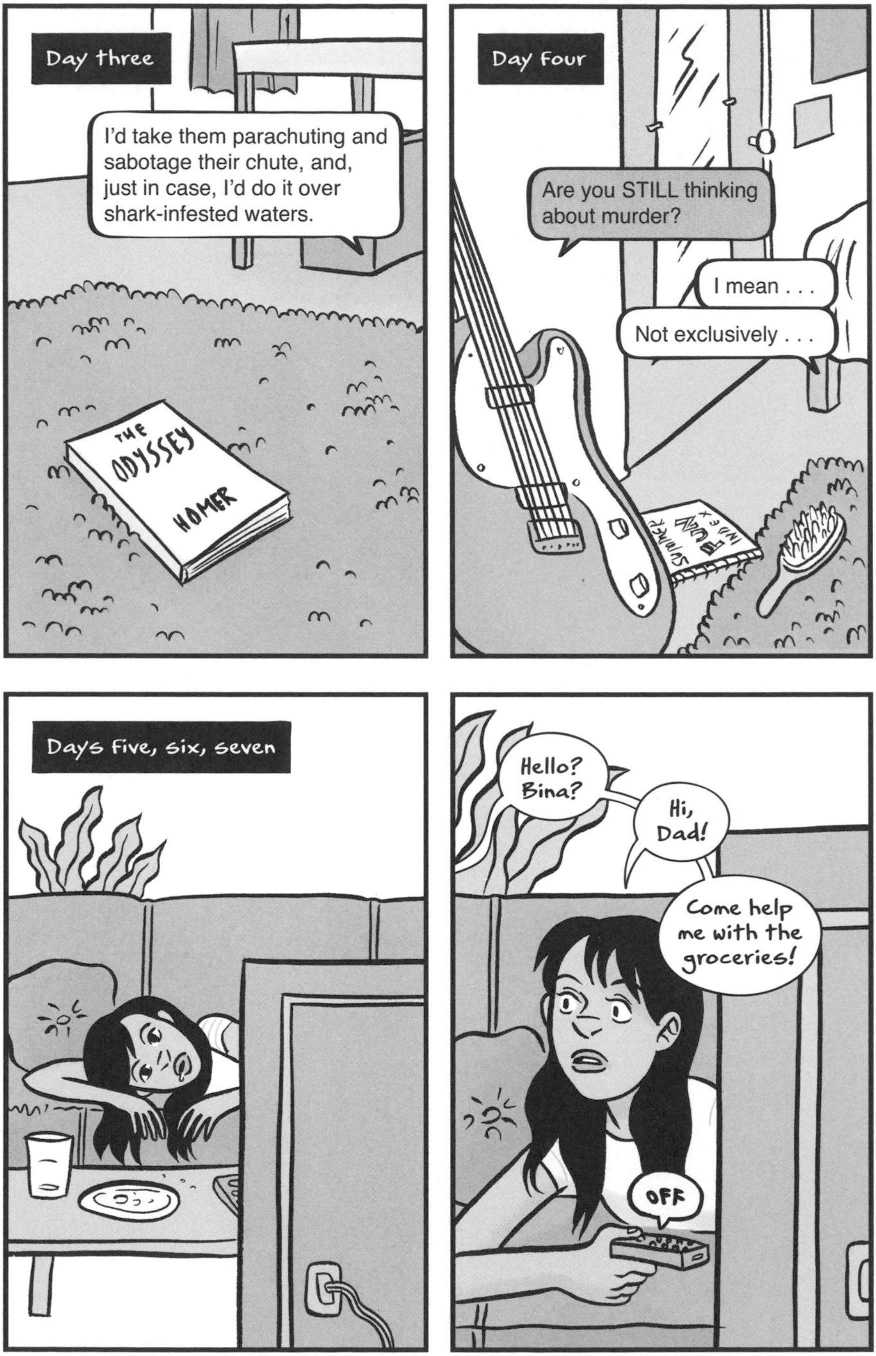
Day three
I'd take them parachuting and sabotage their chute, and, just in case, I'd do it over shark-infested waters.
THE ODYSSEY
HOMER
Day Four
Are you STILL thinking about murder?
I mean . . .
Not exclusively . . .
Days five, six, seven
Hello? Bina?
Hi, Dad!
Come help me with the groceries!
OFF

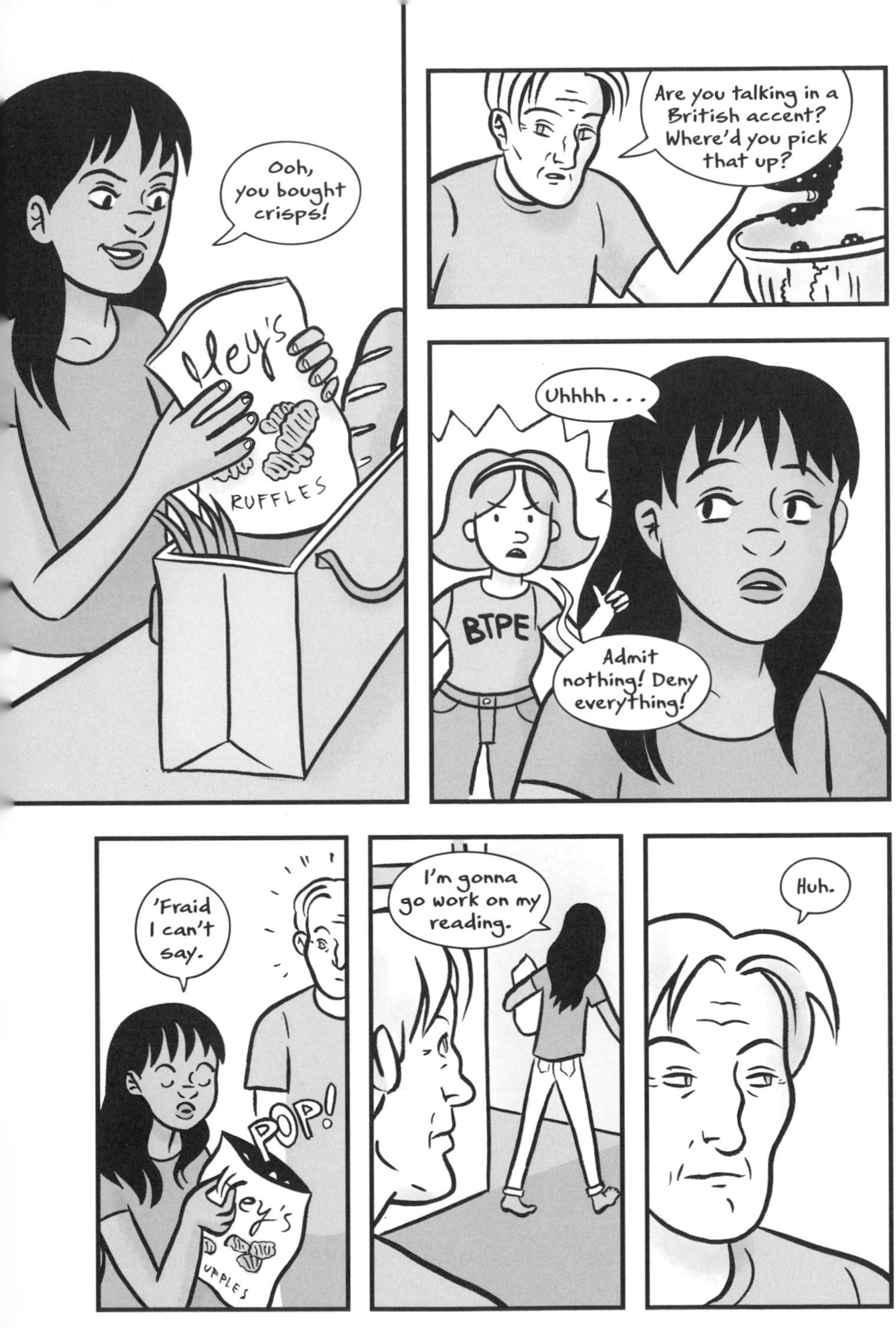
Ooh, you bought crisps!
Hey's
RUFFLES
Are you talking in a British accent? Where'd you pick that up?
Uhhhh . . .
BTPE
Admit nothing! Deny everything!
'Fraid I can't say.
POP!
ey's
UFFLES
I'm gonna go work on my reading.
Huh.

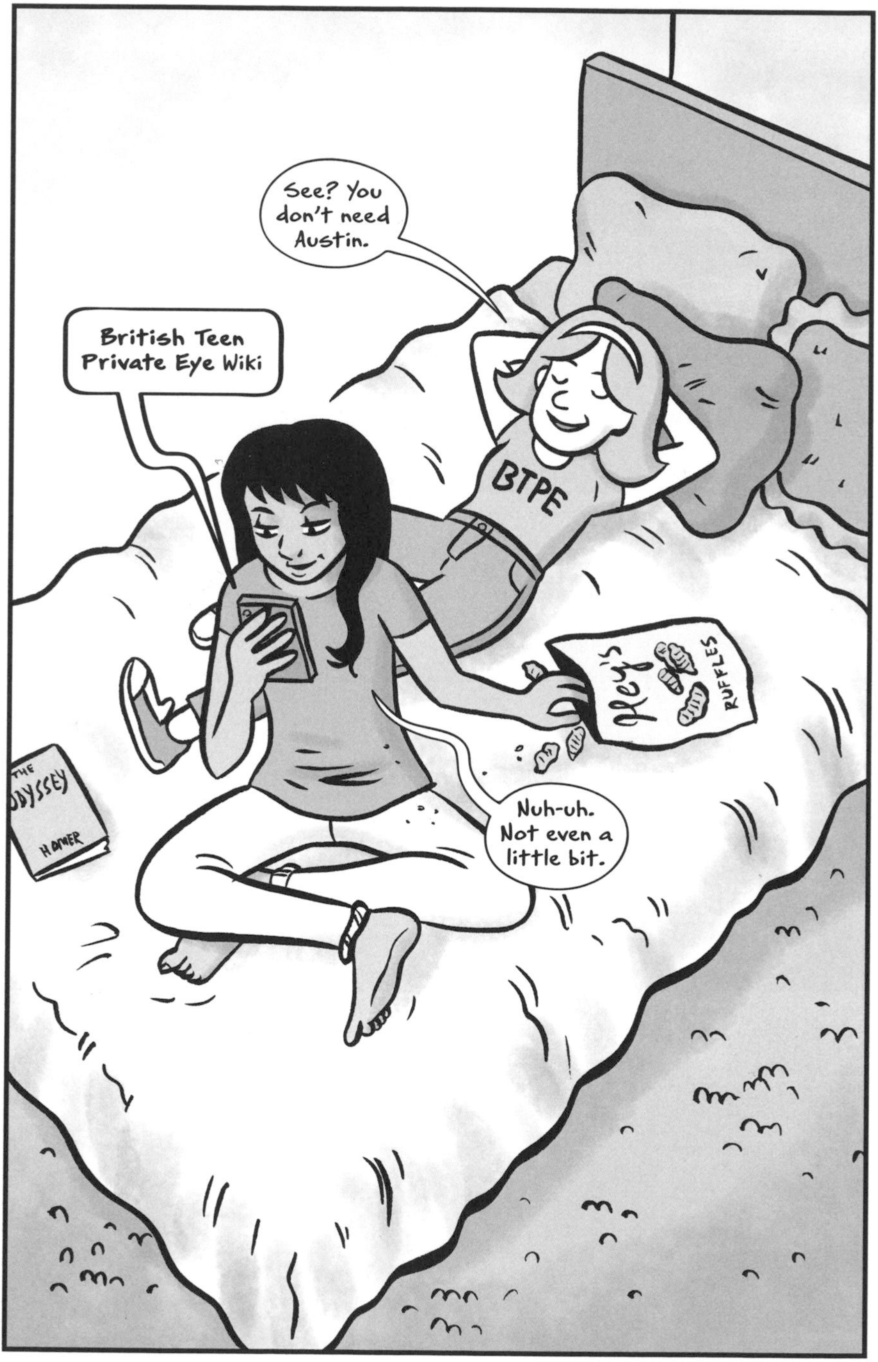
British Teen Private Eye Wiki
See? You don't need Austin.
Nuh-uh. Not even a little bit.
BTPE
THE ODYSSEY
HOMER
Hey's
RUFFLES

Week Two

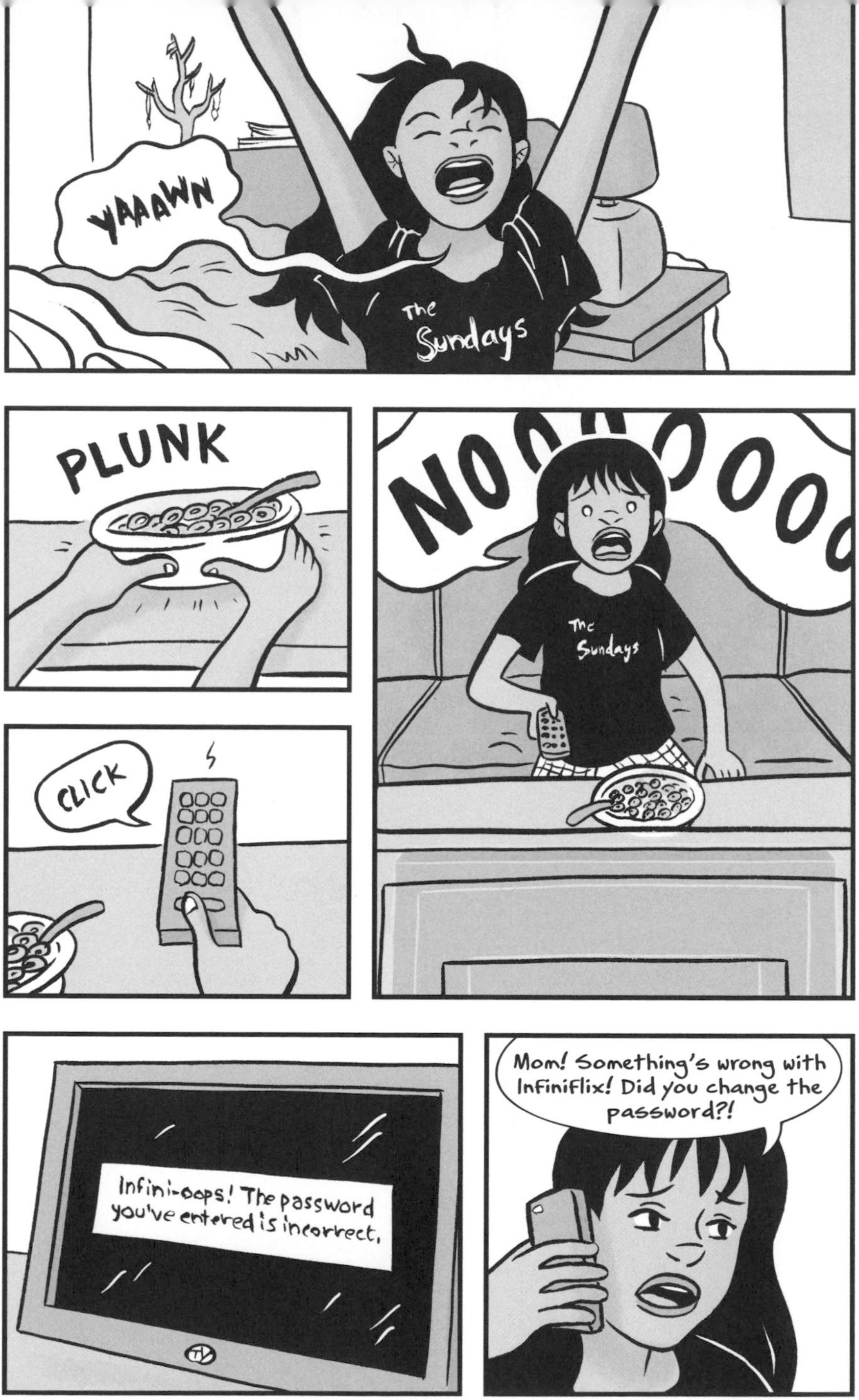
YAAAWN
The Sundays
PLUNK
NOOOOOOO
The Sundays
CLICK
Infini-oops! The password you've entered is incorrect.
Mom! Something's wrong with InfiniFlix! Did you change the password?!

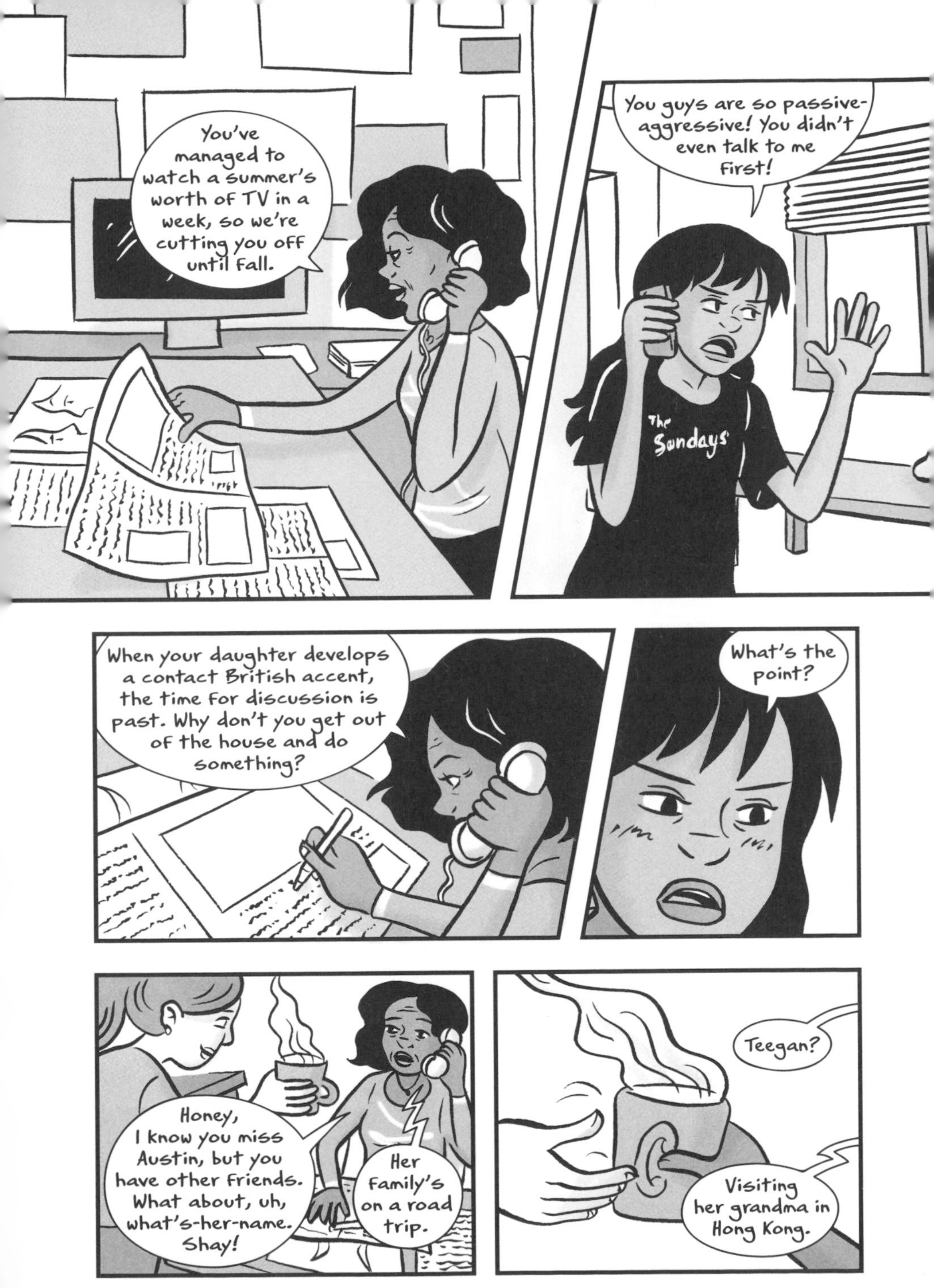
You've managed to watch a summer's worth of TV in a week, so we're cutting you off until fall.
You guys are so passive-aggressive! You didn't even talk to me first!
The Sundays
When your daughter develops a contact British accent, the time for discussion is past. Why don't you get out of the house and do something?
What's the point?
Honey, I know you miss Austin, but you have other friends. What about, uh, what's-her-name. Shay!
Her family's on a road trip.
Teegan?
Visiting her grandma in Hong Kong.

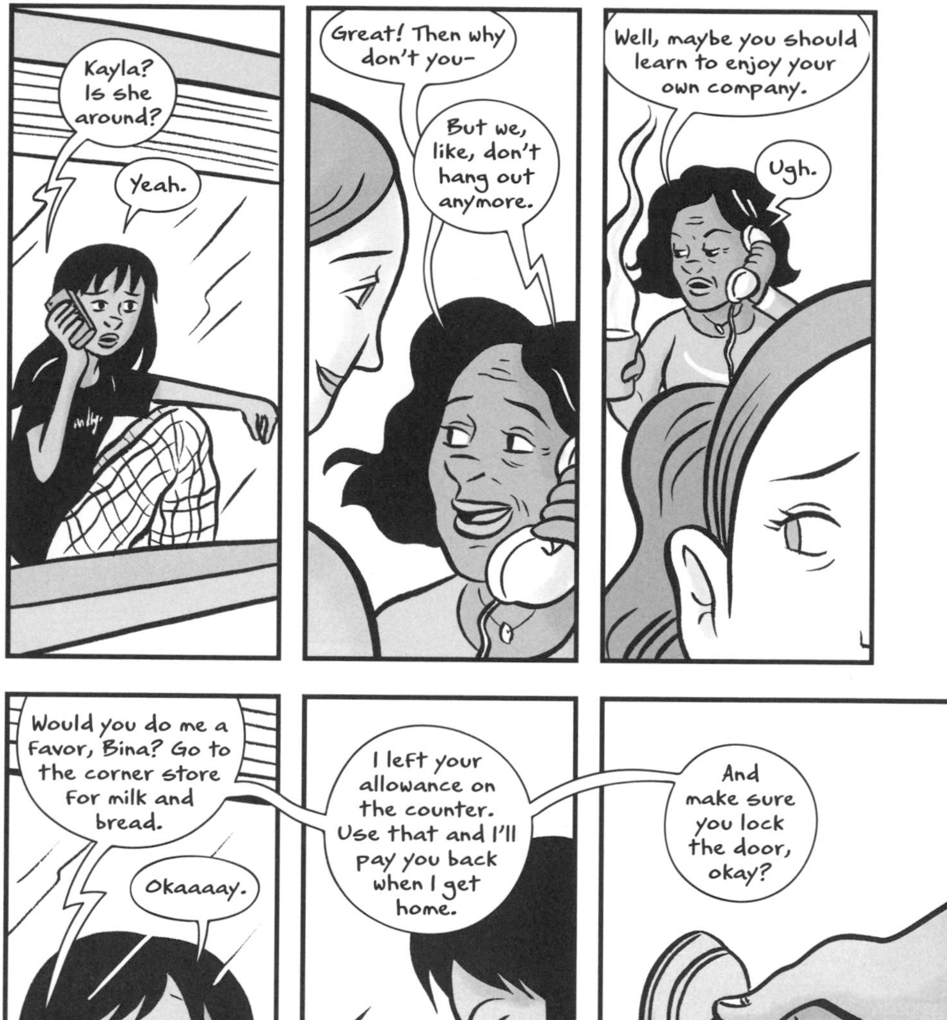

Kayla? Is she around?
Yeah.
Great! Then why don't you-
But we, like, don't hang out anymore.
Well, maybe you should learn to enjoy your own company.
Ugh.
Would you do me a favor, Bina? Go to the corner store for milk and bread.
Okaaaay.
The Sundays
I left your allowance on the counter. Use that and I'll pay you back when I get home.
And make sure you lock the door, okay?
CLICK

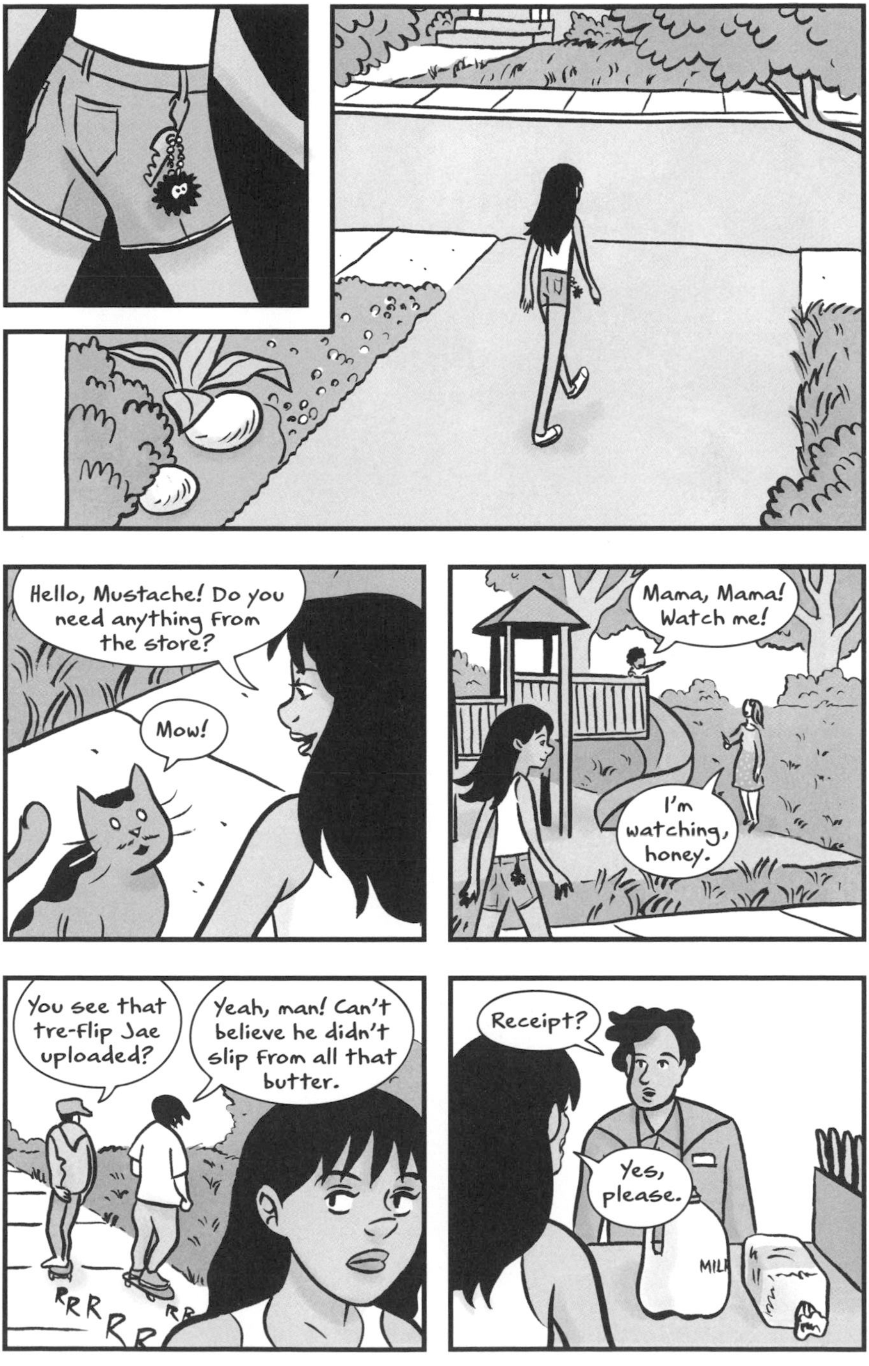
Hello, Mustache! Do you need anything from the store?
Mow!
Mama, Mama! Watch me!
I'm watching, honey.
You see that tre-flip Jae uploaded?
Yeah, man! Can't believe he didn't slip from all that butter.
RRRRR
RR
Receipt?
Yes, please.
MILK

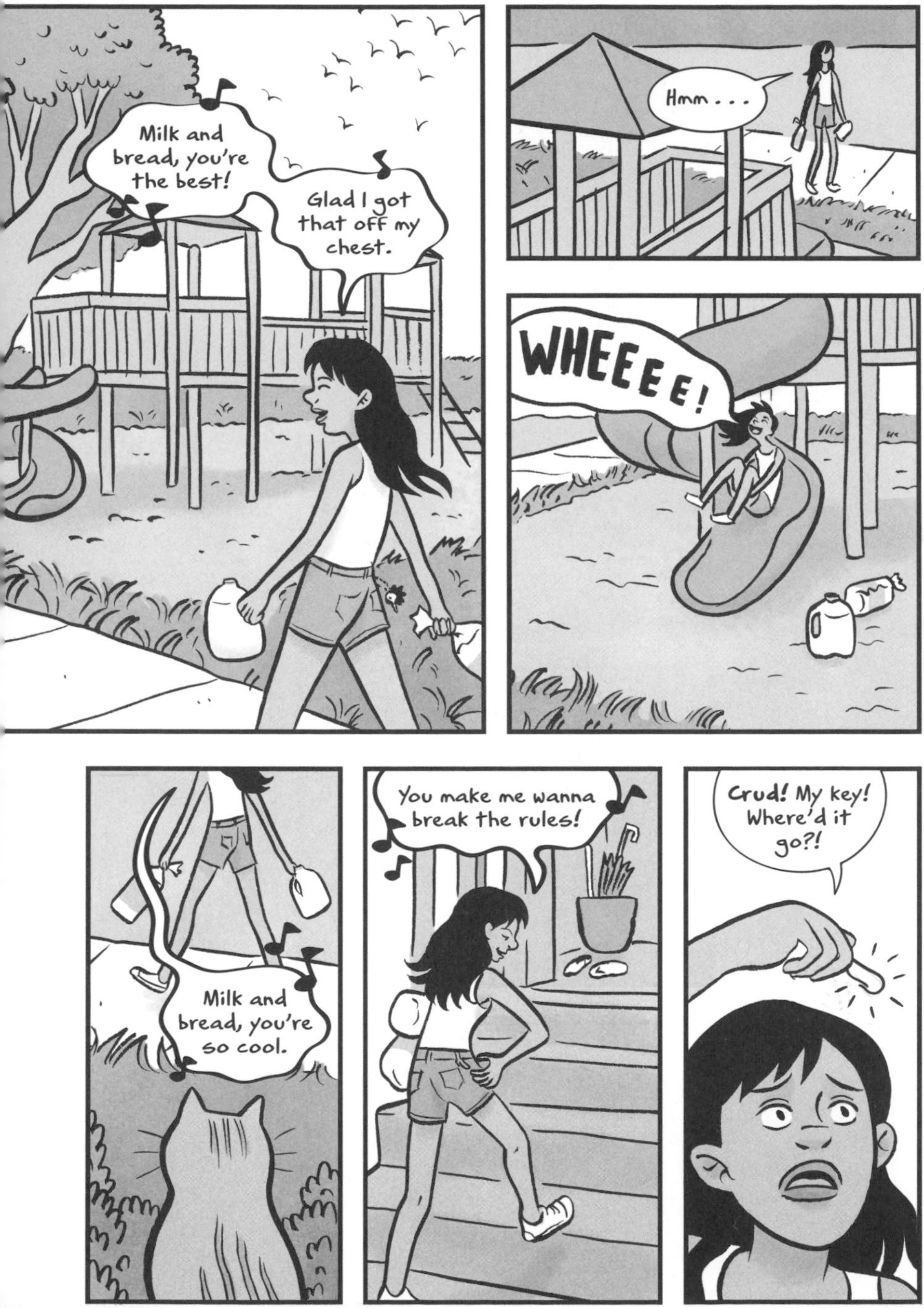

Milk and bread, you're the best!
Glad I got that off my chest.
Hmm . . .
WHEEEEE!
Milk and bread, you're so cool.
You make me wanna break the rules!
Crud! My key! Where'd it go?!

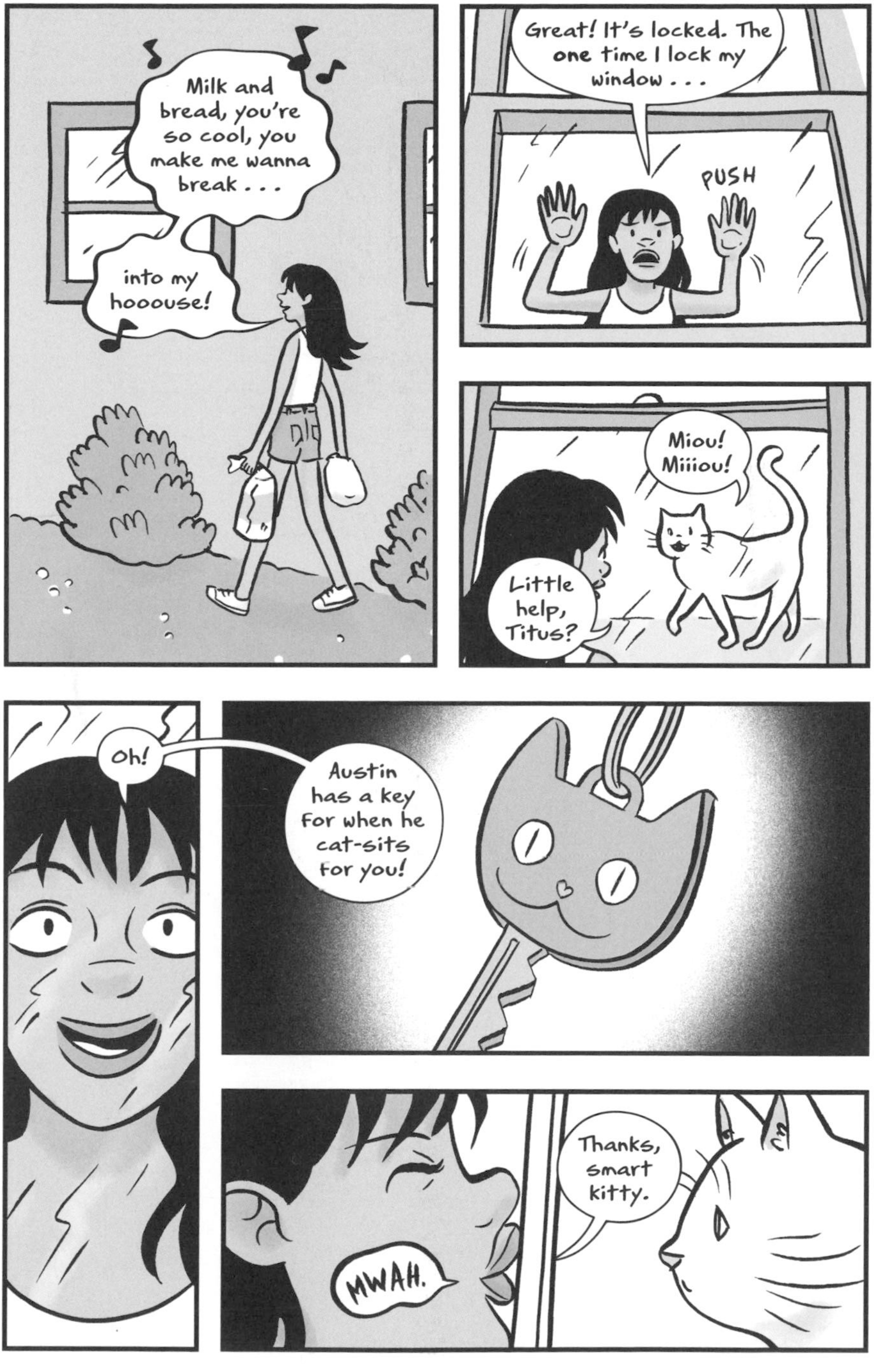

Milk and bread, you're so cool, you make me wanna break . . .
into my hooouse!
Great! It's locked. The one time I lock my window . . .
PUSH
Miou! Miiiou!
Little help, Titus?
Oh!
Austin has a key for when he cat-sits for you!
MWAH.
Thanks, smart kitty.

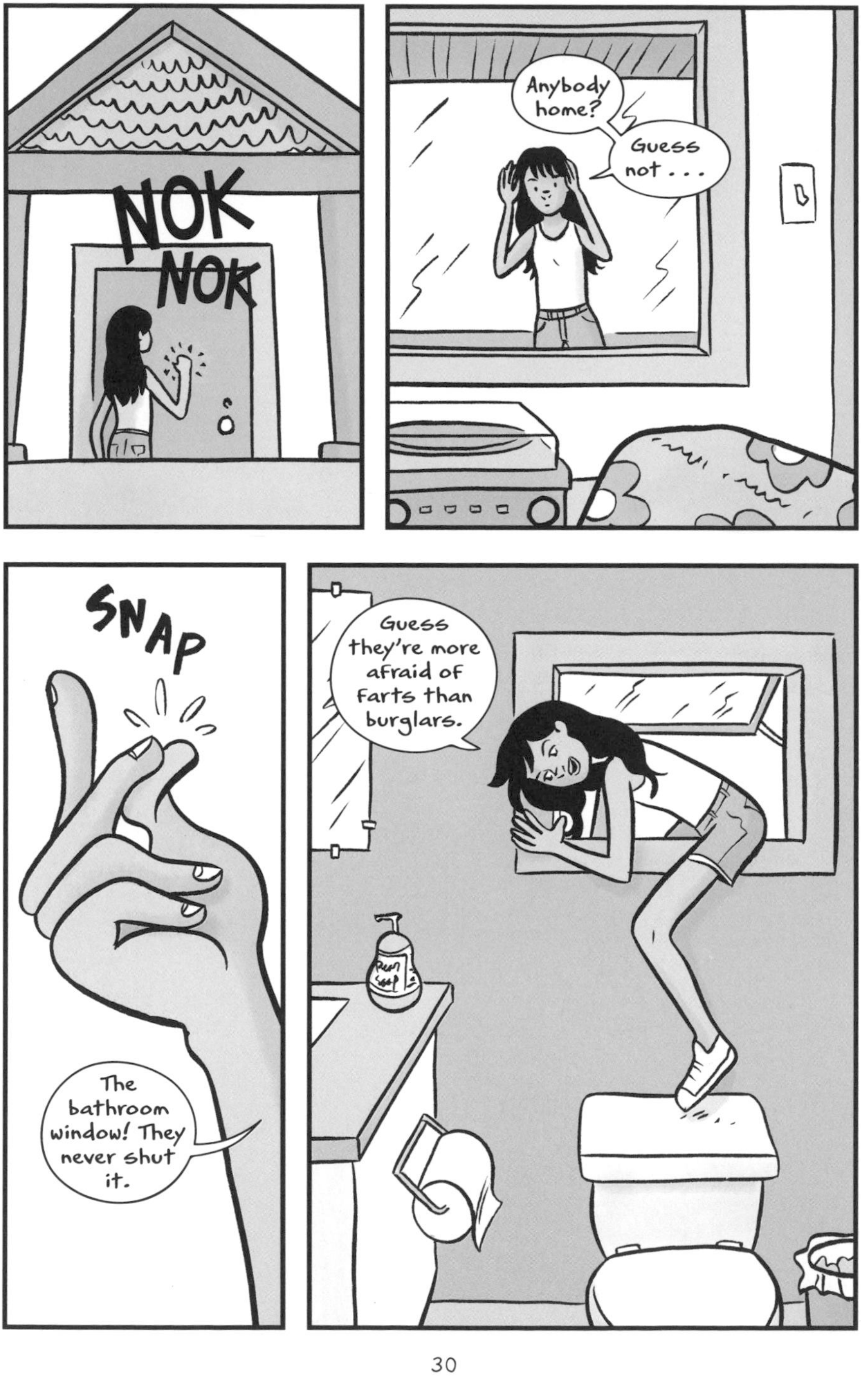
NOK
NOK
Anybody home?
Guess not . . .
SNAP
The bathroom window! They never shut it.
Guess they're more afraid of farts than burglars.

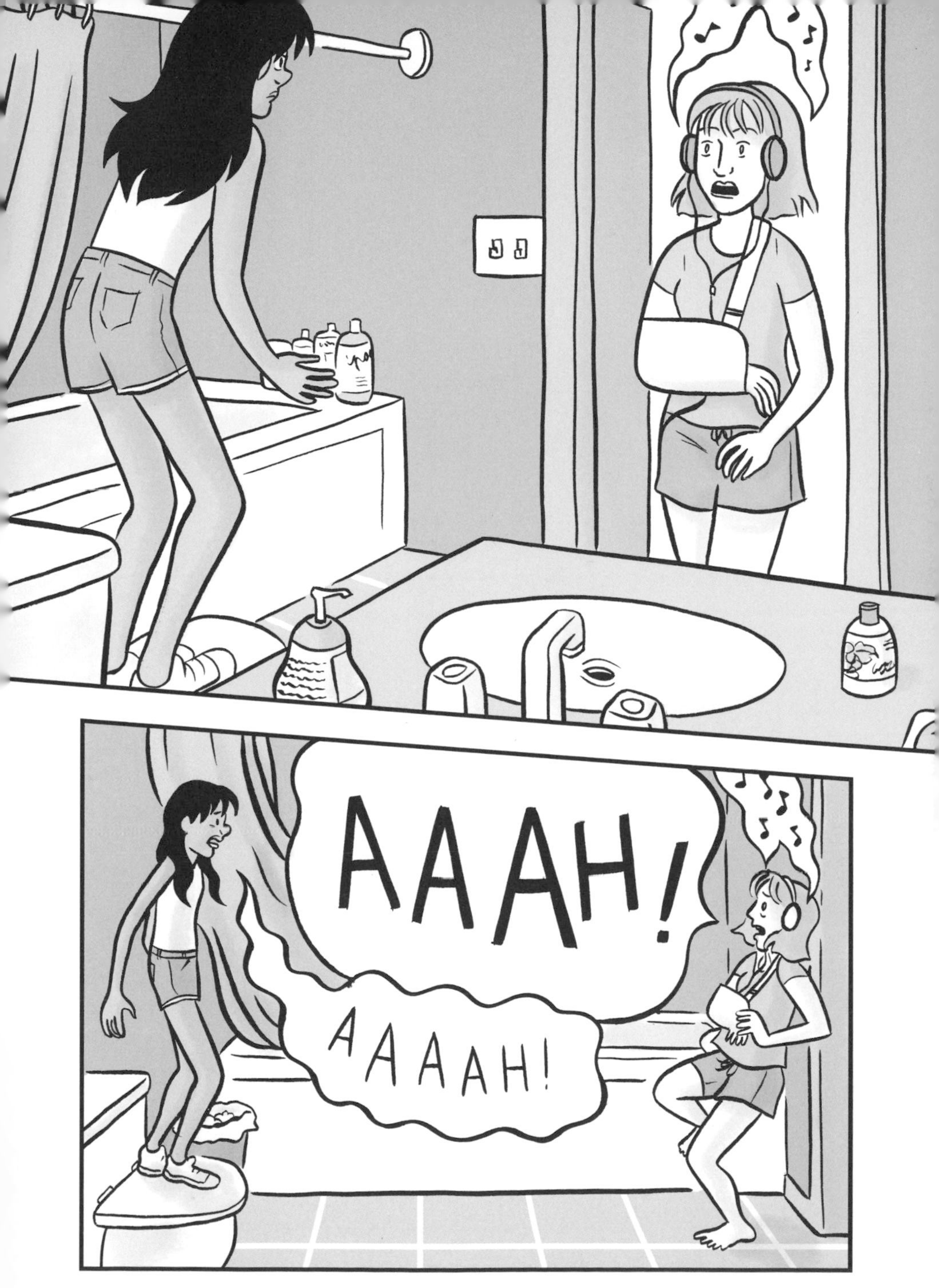
AAAH!
AAAAH!

I'm sorry! I-I didn't think anyone was home!
So you thought, "Hey! I'll just **break in**!"?
I'm locked out of my house, Charlie!
So go break in **there!**
I can't! It's like Fort Knox! But Austin has a key in his room. For cat-sitting.
SQUINT
Get down off the toilet. You're a stone-cold psycho and I kinda admire that.
Come get your dumb key.

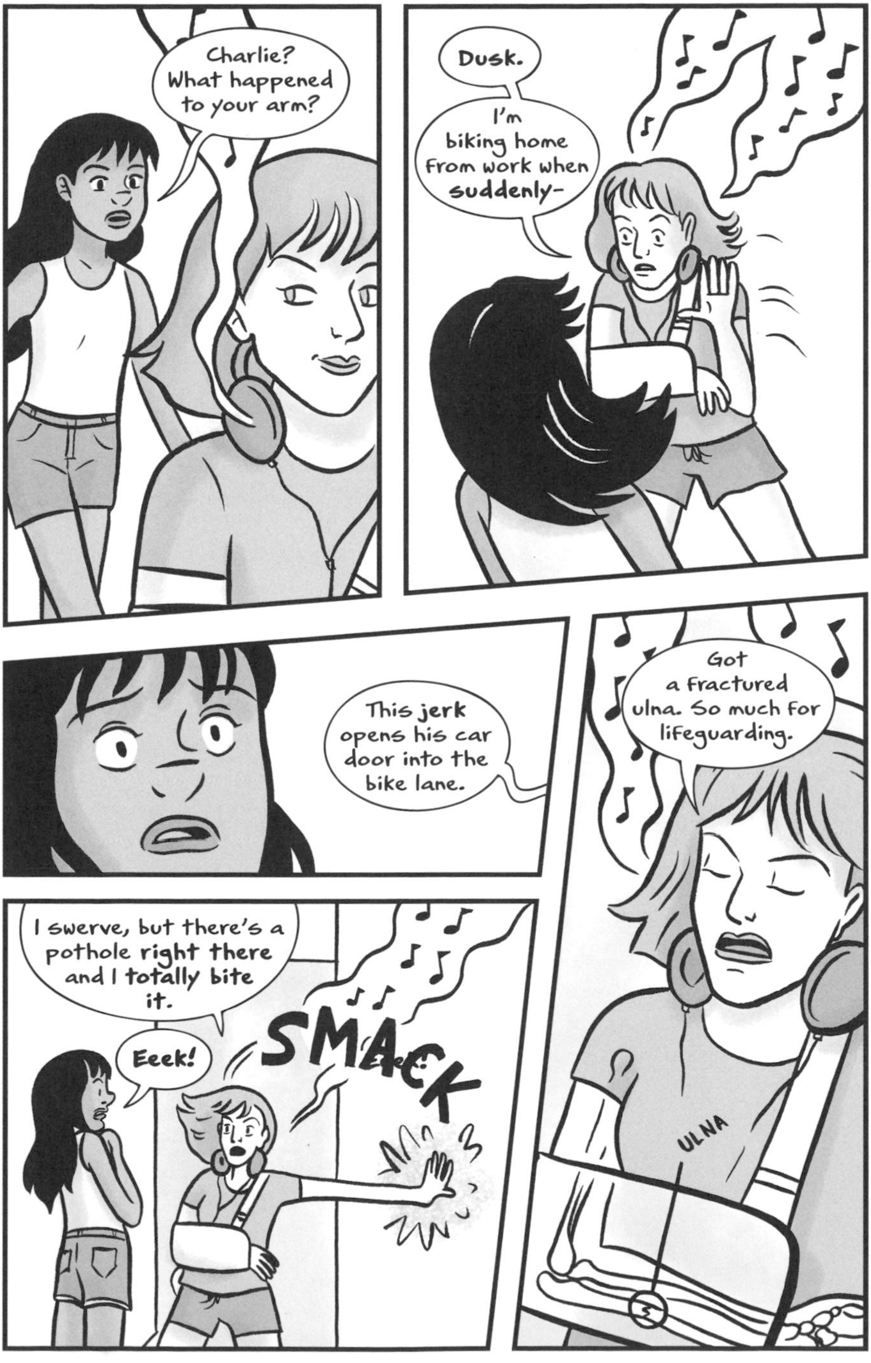
Charlie? What happened to your arm?
Dusk.
I'm biking home from work when suddenly-
This jerk opens his car door into the bike lane.
Got a fractured ulna. So much for lifeguarding.
ULNA
I swerve, but there's a pothole right there and I totally bite it.
Eeek!
SMACK

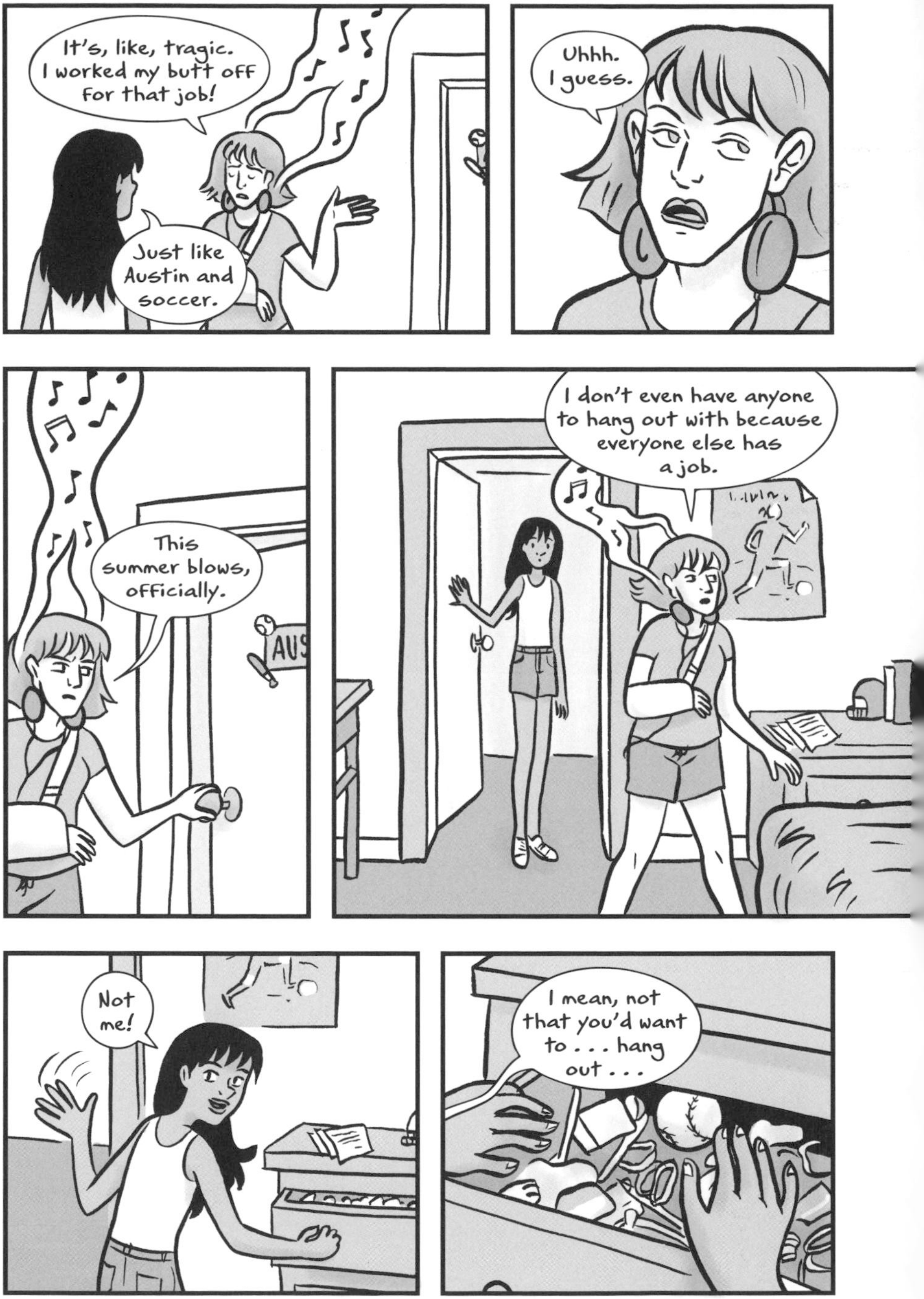
It's, like, tragic. I worked my butt off for that job!
Just like Austin and soccer.
Uhhh. I guess.
This summer blows, officially.
AUS
I don't even have anyone to hang out with because everyone else has a job.
Not me!
I mean, not that you'd want to . . . hang out . . .

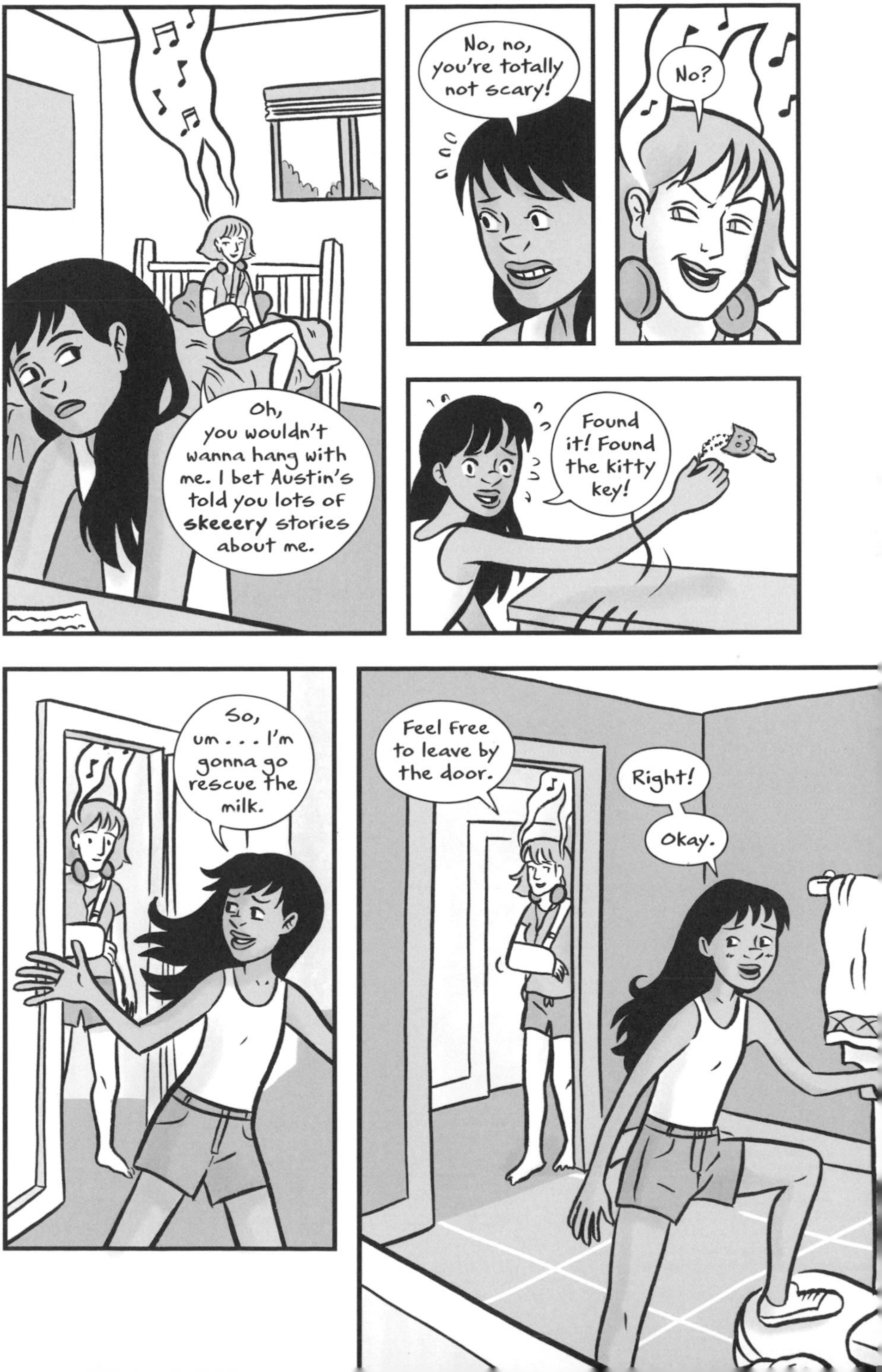
Oh, you wouldn't wanna hang with me. I bet Austin's told you lots of skeeery stories about me.
No, no, you're totally not scary!
No?
Found it! Found the kitty key!
So, um . . . I'm gonna go rescue the milk.
Feel free to leave by the door.
Right!
Okay.

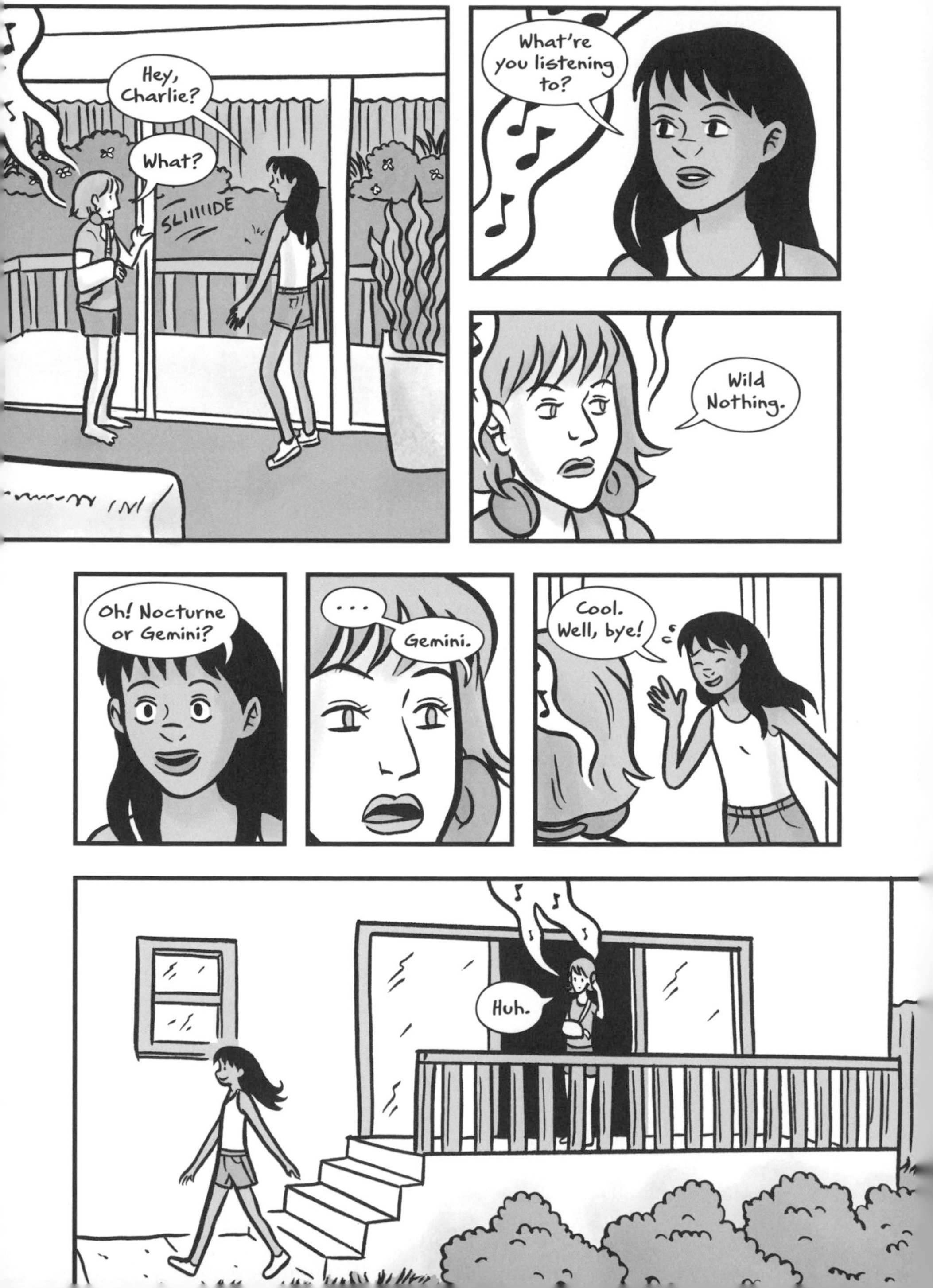

Hey, Charlie?
What?
SLIIIIIDE
What're you listening to?
Wild Nothing.
Oh! Nocturne or Gemini?
...
Gemini.
Cool. Well, bye!
Huh.

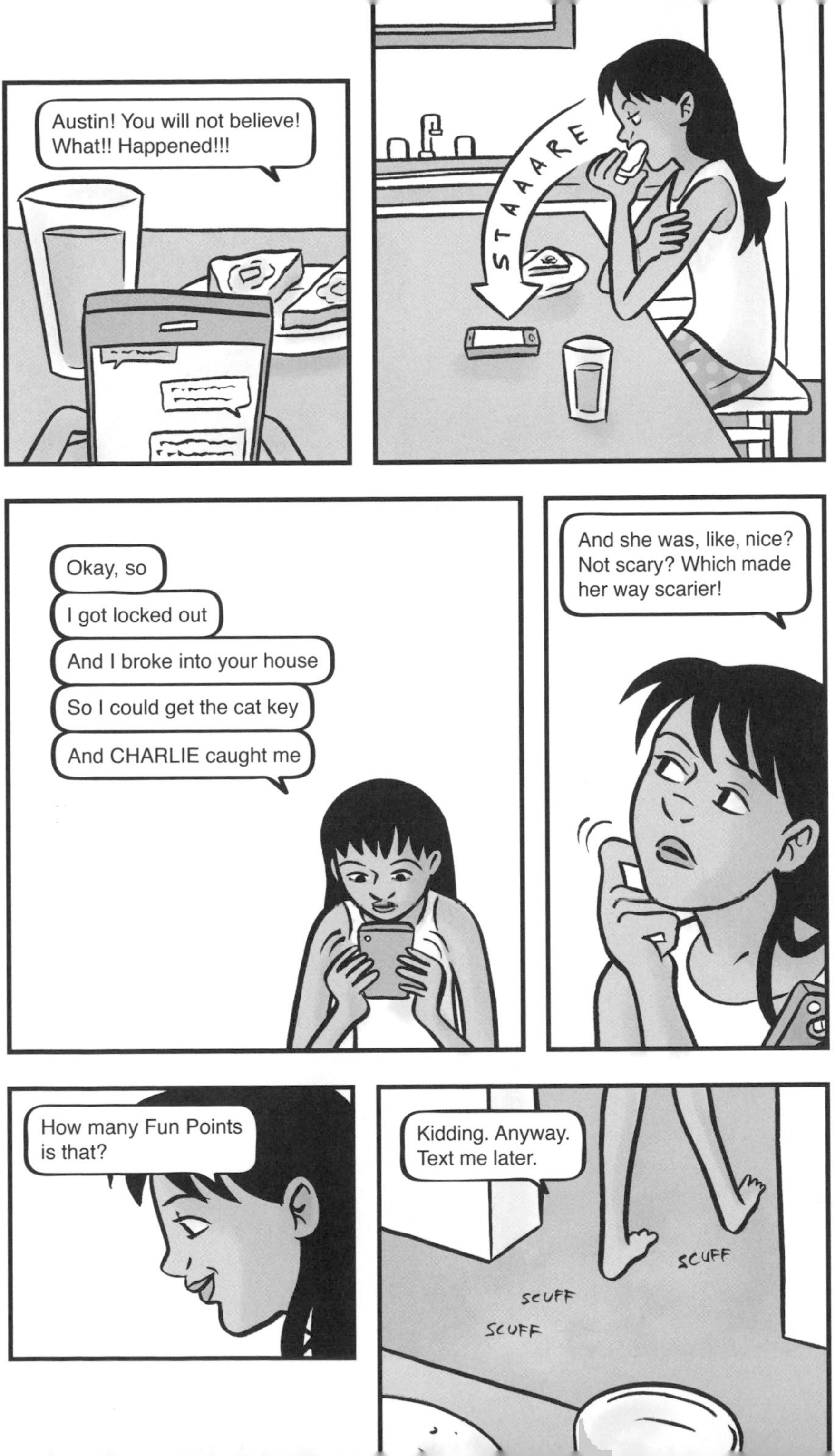
Austin! You will not believe! What!! Happened!!!
STAAARE
Okay, so
I got locked out
And I broke into your house
So I could get the cat key
And CHARLIE caught me
And she was, like, nice? Not scary? Which made her way scarier!
How many Fun Points is that?
Kidding. Anyway. Text me later.
SCUFF
SCUFF
SCUFF

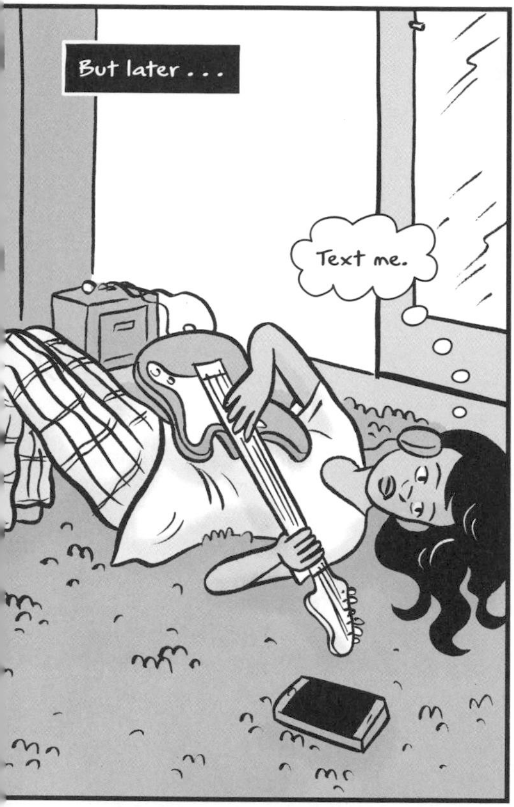
But later . . .
Text me.

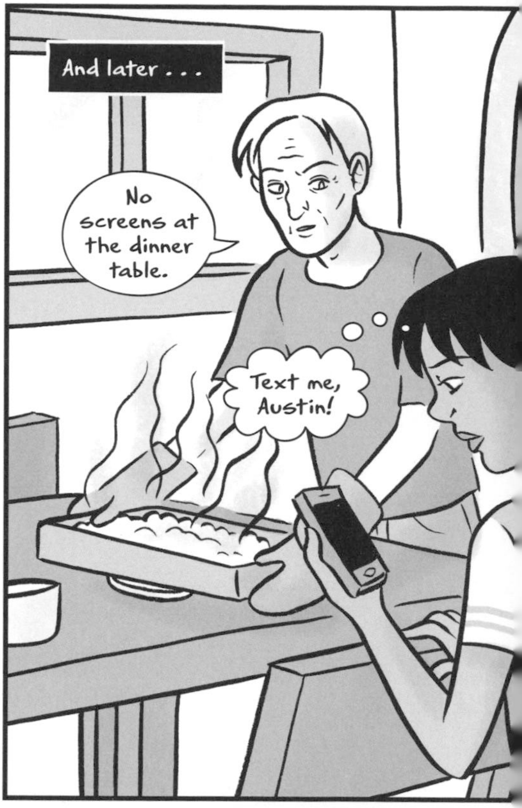
And later . . .
No screens at the dinner table.
Text me, Austin!

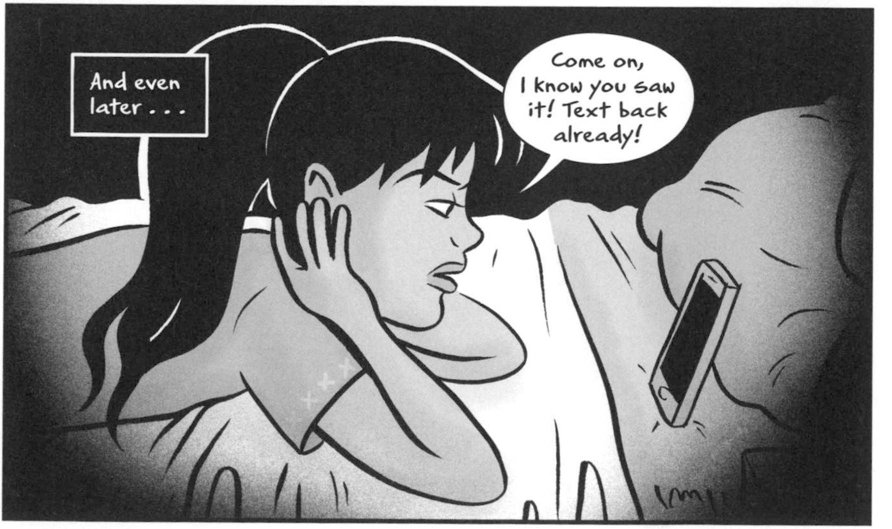
And even later . . .
Come on, I know you saw it! Text back already!

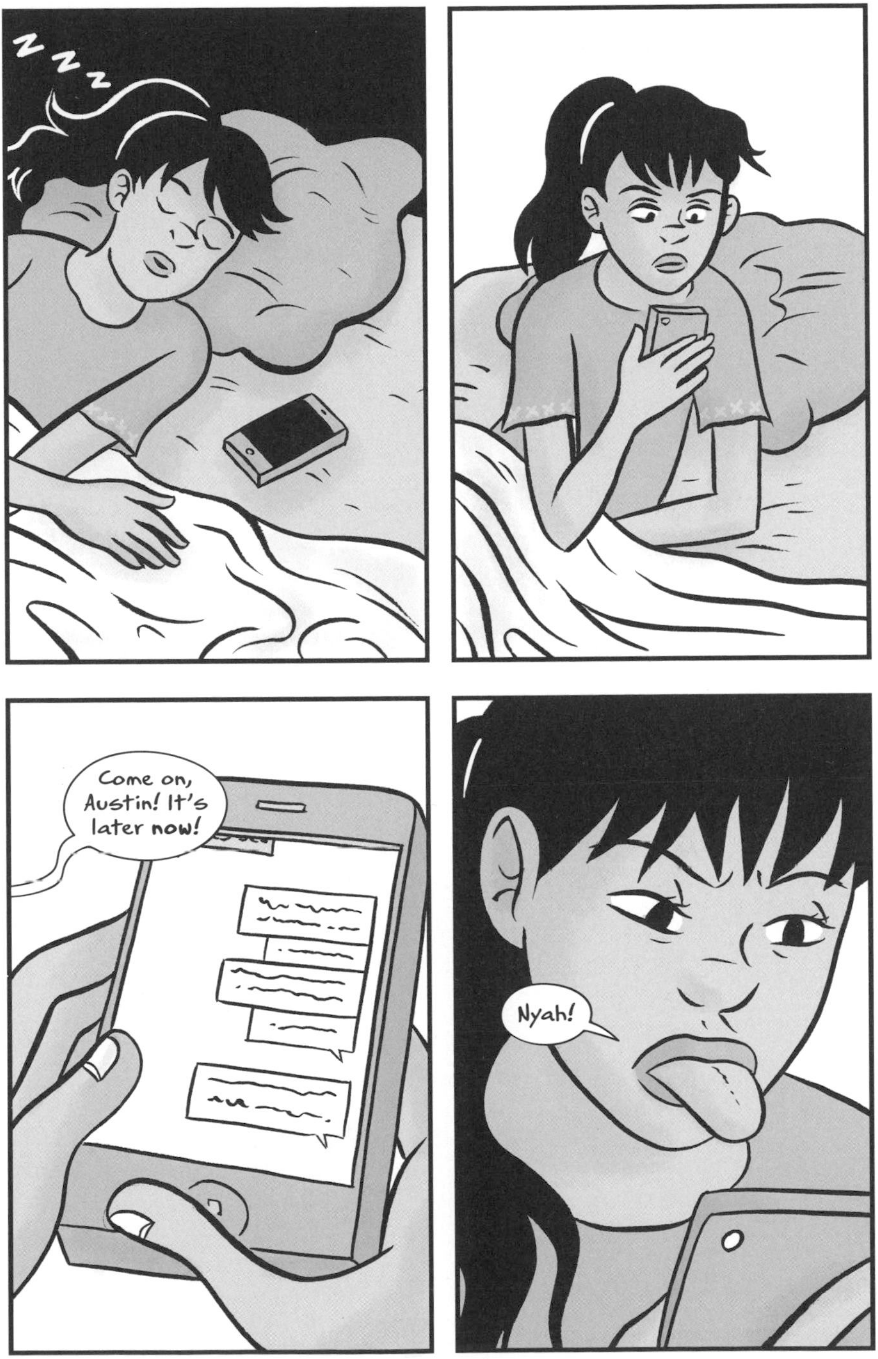
Z Z Z
Come on, Austin! It's later now!
Nyah!

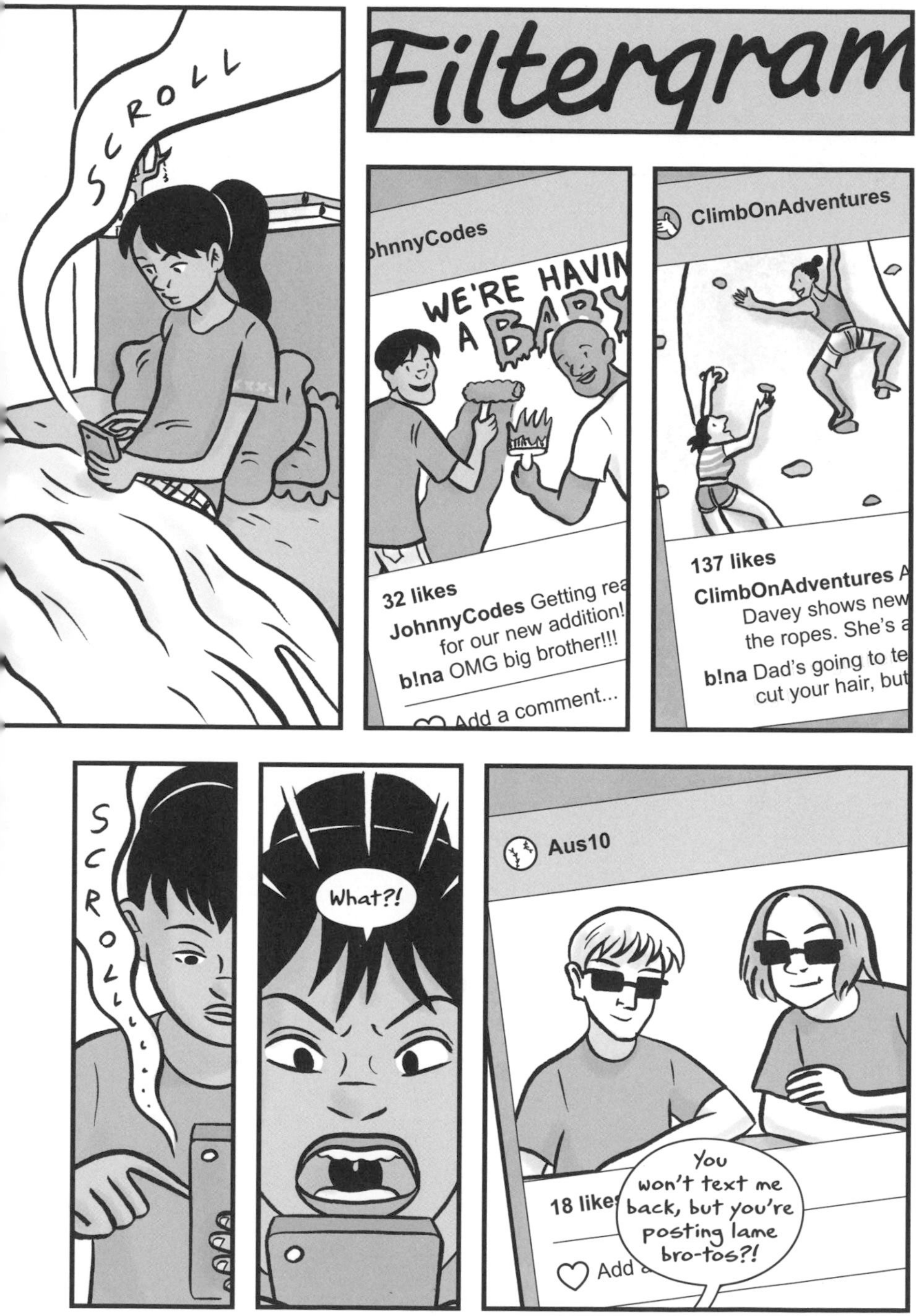
SCROLL
Filtergram
ohnnyCodes
WE'RE HAVIN
A BABY
32 likes
JohnnyCodes Getting rea
for our new addition!
b!na OMG big brother!!!
Add a comment...
ClimbOnAdventures
137 likes
ClimbOnAdventures A
Davey shows new
the ropes. She's a
b!na Dad's going to te
cut your hair, but
SCROLL...
What?!
Aus10
18 likes
Add a
You won't text me back, but you're posting lame bro-tos?!

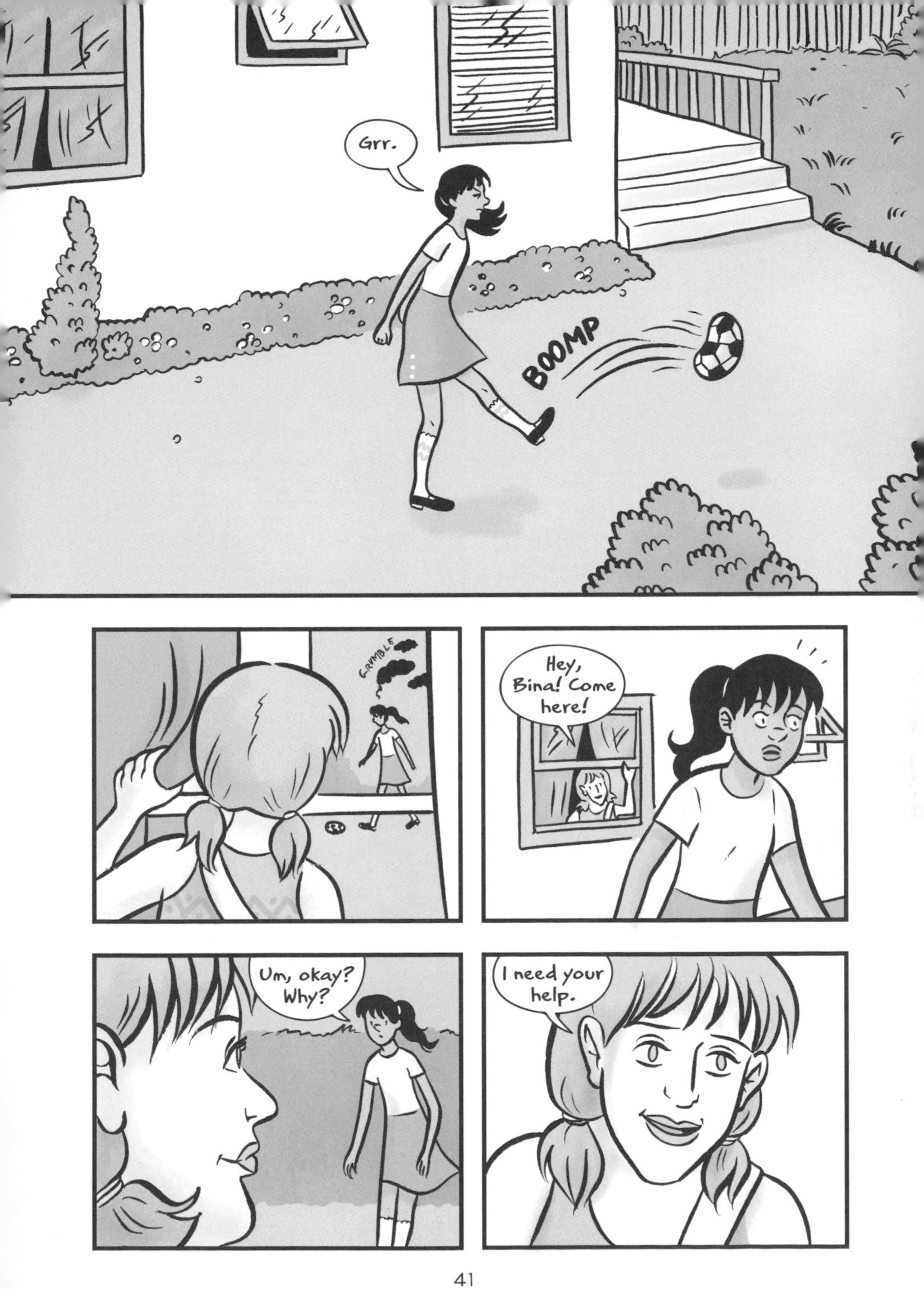
Grr.
BOOMP
GRUMBLE
Hey, Bina! Come here!
Um, okay? Why?
I need your help.

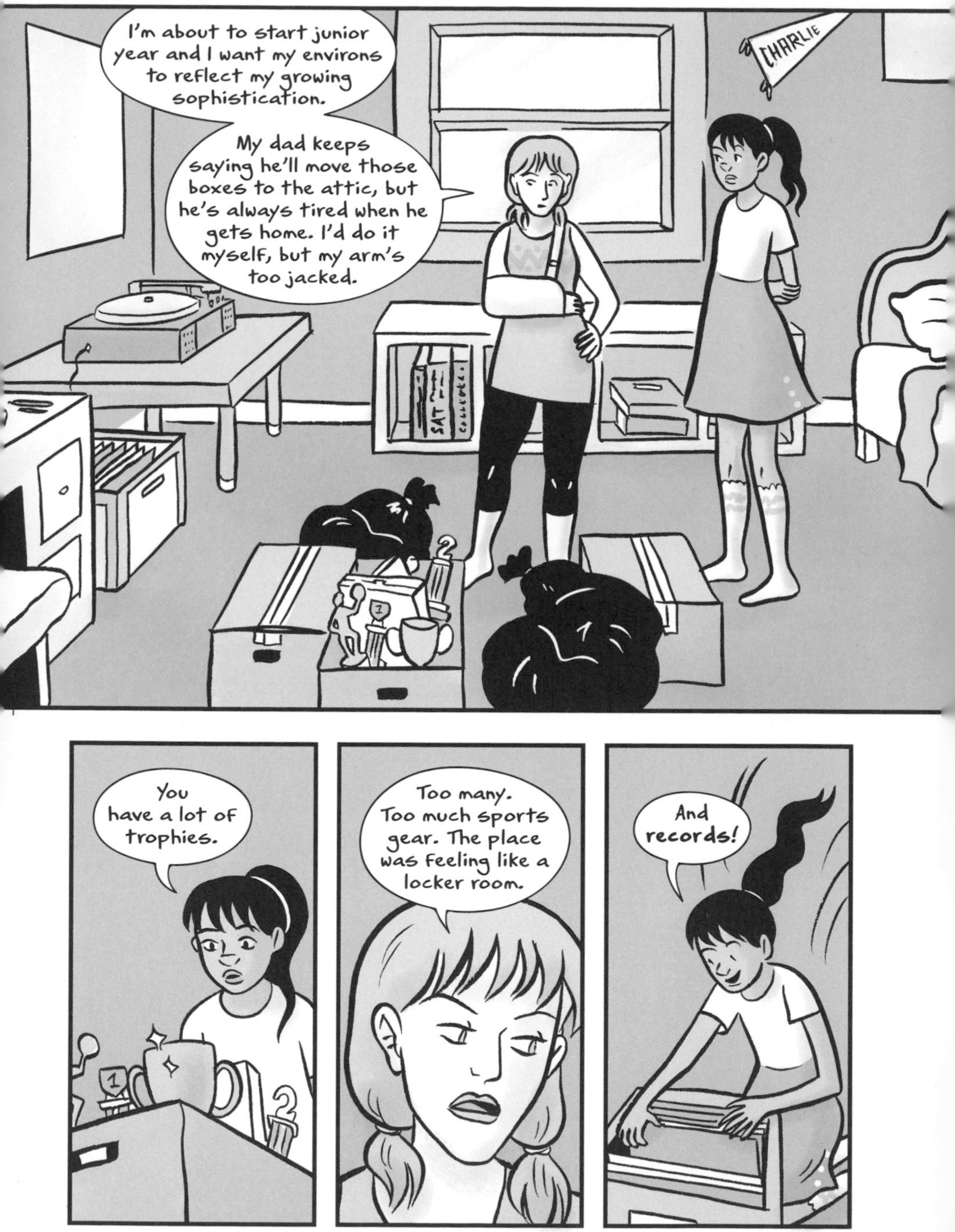

I'm about to start junior year and I want my environs to reflect my growing sophistication.
My dad keeps saying he'll move those boxes to the attic, but he's always tired when he gets home. I'd do it myself, but my arm's too jacked.
CHARLIE
SAT
COLLEGES
You have a lot of trophies.
Too many. Too much sports gear. The place was feeling like a locker room.
And records!

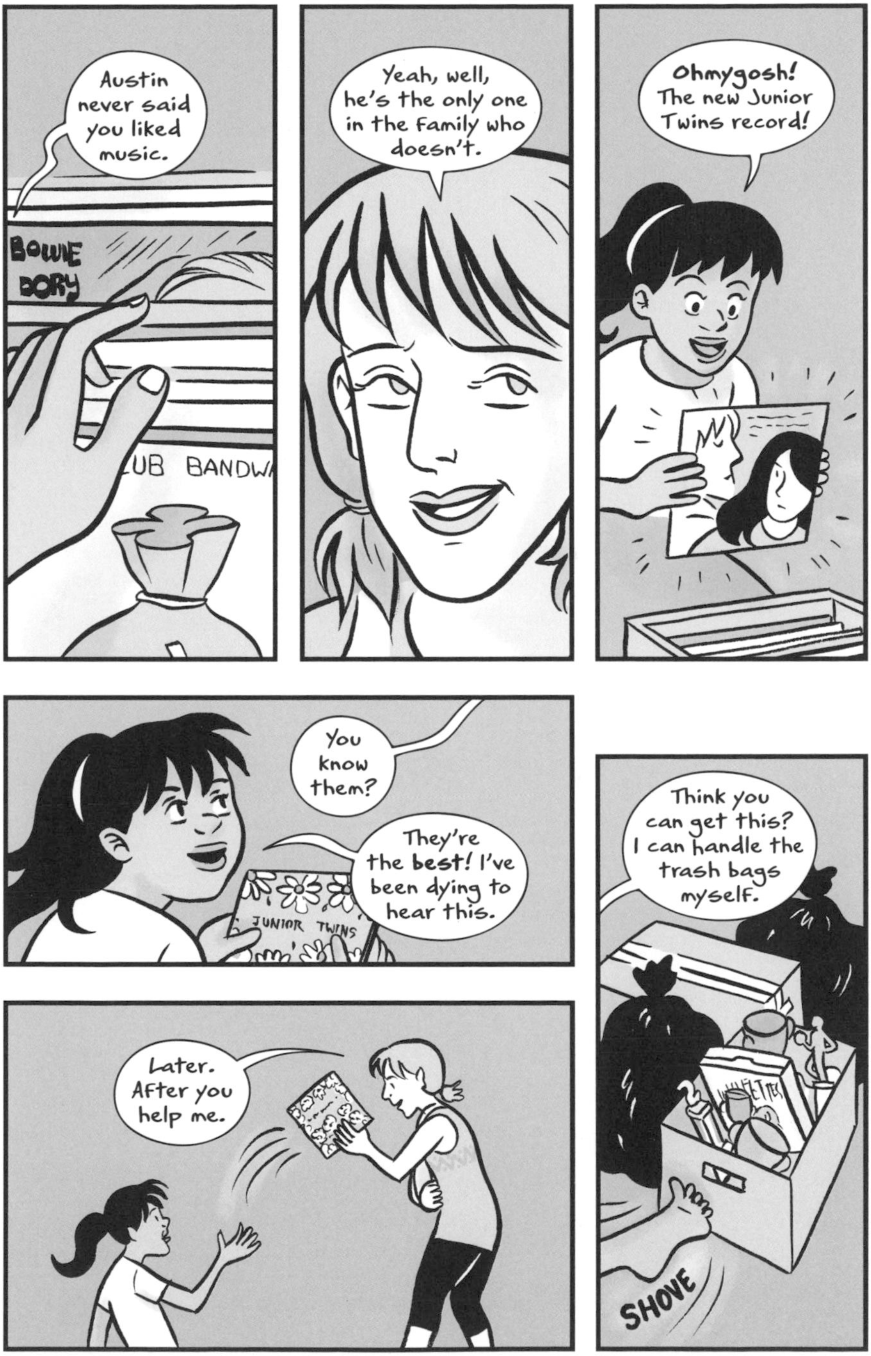
Austin never said you liked music.
BOWIE
BORY
UB BANDW
Yeah, well, he's the only one in the family who doesn't.
Ohmygosh! The new Junior Twins record!
You know them?
They're the **best**! I've been dying to hear this.
JUNIOR TWINS
Later. After you help me.
Think you can get this? I can handle the trash bags myself.
SHOVE

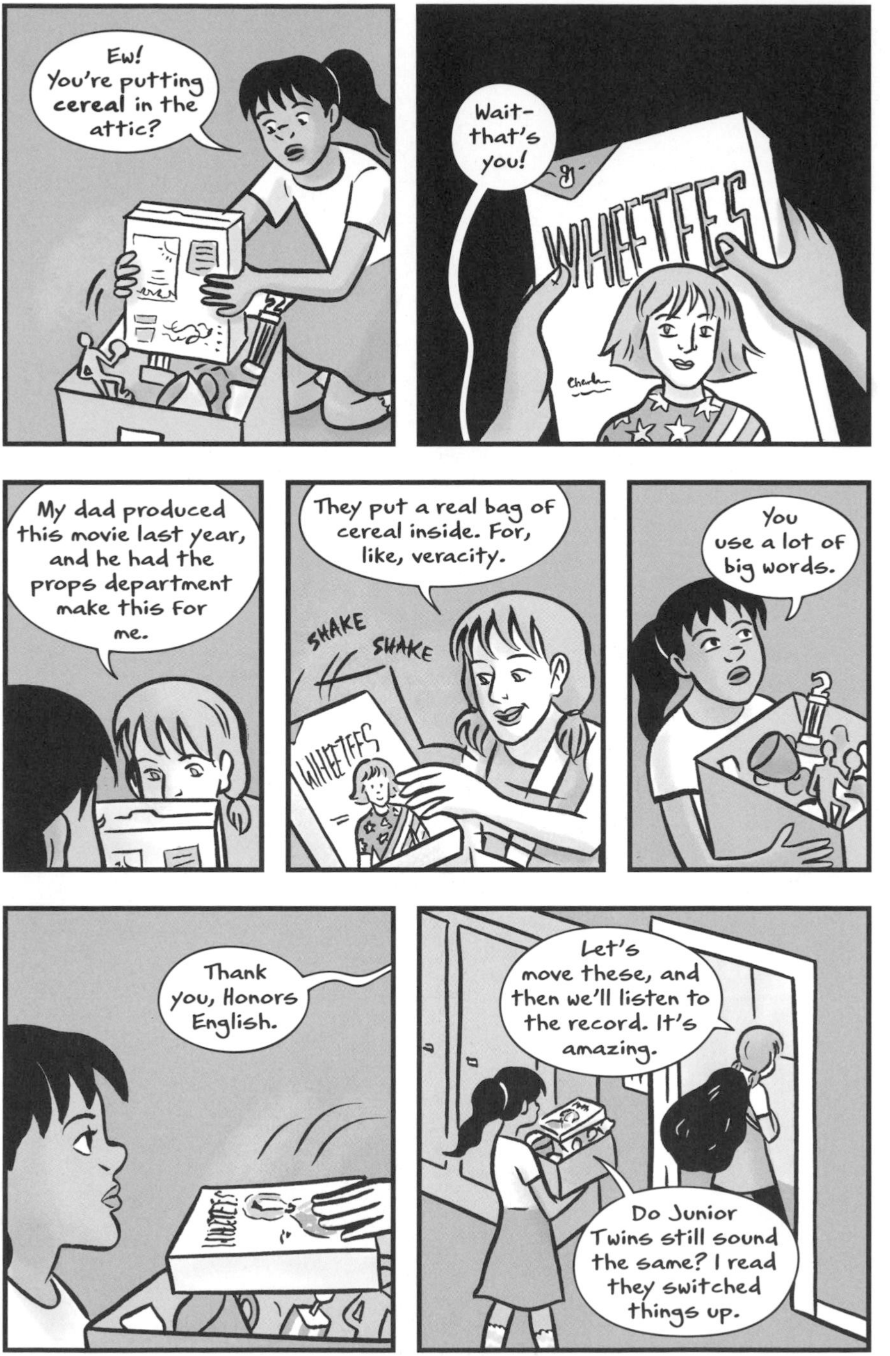

Ew! You're putting cereal in the attic?
Wait- that's you!
WHEETFES
My dad produced this movie last year, and he had the props department make this for me.
They put a real bag of cereal inside. For, like, veracity.
SHAKE
SHAKE
WHEETFES
You use a lot of big words.
Thank you, Honors English.
Let's move these, and then we'll listen to the record. It's amazing.
Do Junior Twins still sound the same? I read they switched things up.

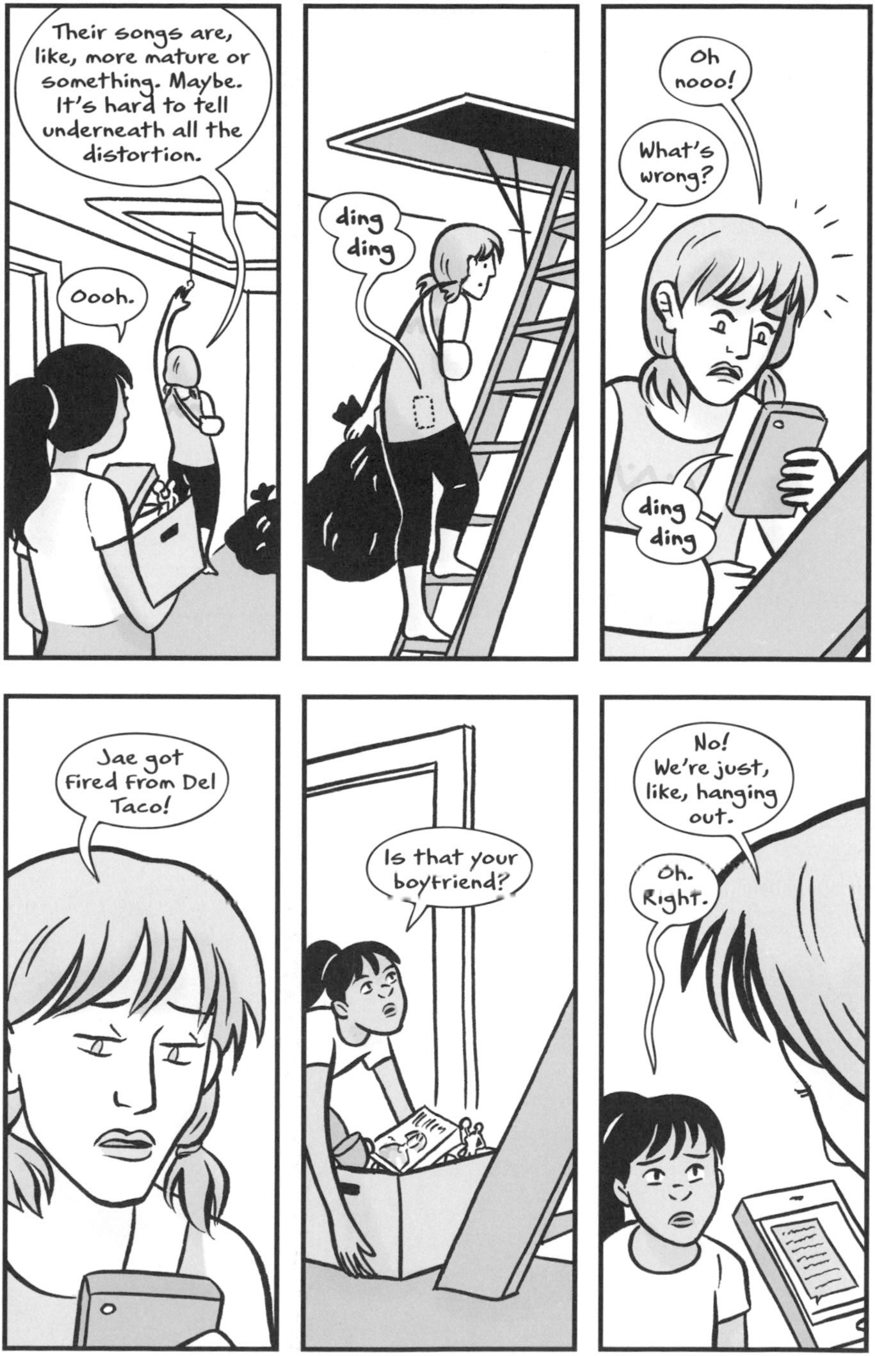
Their songs are, like, more mature or something. Maybe. It's hard to tell underneath all the distortion.
Oooh.
ding ding
Oh nooo!
What's wrong?
ding ding
Jae got fired from Del Taco!
Is that your boyfriend?
No! We're just, like, hanging out.
Oh. Right.

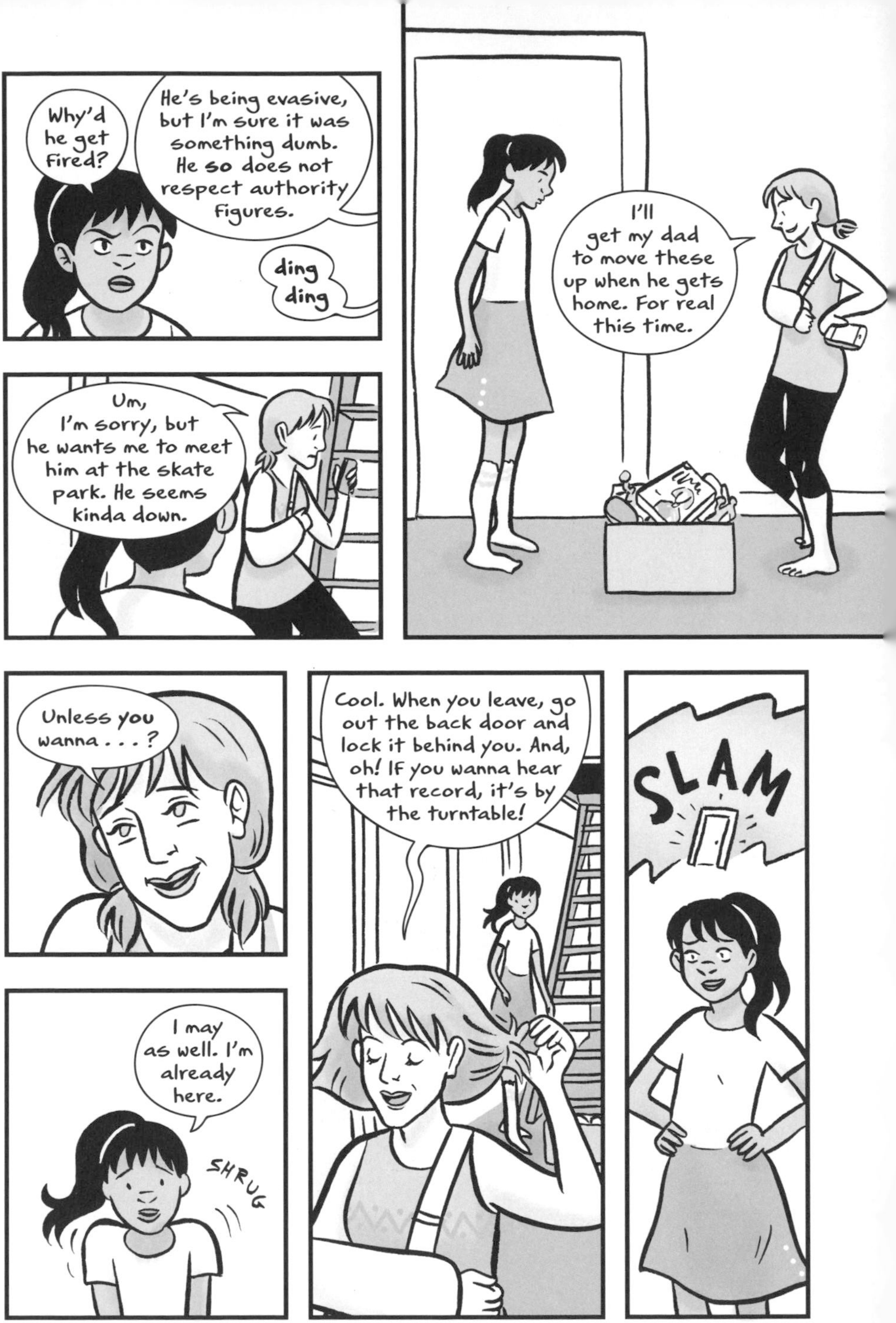
Why'd he get fired?
He's being evasive, but I'm sure it was something dumb. He so does not respect authority figures.
ding ding
Um, I'm sorry, but he wants me to meet him at the skate park. He seems kinda down.
I'll get my dad to move these up when he gets home. For real this time.
Unless you wanna . . . ?
I may as well. I'm already here.
SHRUG
Cool. When you leave, go out the back door and lock it behind you. And, oh! If you wanna hear that record, it's by the turntable!
SLAM

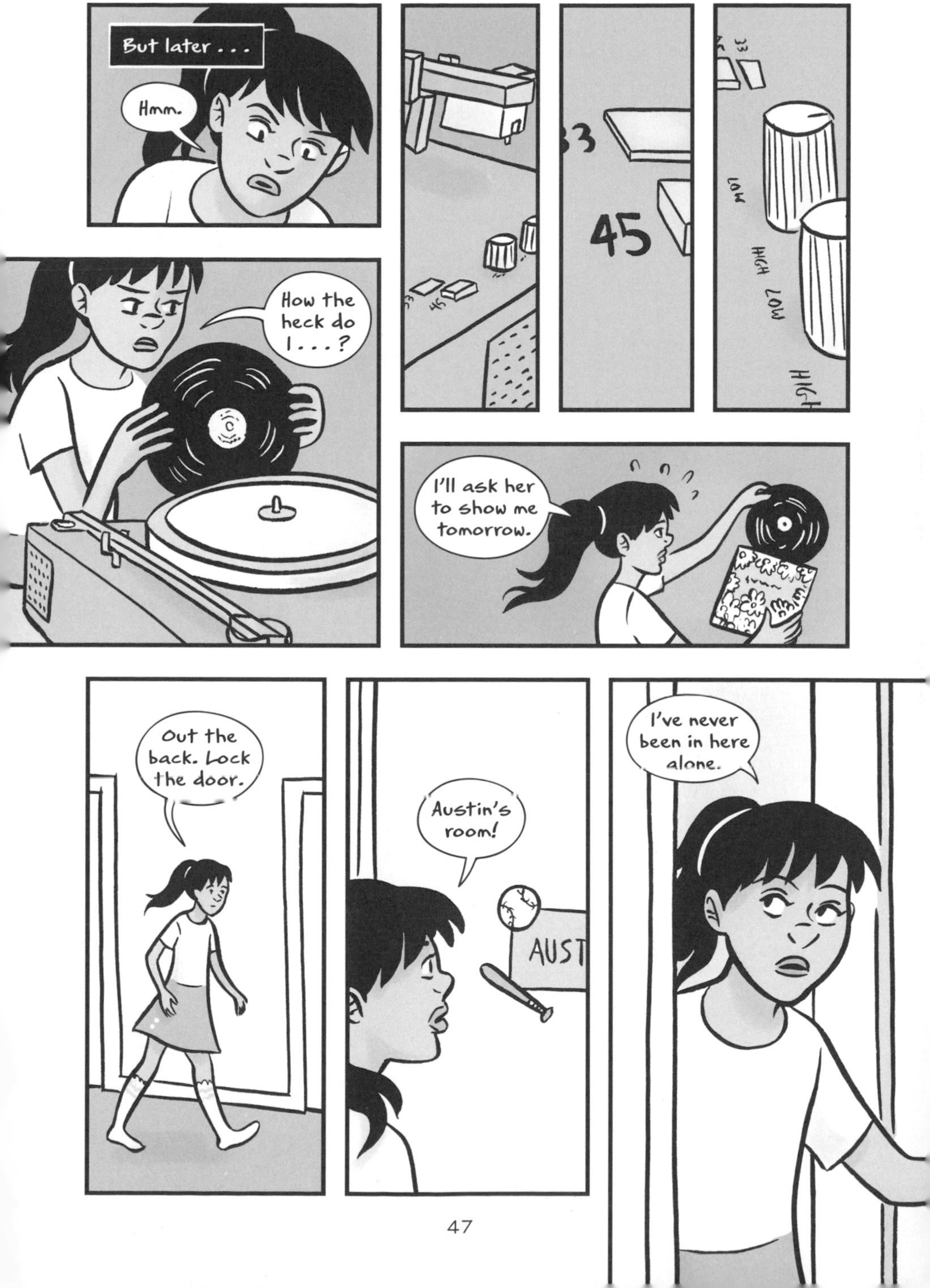
But later . . .
Hmm.
How the heck do I . . . ?
33
45
LOW
HIGH
LOW
HIGH
I'll ask her to show me tomorrow.
Out the back. Lock the door.
Austin's room!
AUST
I've never been in here alone.

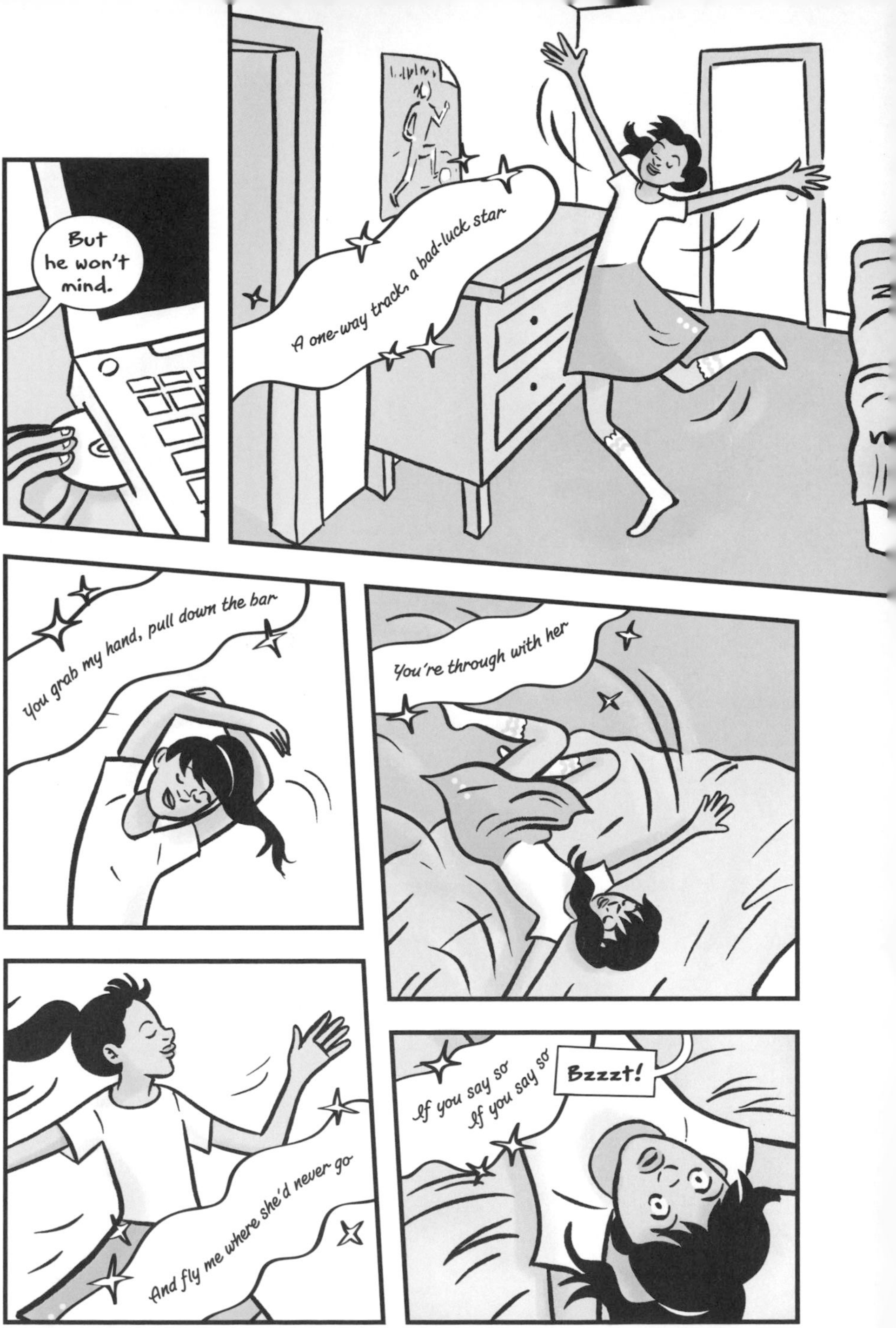
But he won't mind.
A one-way track, a bad-luck star
You grab my hand, pull down the bar
You're through with her
And fly me where she'd never go
If you say so
If you say so
Bzzzt!

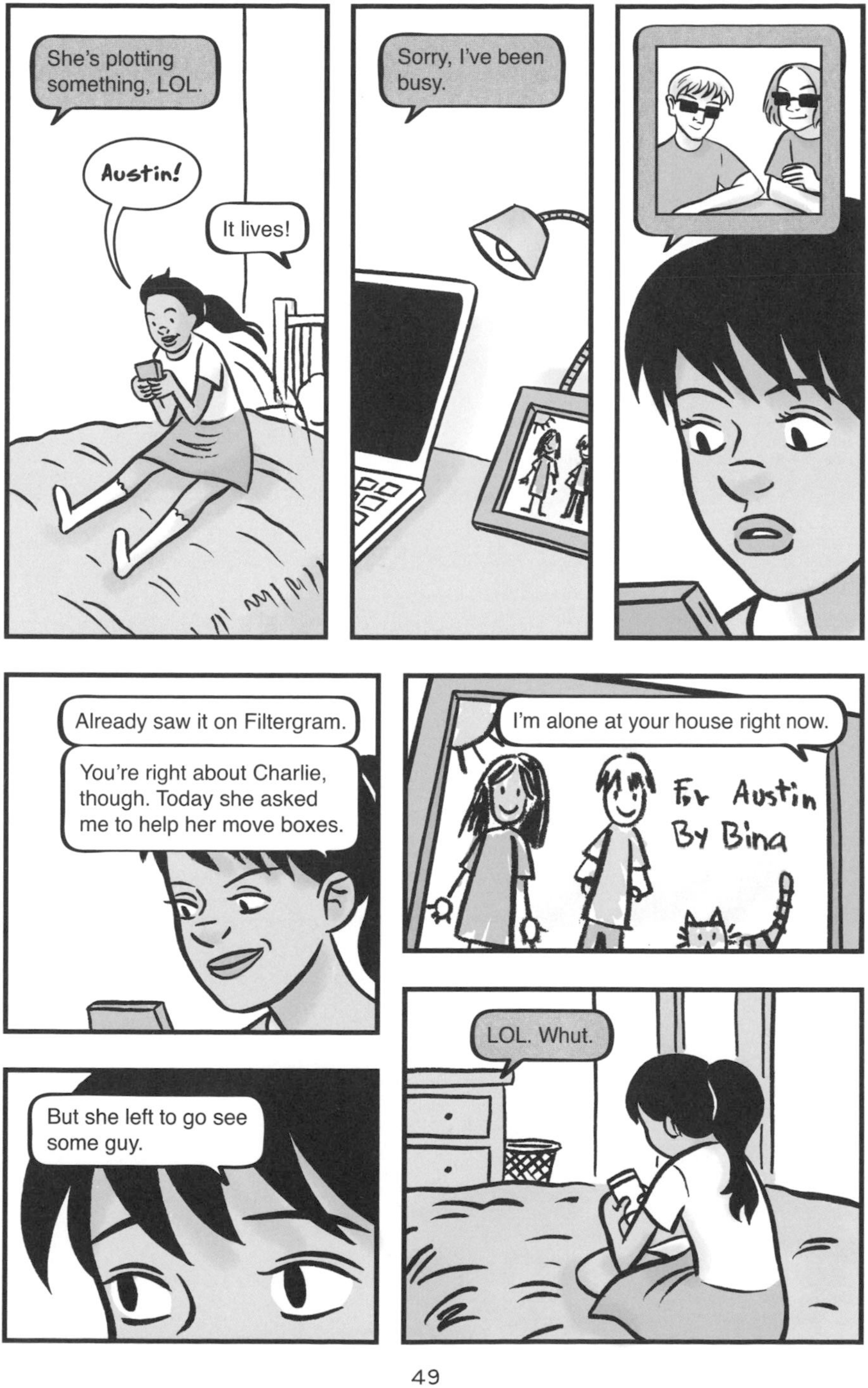

She's plotting something, LOL.
Austin!
It lives!
Sorry, I've been busy.
Already saw it on Filtergram.
You're right about Charlie, though. Today she asked me to help her move boxes.
I'm alone at your house right now.
For Austin
By Bina
But she left to go see some guy.
LOL. Whut.

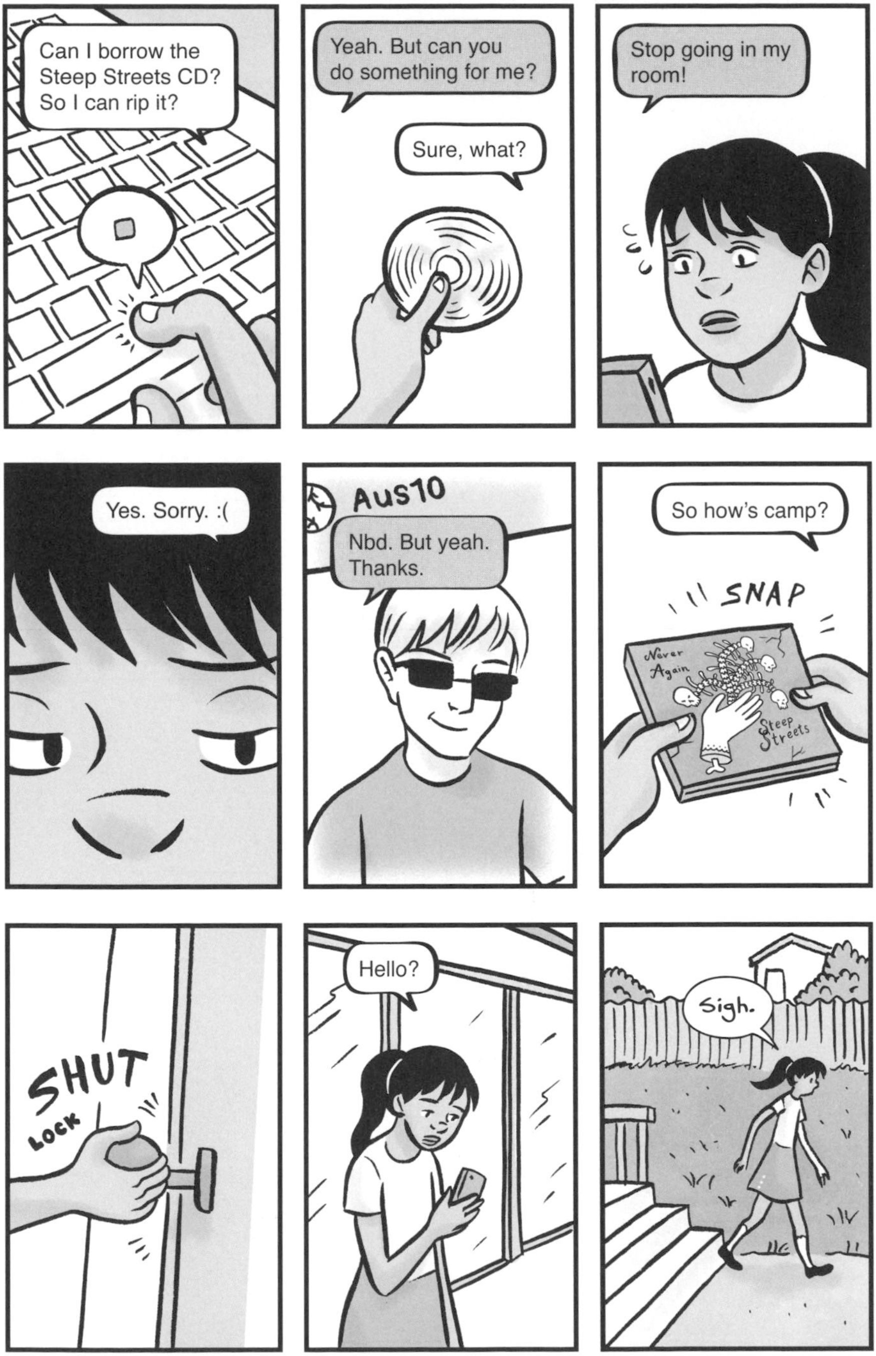
Can I borrow the Steep Streets CD? So I can rip it?
Yeah. But can you do something for me?
Sure, what?
Stop going in my room!
Yes. Sorry. :(
AUS10
Nbd. But yeah. Thanks.
So how's camp?
SNAP
Never Again
Steep Streets
SHUT
LOCK
Hello?
Sigh.

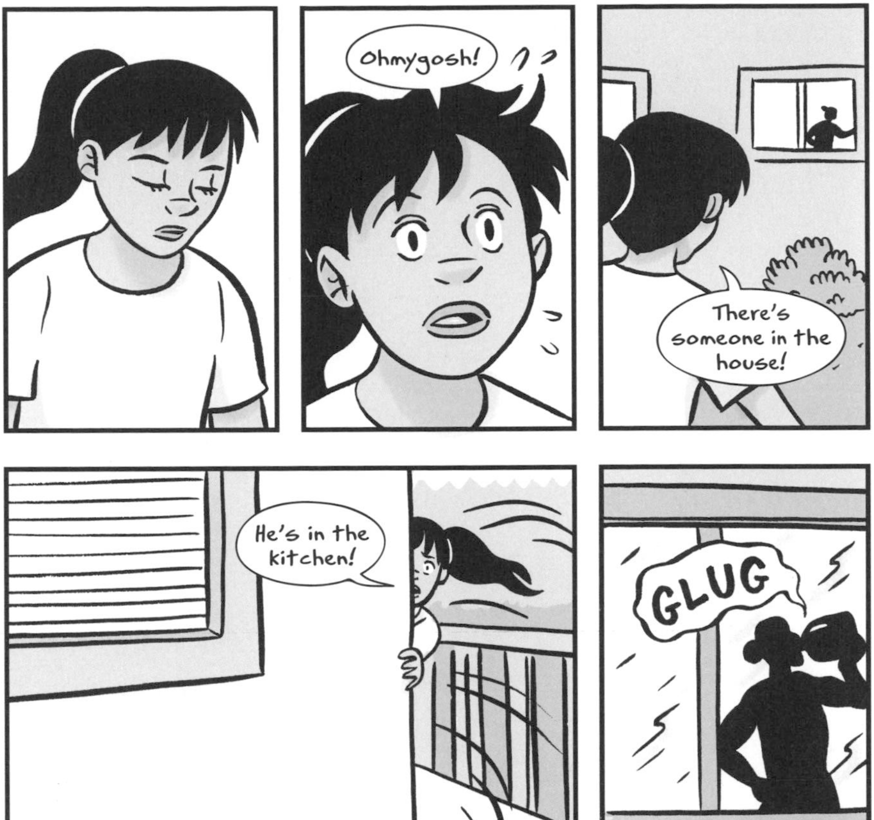
Ohmygosh!
There's someone in the house!
He's in the kitchen!
GLUG
No! Not my milk!
Hold on . . .
I know that stupid topknot!
GLU
GLU
GLU

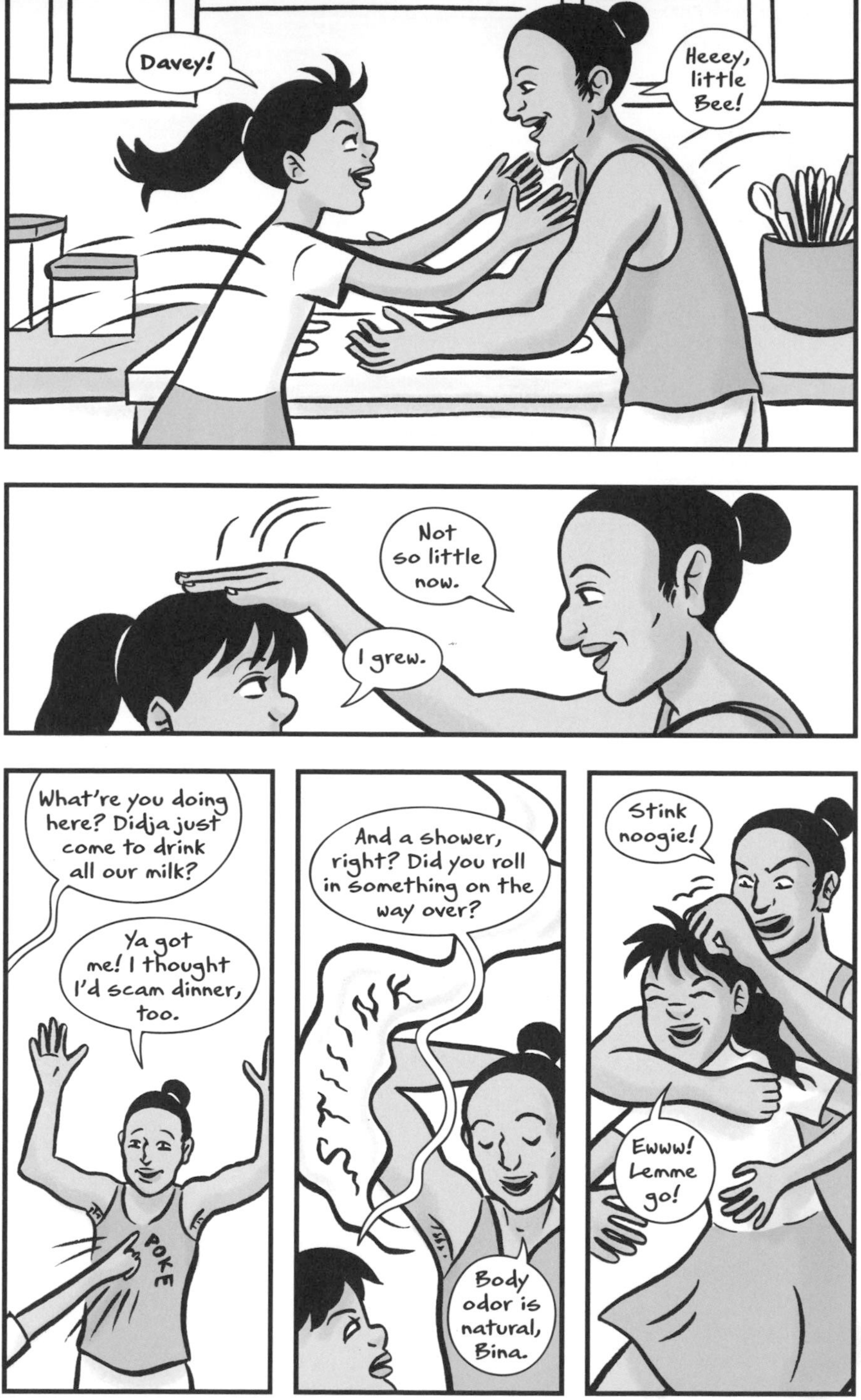
Davey!
Heeey, little Bee!
Not so little now.
I grew.
What're you doing here? Didja just come to drink all our milk?
Ya got me! I thought I'd scam dinner, too.
POKE
And a shower, right? Did you roll in something on the way over?
STIIINK
Body odor is natural, Bina.
Stink noogie!
Ewww! Lemme go!

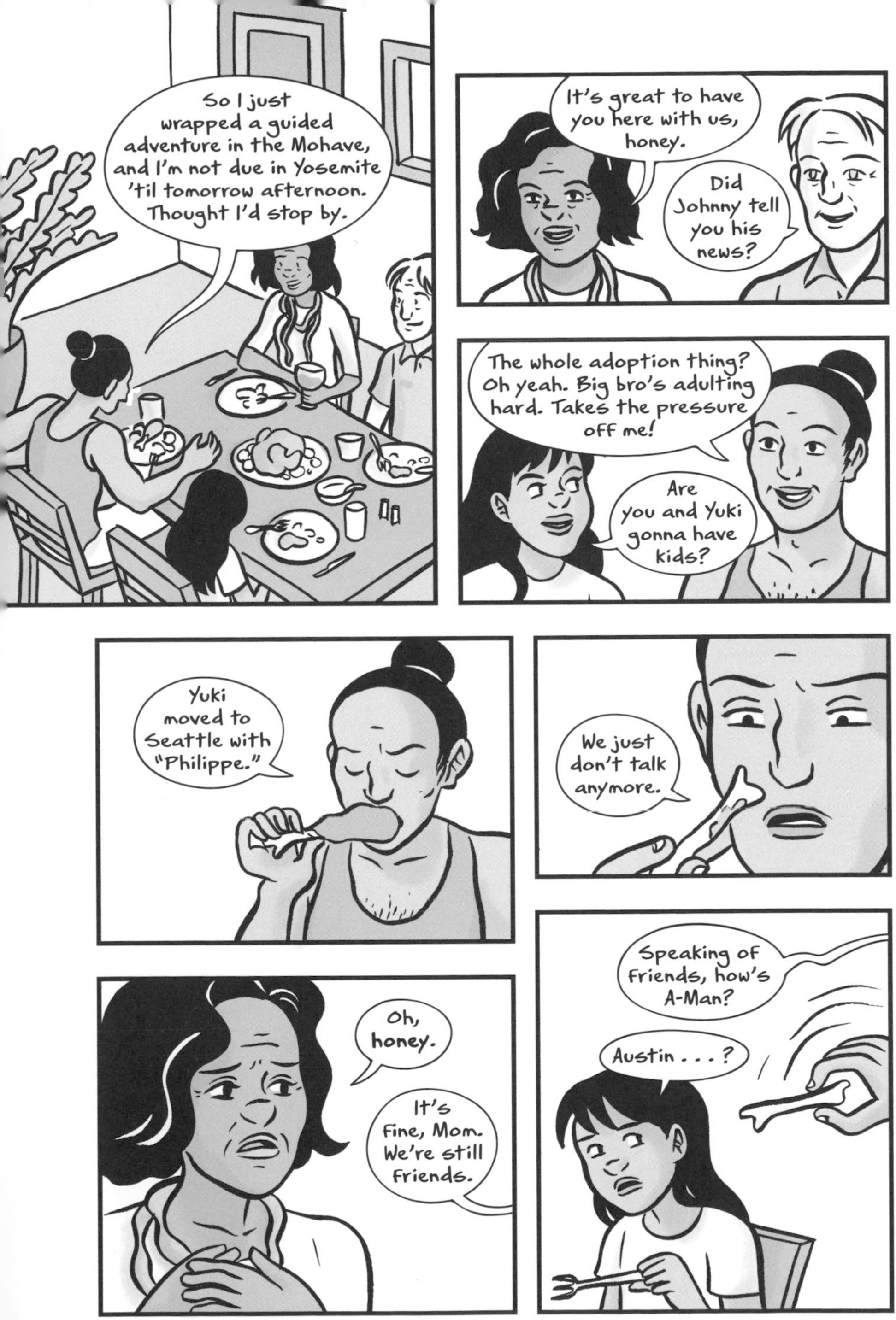
So I just wrapped a guided adventure in the Mohave, and I'm not due in Yosemite 'til tomorrow afternoon. Thought I'd stop by.
It's great to have you here with us, honey.
Did Johnny tell you his news?
The whole adoption thing? Oh yeah. Big bro's adulting hard. Takes the pressure off me!
Are you and Yuki gonna have kids?
Yuki moved to Seattle with "Philippe."
We just don't talk anymore.
Oh, honey.
It's fine, Mom. We're still friends.
Speaking of friends, how's A-Man?
Austin . . . ?

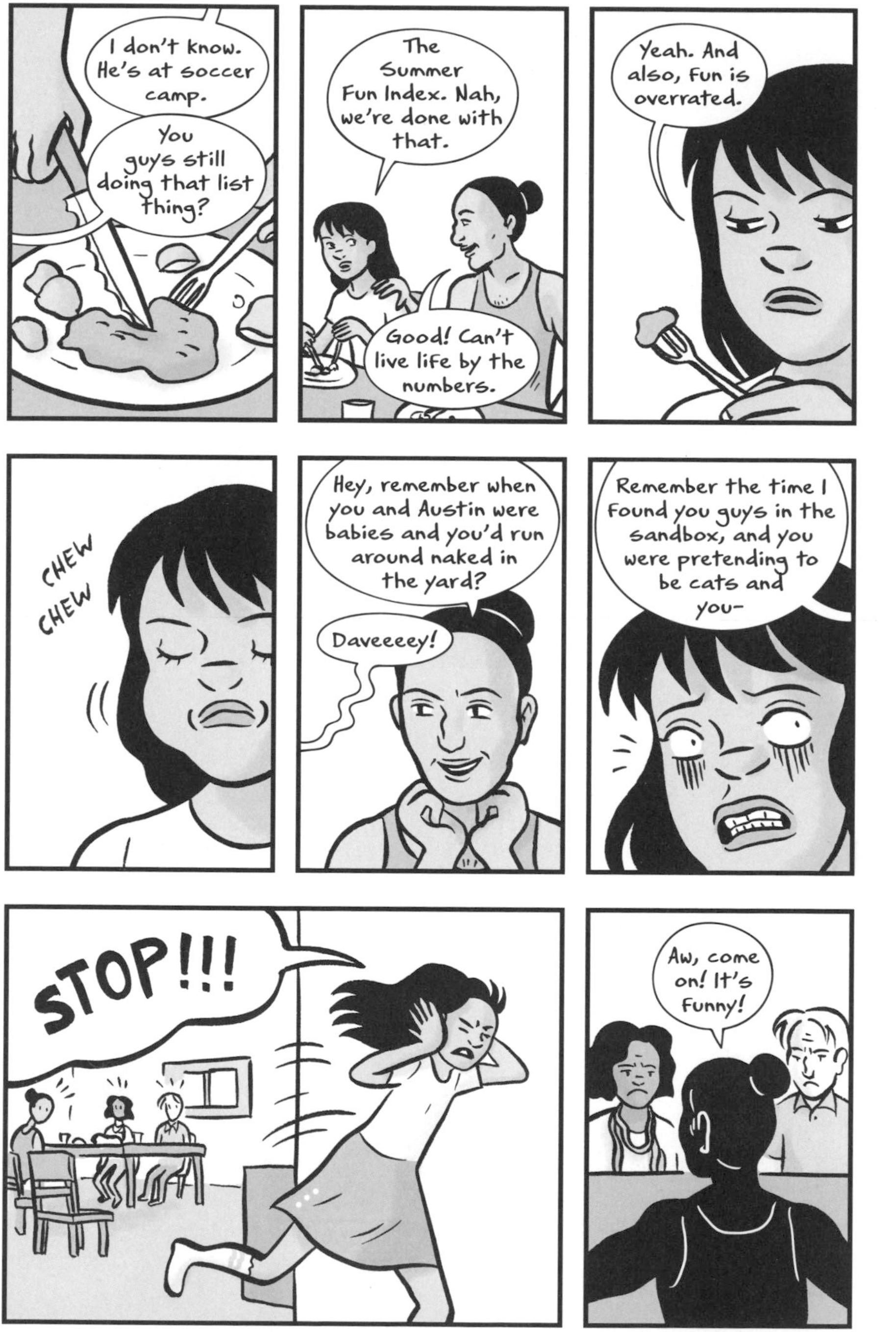
I don't know. He's at soccer camp.
You guys still doing that list thing?
The Summer Fun Index. Nah, we're done with that.
Good! Can't live life by the numbers.
Yeah. And also, Fun is overrated.
CHEW CHEW
Hey, remember when you and Austin were babies and you'd run around naked in the yard?
Daveeeey!
Remember the time I found you guys in the sandbox, and you were pretending to be cats and you-
STOP!!!
Aw, come on! It's funny!

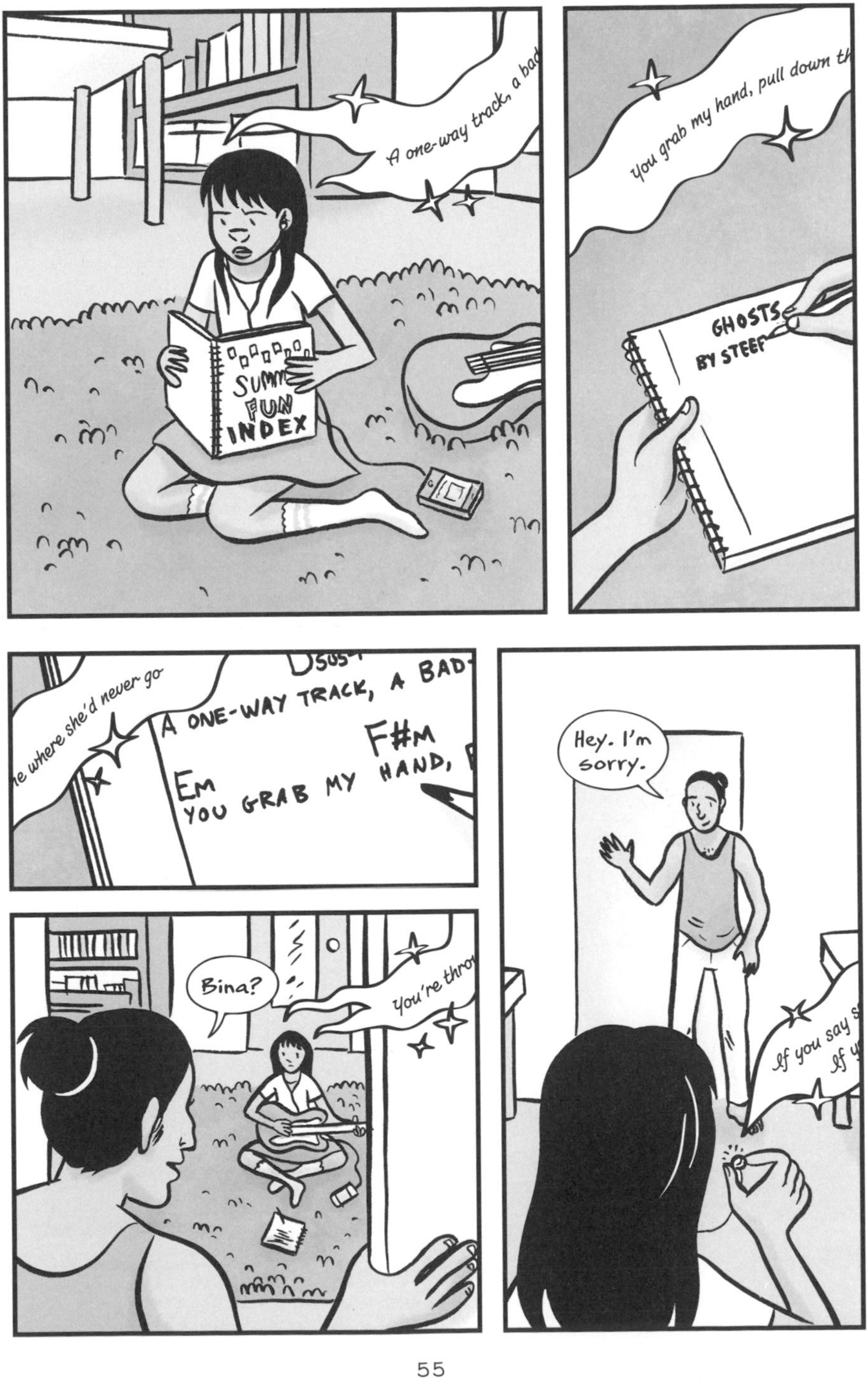
A one-way track, a bad
SUMM FUN INDEX
You grab my hand, pull down th
GHOSTS
BY STEEF
the where she'd never go
A ONE-WAY TRACK, A BAD-
F#M
EM
YOU GRAB MY HAND,
Hey. I'm sorry.
Bina?
You're thro
If you say s

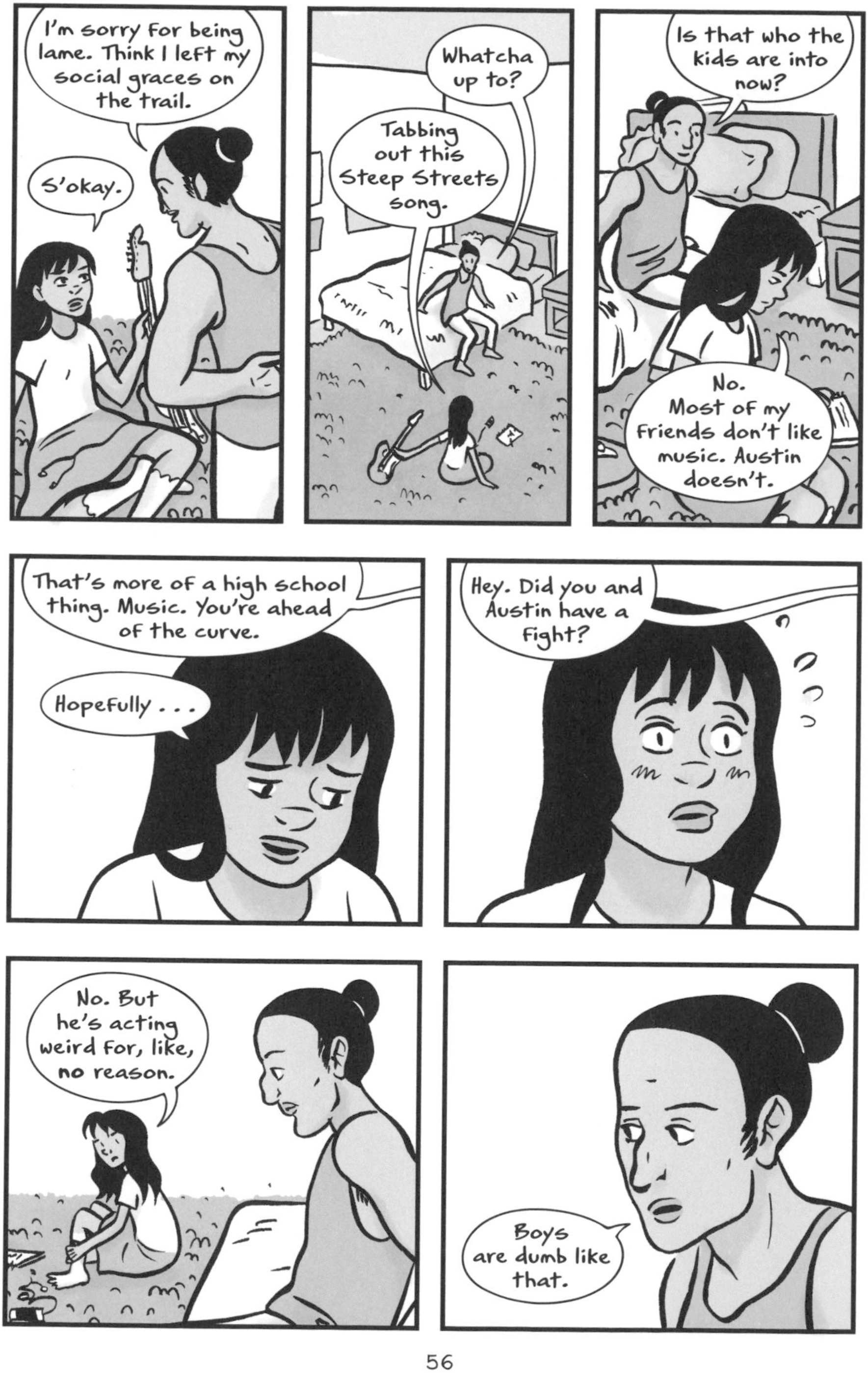

I'm sorry for being lame. Think I left my social graces on the trail.
S'okay.
Whatcha up to?
Tabbing out this Steep Streets song.
Is that who the kids are into now?
No. Most of my friends don't like music. Austin doesn't.
That's more of a high school thing. Music. You're ahead of the curve.
Hopefully . . .
Hey. Did you and Austin have a fight?
No. But he's acting weird for, like, no reason.
Boys are dumb like that.

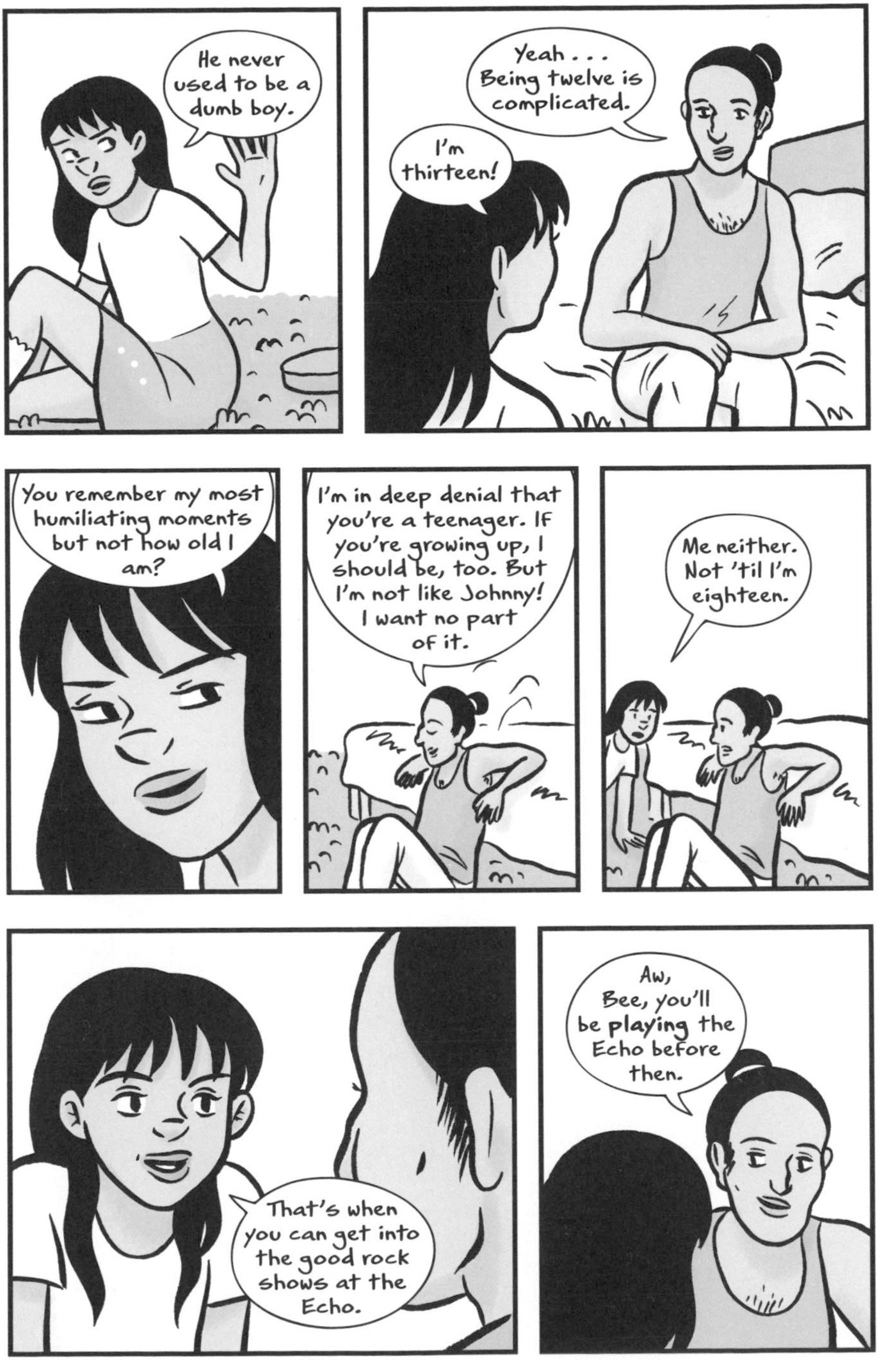
He never used to be a dumb boy.
Yeah . . . Being twelve is complicated.
I'm thirteen!
You remember my most humiliating moments but not how old I am?
I'm in deep denial that you're a teenager. If you're growing up, I should be, too. But I'm not like Johnny! I want no part of it.
Me neither. Not 'til I'm eighteen.
That's when you can get into the good rock shows at the Echo.
Aw, Bee, you'll be playing the Echo before then.

Week Three

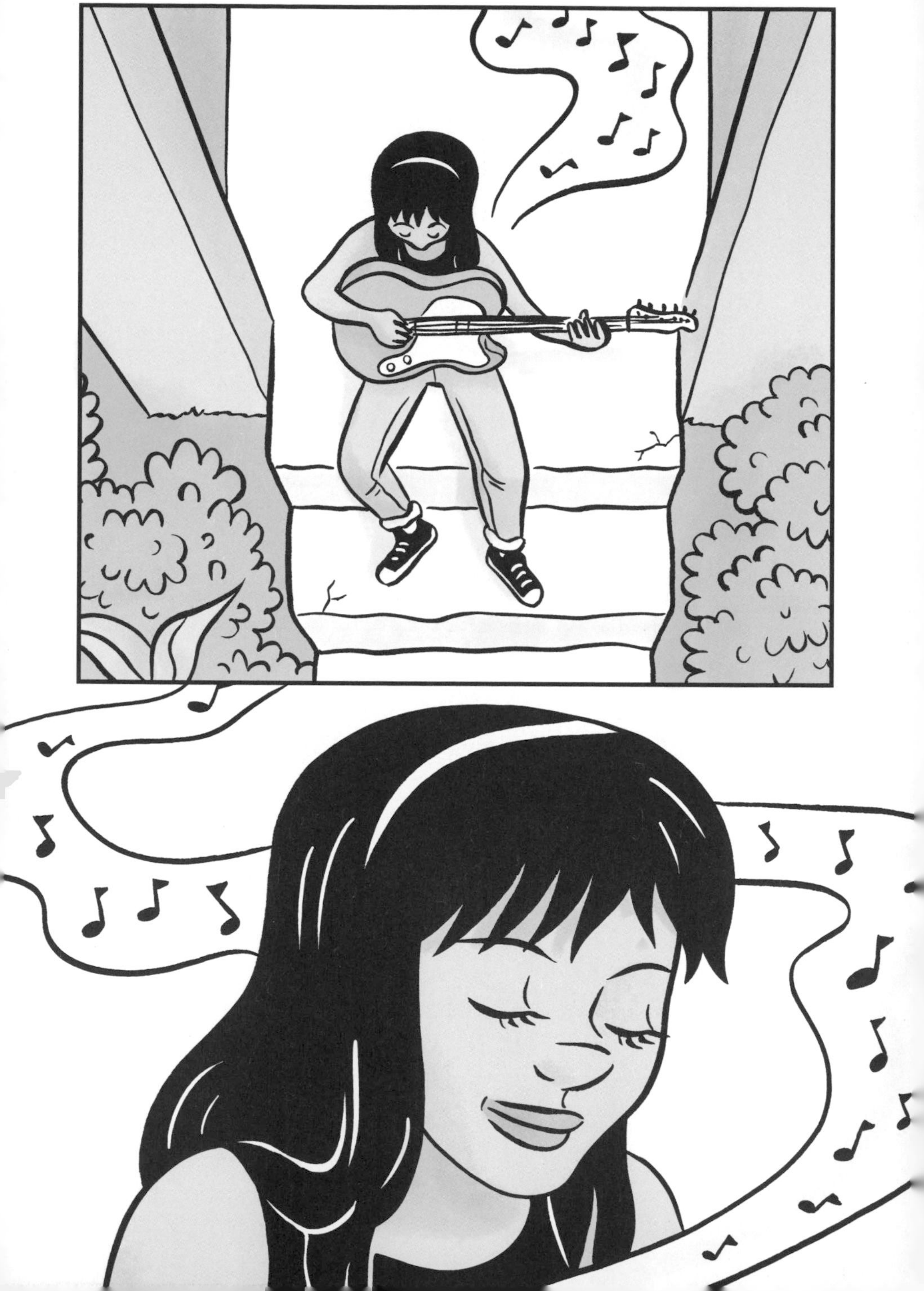

61

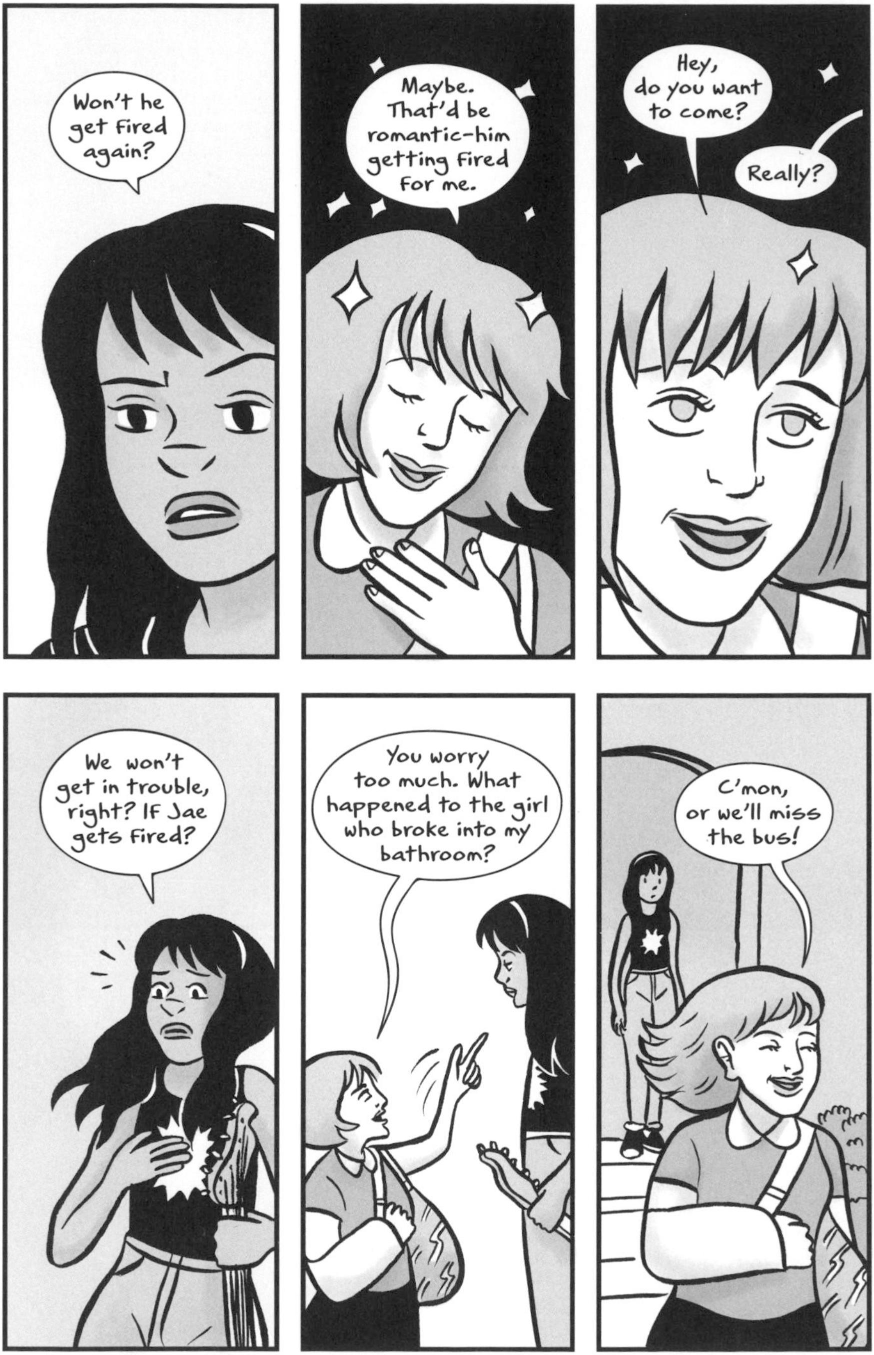
Won't he get fired again?
Maybe. That'd be romantic—him getting fired for me.
Hey, do you want to come?
Really?
We won't get in trouble, right? If Jae gets fired?
You worry too much. What happened to the girl who broke into my bathroom?
C'mon, or we'll miss the bus!

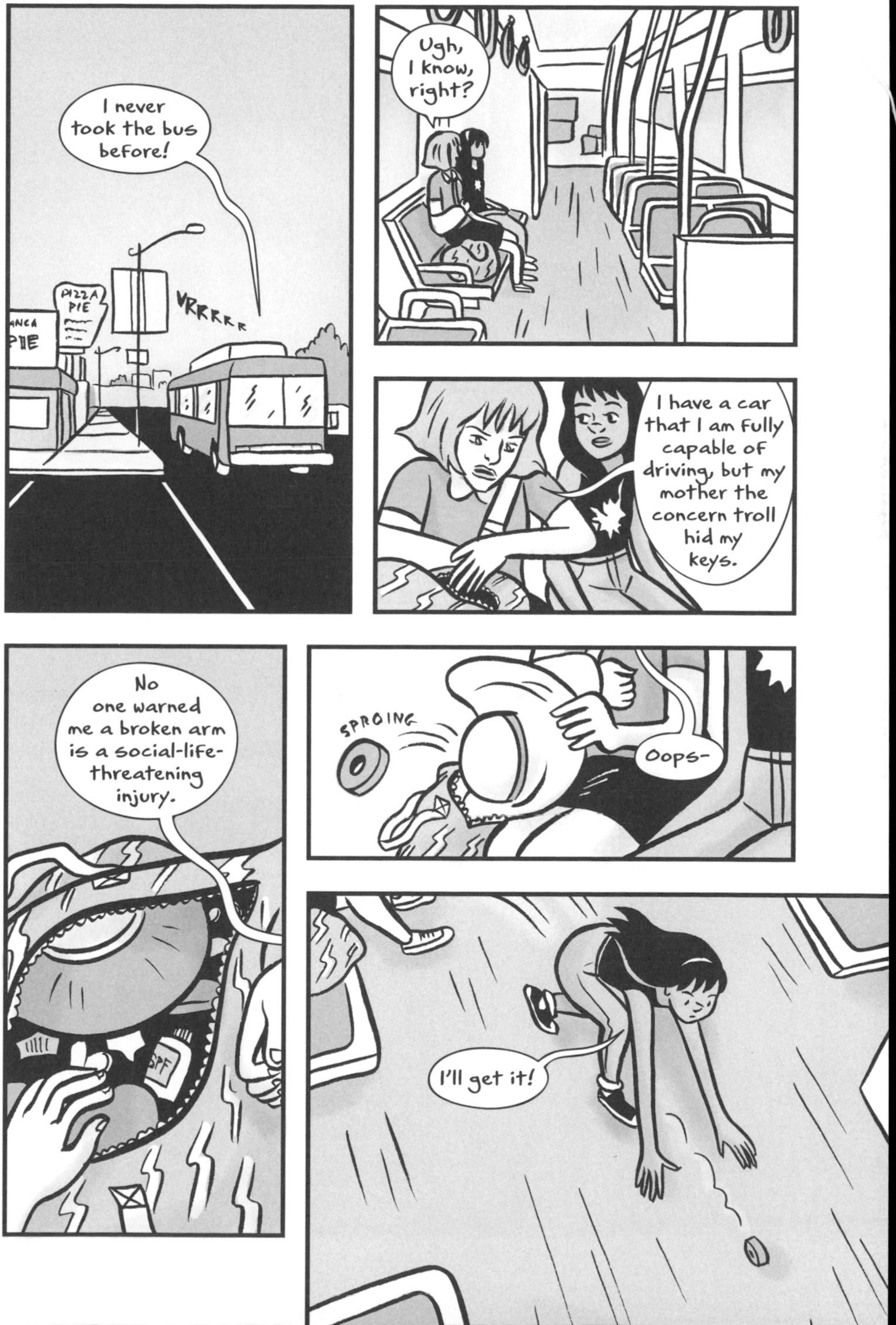
I never took the bus before!
PIZZA PIE
VRRRRRR
Ugh, I know, right?
I have a car that I am fully capable of driving, but my mother the concern troll hid my keys.
No one warned me a broken arm is a social-life-threatening injury.
SPROING
Oops-
SPF
I'll get it!

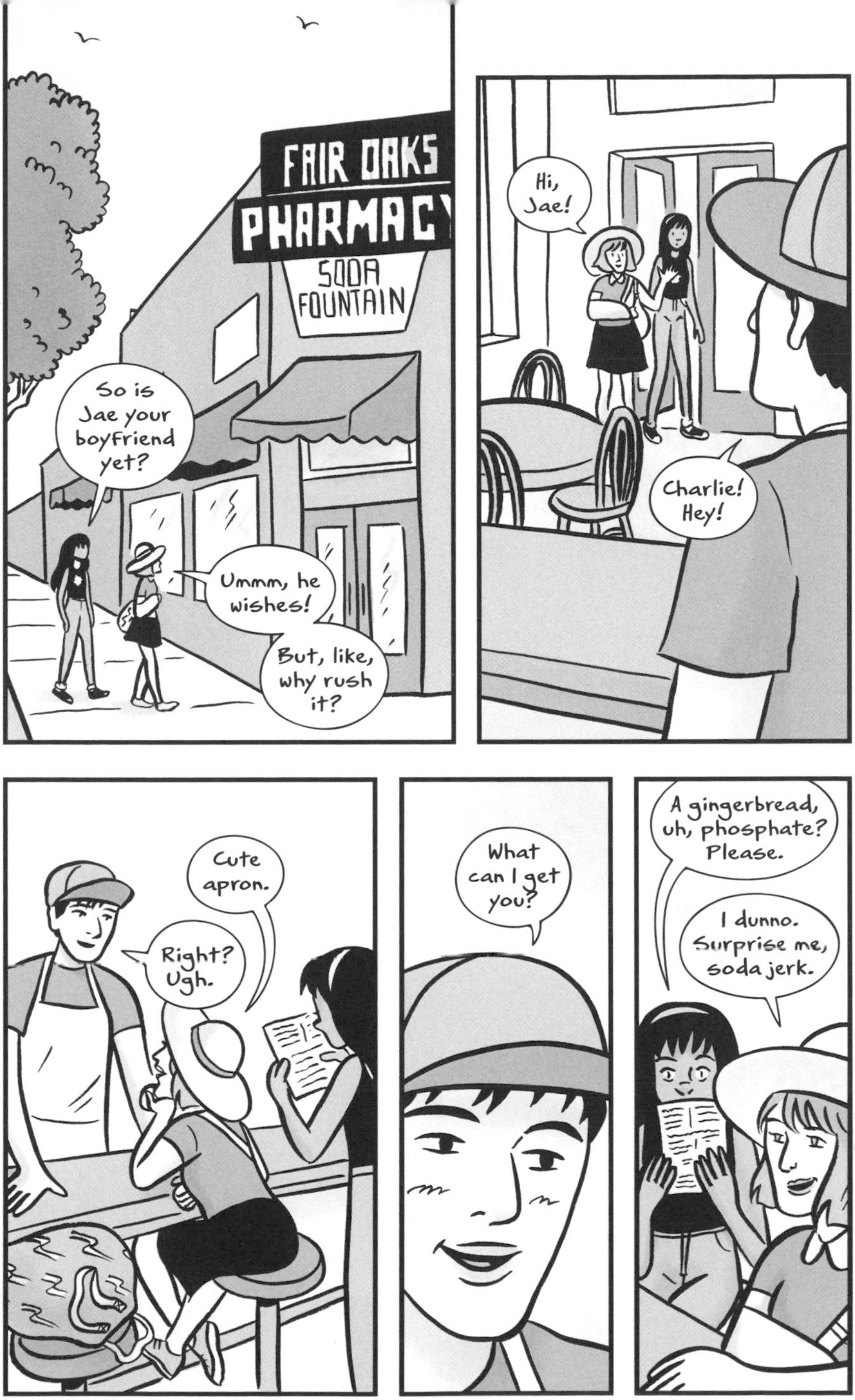
FAIR OAKS
PHARMACY
SODA FOUNTAIN
So is Jae your boyfriend yet?
Ummm, he wishes!
But, like, why rush it?
Hi, Jae!
Charlie! Hey!
Cute apron.
Right? Ugh.
What can I get you?
A gingerbread, uh, phosphate? Please.
I dunno. Surprise me, soda jerk.

69

72

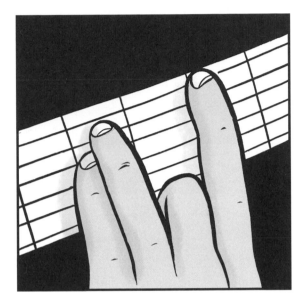

Week Four

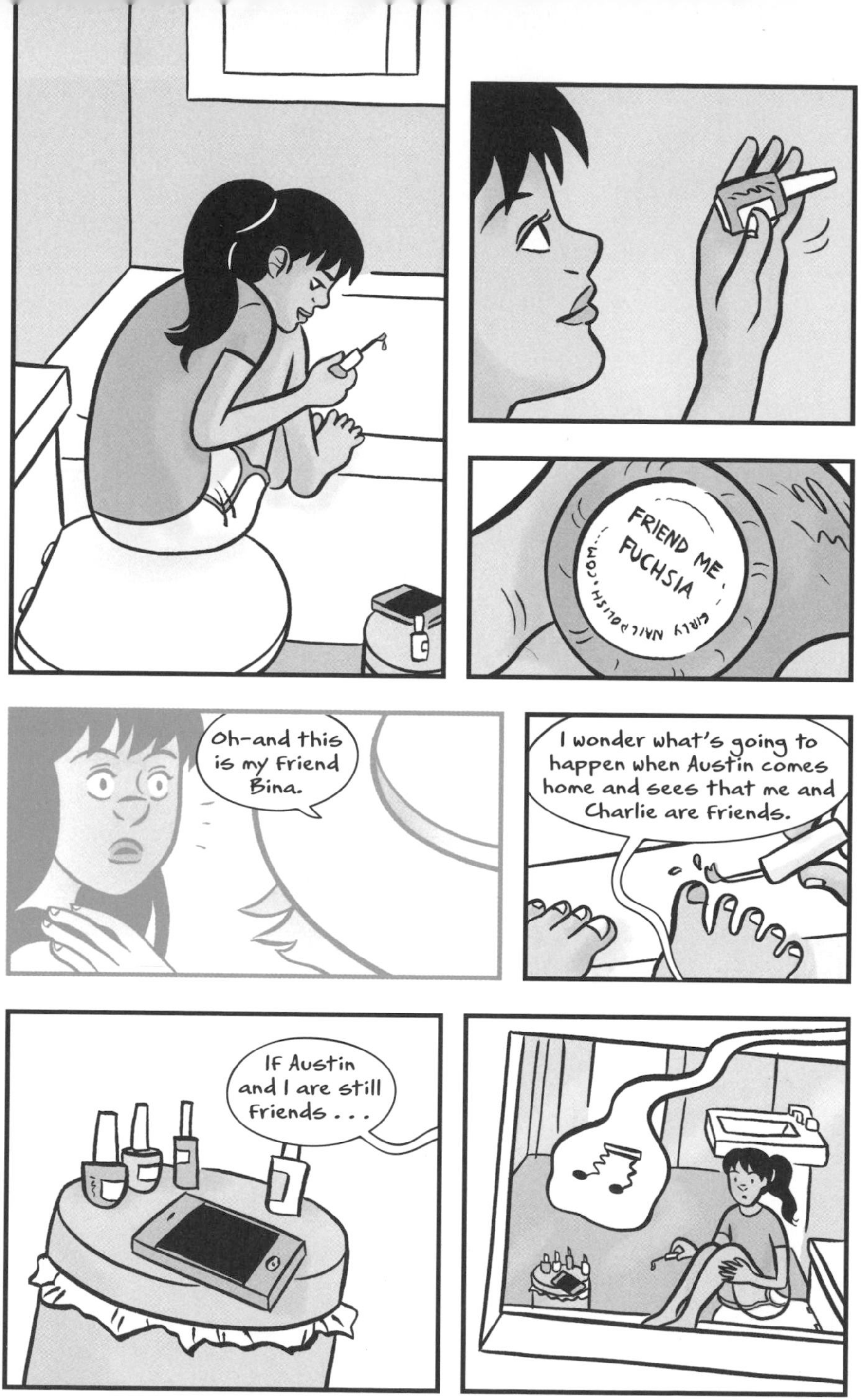
FRIEND ME FUCHSIA
GIRLY NAIL POLISH.COM
Oh-and this is my friend Bina.
I wonder what's going to happen when Austin comes home and sees that me and Charlie are friends.
If Austin and I are still friends . . .

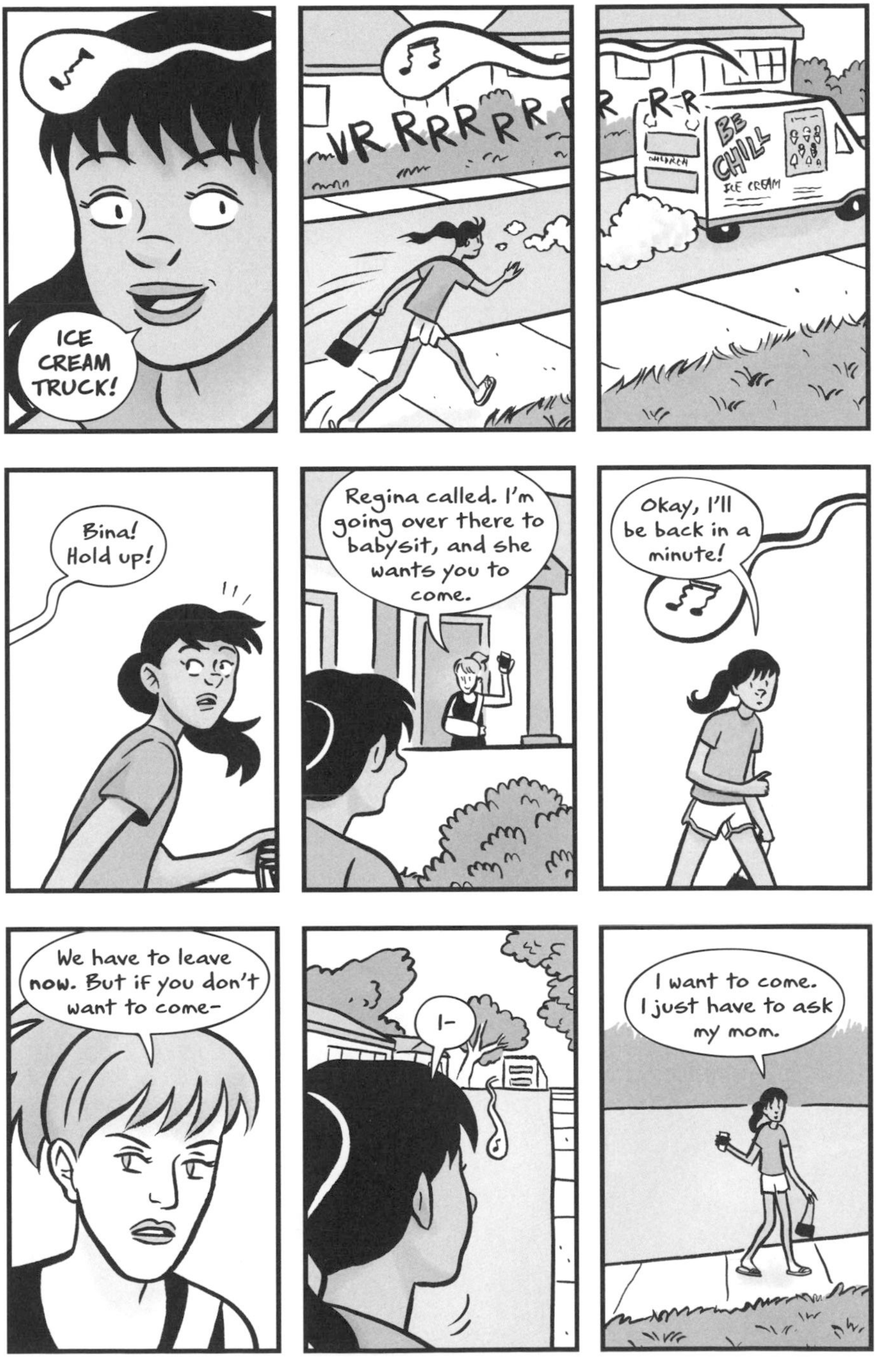
ICE CREAM TRUCK!
VRRRRRRRR-R-R
BE CHILL ICE CREAM
CHILDREN
Bina! Hold up!
Regina called. I'm going over there to babysit, and she wants you to come.
Okay, I'll be back in a minute!
We have to leave now. But if you don't want to come-
I-
I want to come. I just have to ask my mom.

78

79

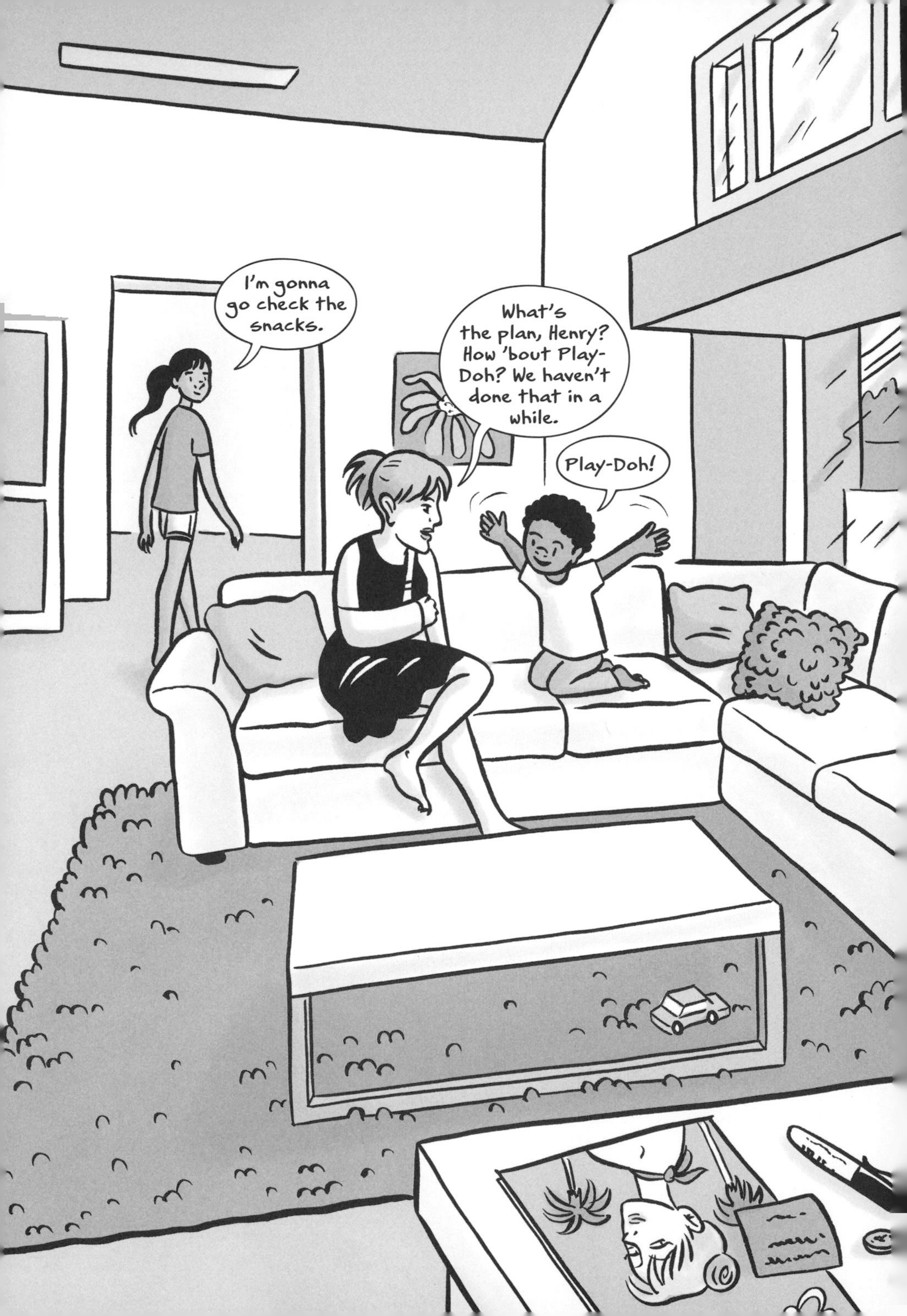
I'm gonna go check the snacks.
What's the plan, Henry? How 'bout Play-Doh? We haven't done that in a while.
Play-Doh!

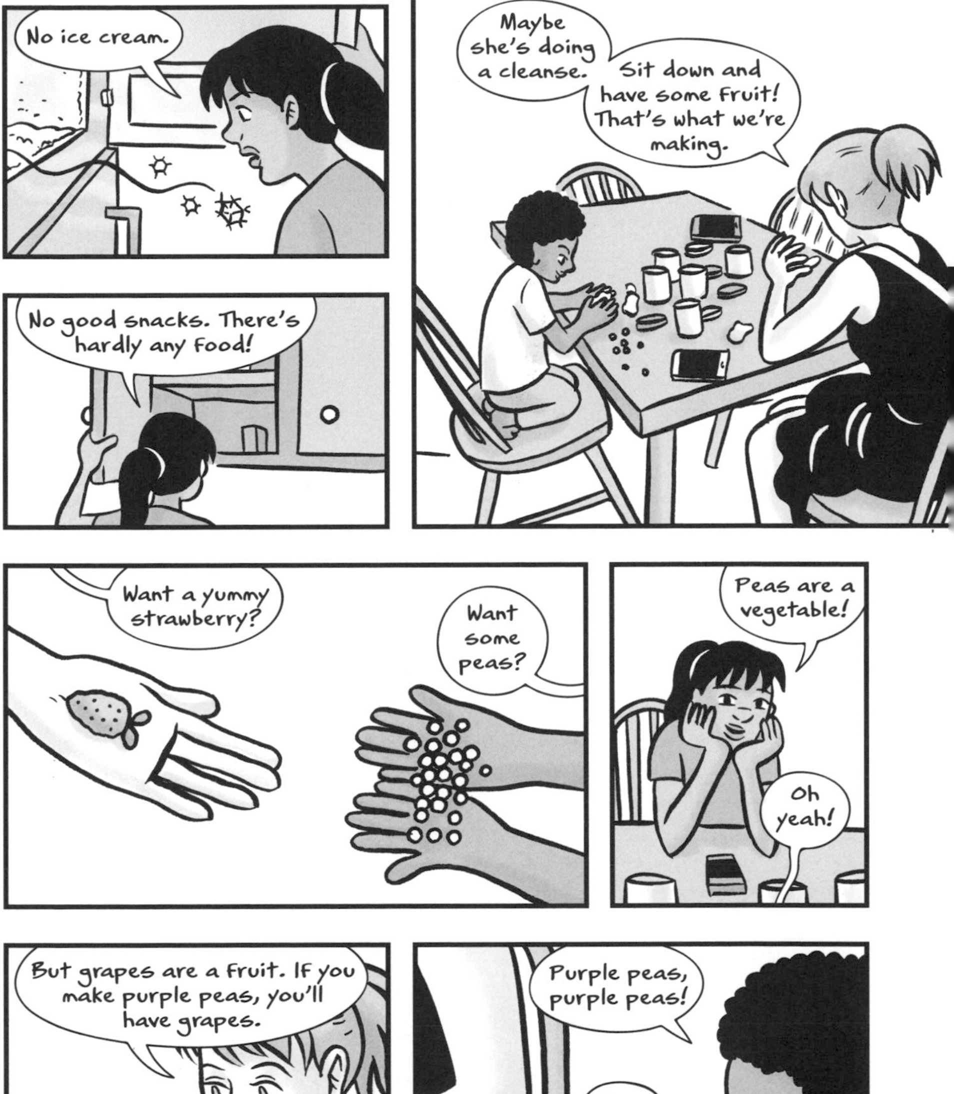
No ice cream.
No good snacks. There's hardly any food!
Maybe she's doing a cleanse.
Sit down and have some fruit! That's what we're making.
Want a yummy strawberry?
Want some peas?
Peas are a vegetable!
Oh yeah!
But grapes are a fruit. If you make purple peas, you'll have grapes.
doh
PURPLE
Purple peas, purple peas!
ding ding

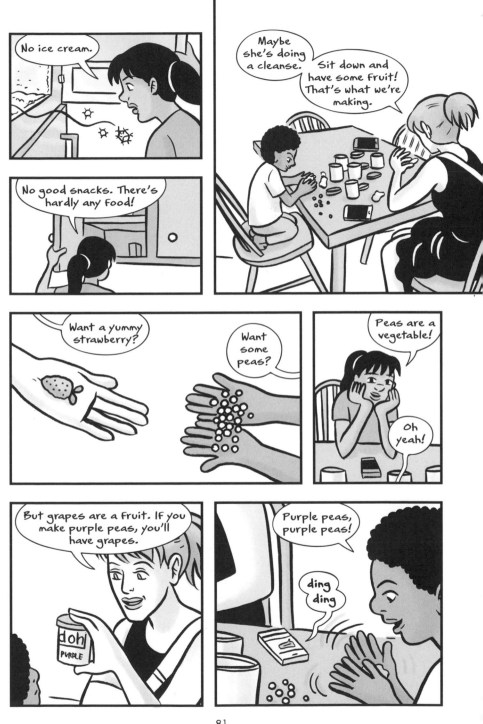

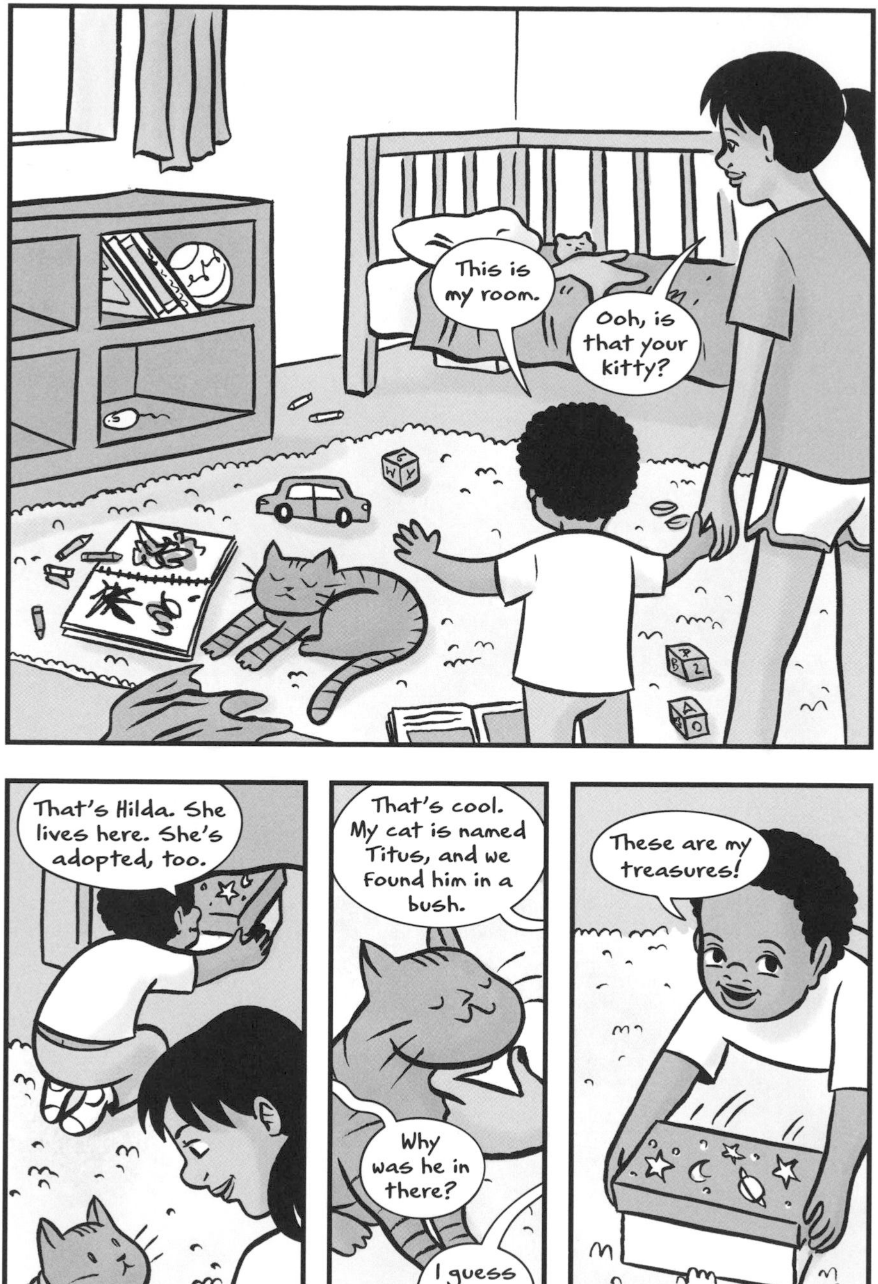
This is my room.
Ooh, is that your kitty?
That's Hilda. She lives here. She's adopted, too.
That's cool. My cat is named Titus, and we found him in a bush.
Why was he in there?
I guess he got lost.
These are my treasures!

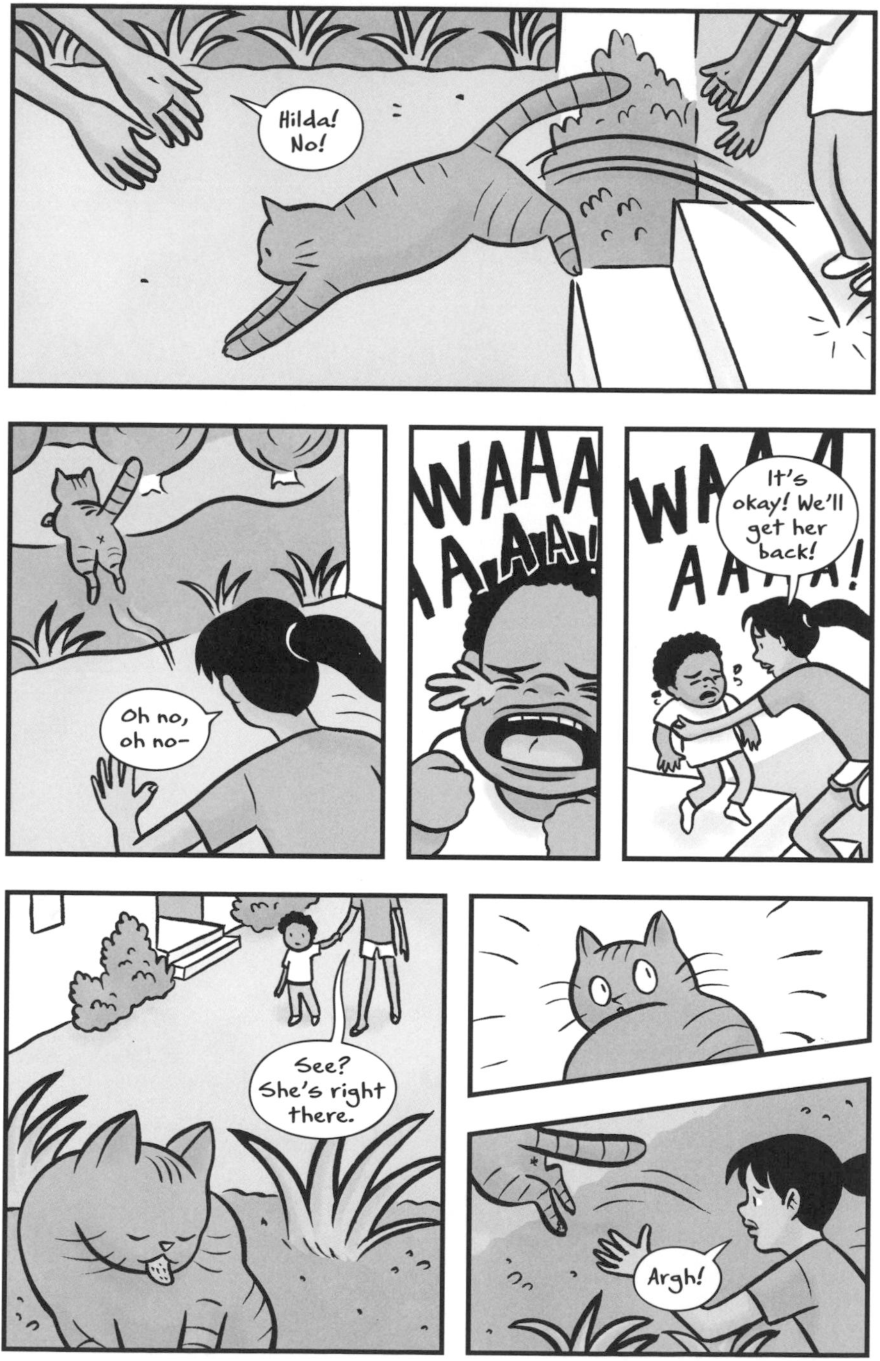
Hilda! No!
Oh no, oh no-
WAAAAAA!
WAAAAAA!
It's okay! We'll get her back!
See? She's right there.
Argh!

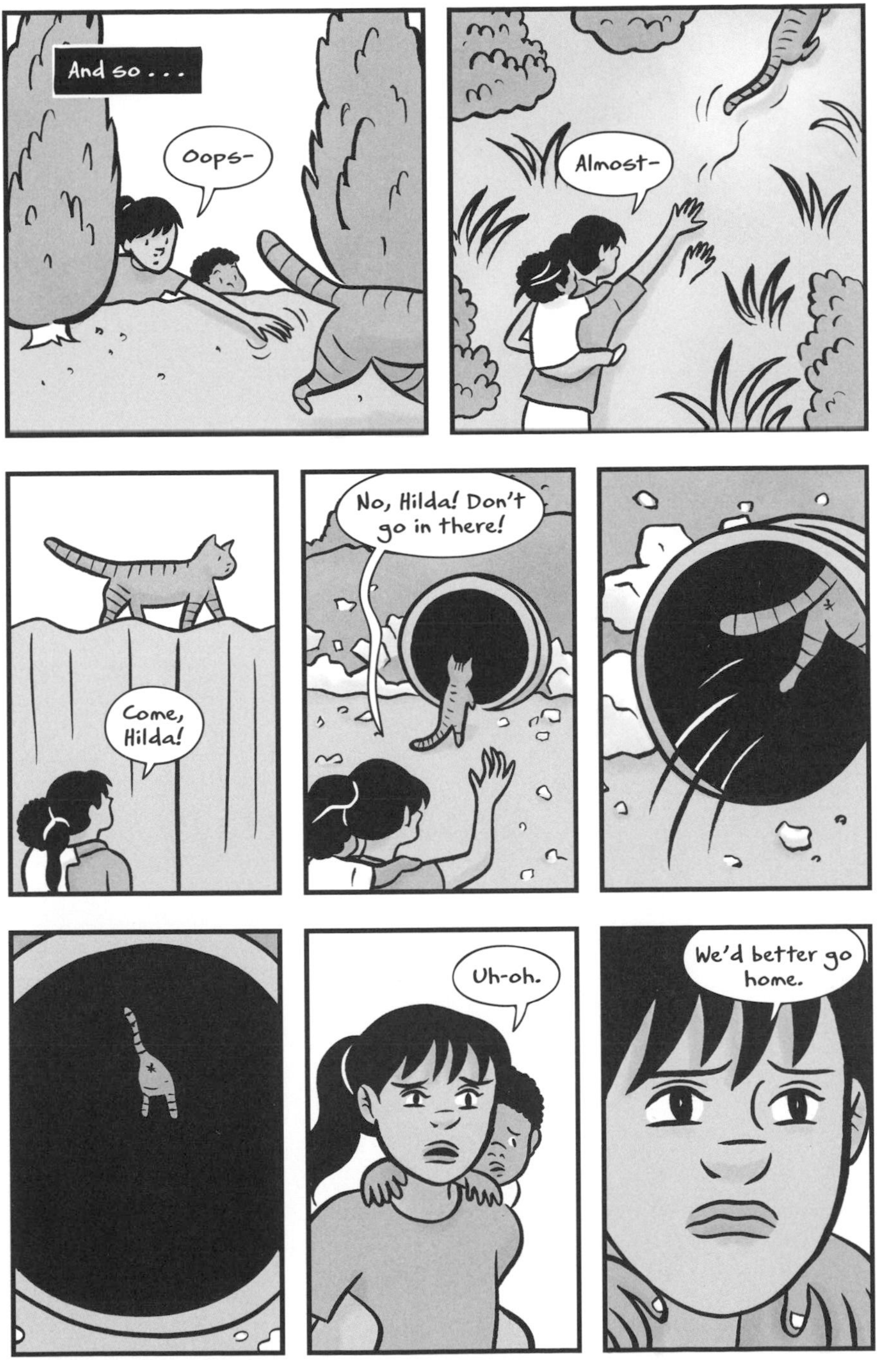
And so . . .
Oops-
Almost-
Come, Hilda!
No, Hilda! Don't go in there!
Uh-oh.
We'd better go home.

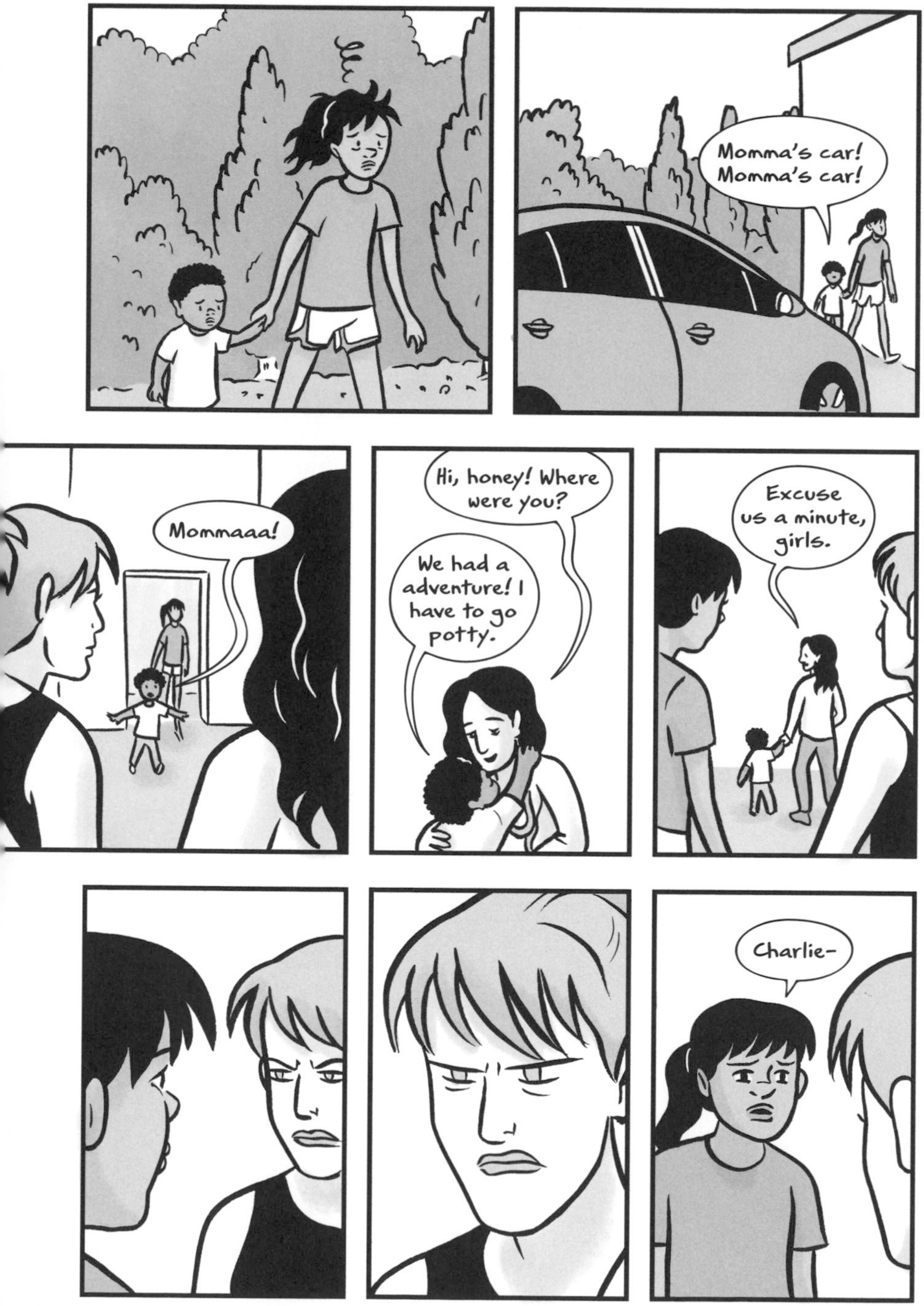
Momma's car! Momma's car!
Mommaaa!
Hi, honey! Where were you?
We had a adventure! I have to go potty.
Excuse us a minute, girls.
Charlie-

93

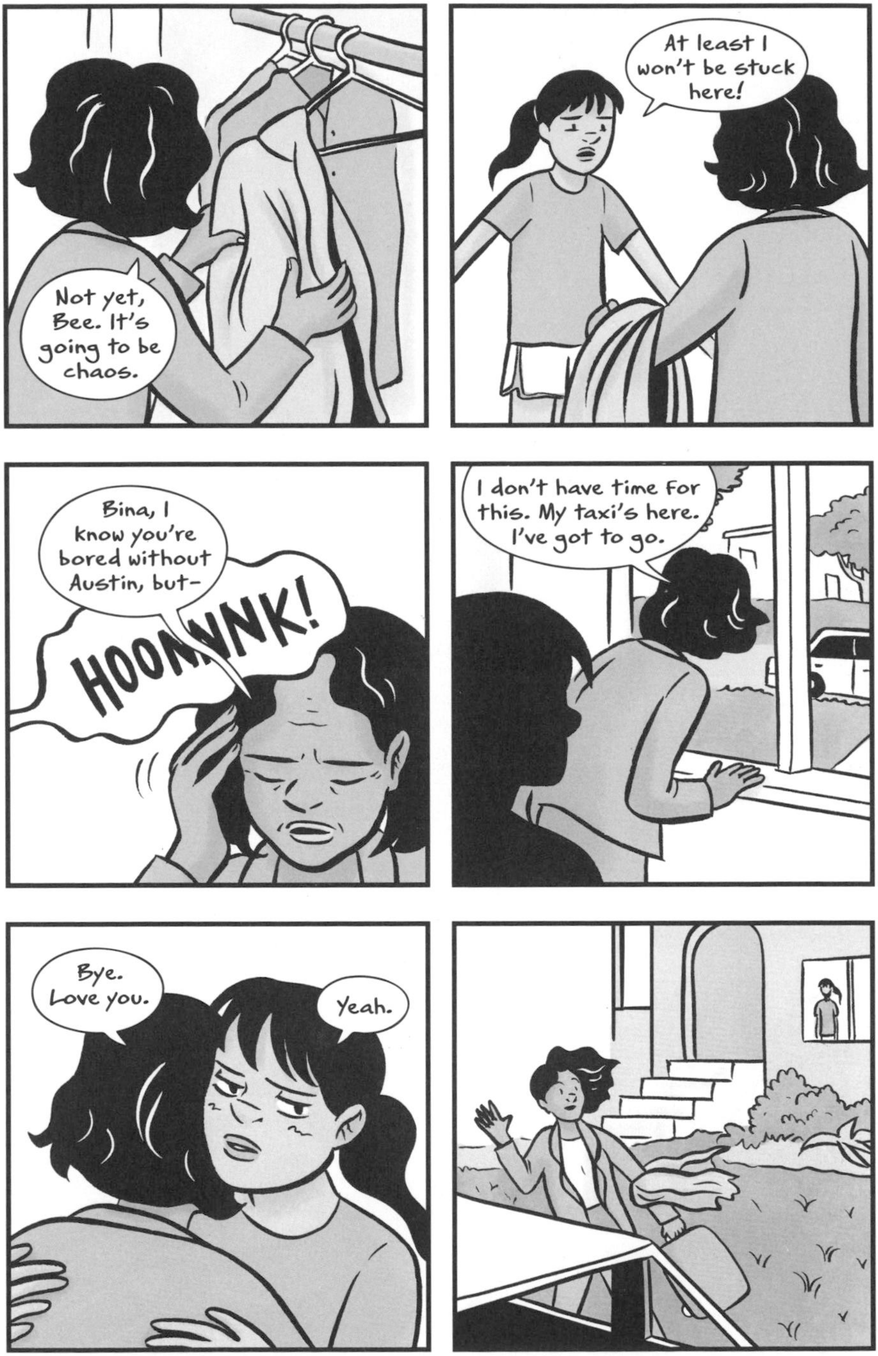

Not yet, Bee. It's going to be chaos.
At least I won't be stuck here!
Bina, I know you're bored without Austin, but-
HOONNNK!
I don't have time for this. My taxi's here. I've got to go.
Bye. Love you.
Yeah.

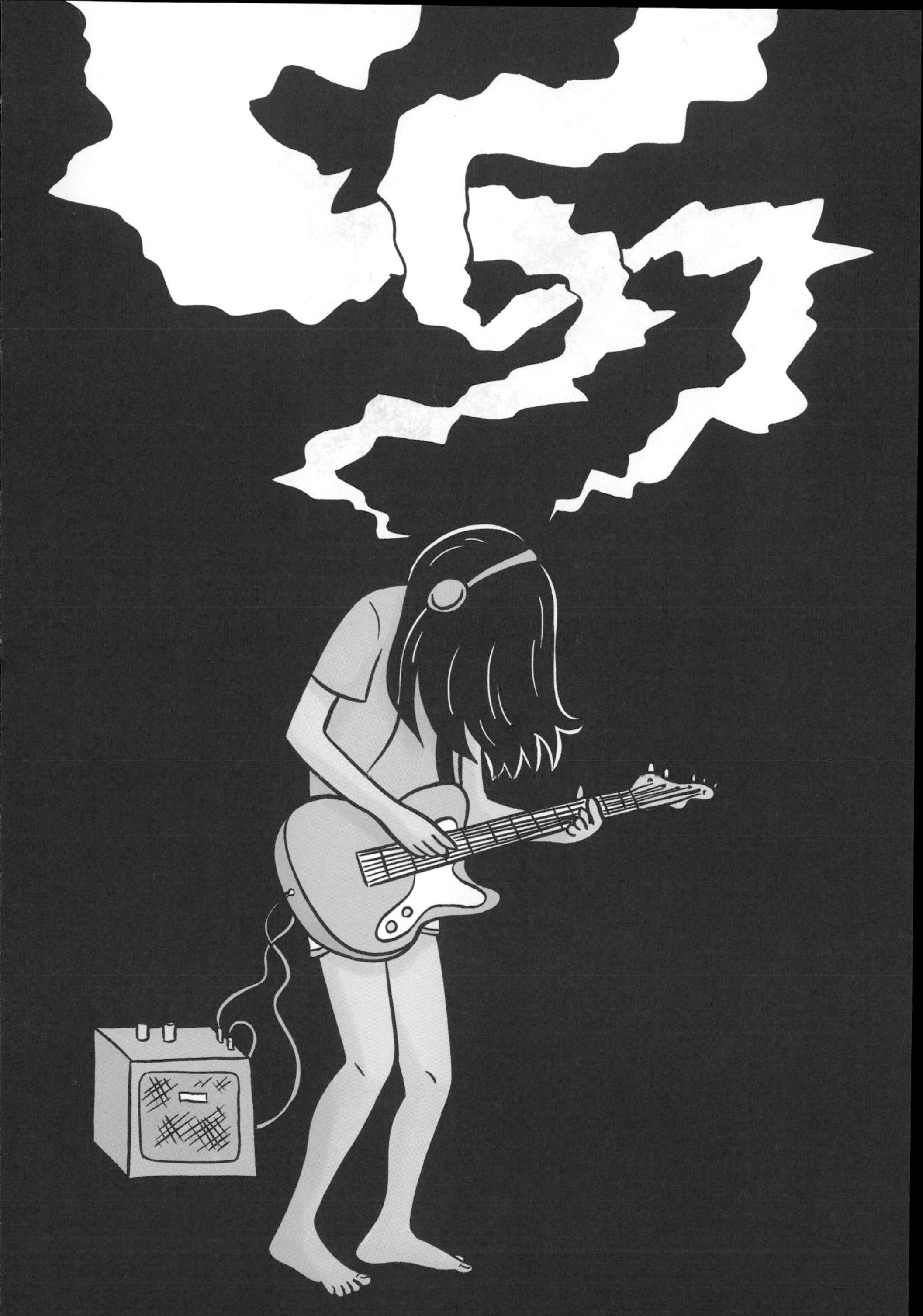

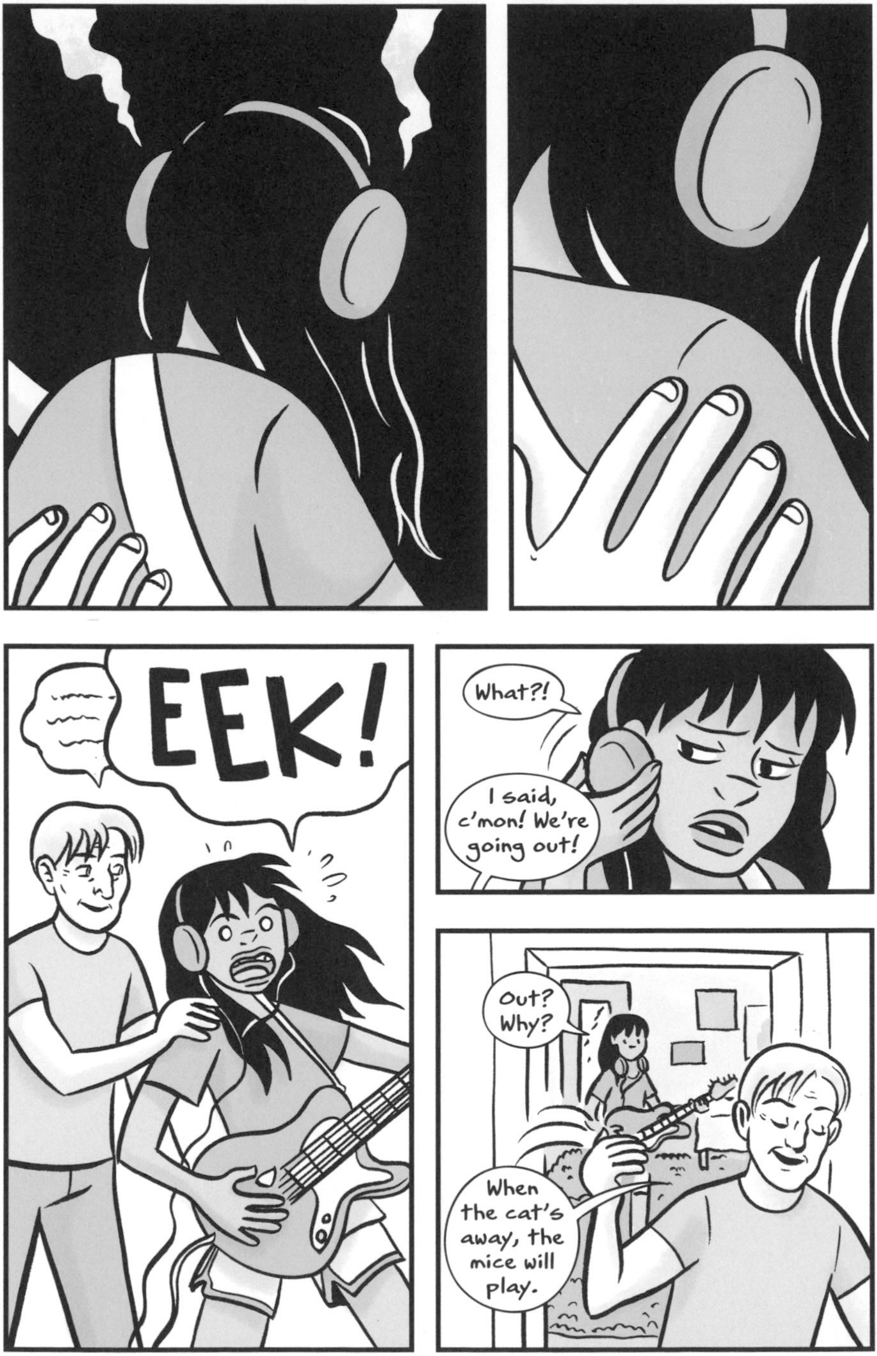
EEK!
What?!
I said, c'mon! We're going out!
Out? Why?
When the cat's away, the mice will play.

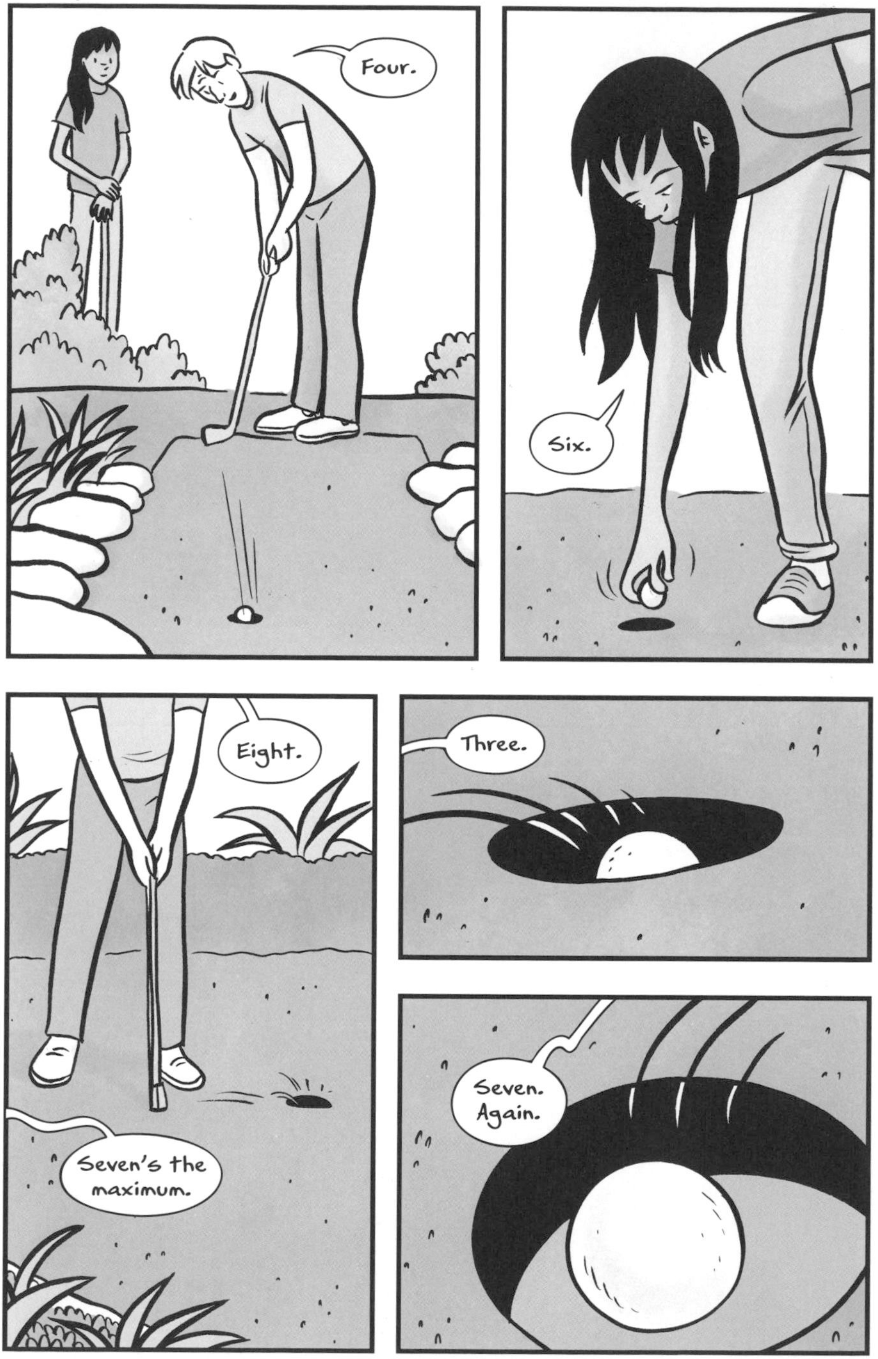
Four.
Six.
Eight.
Seven's the maximum.
Three.
Seven. Again.

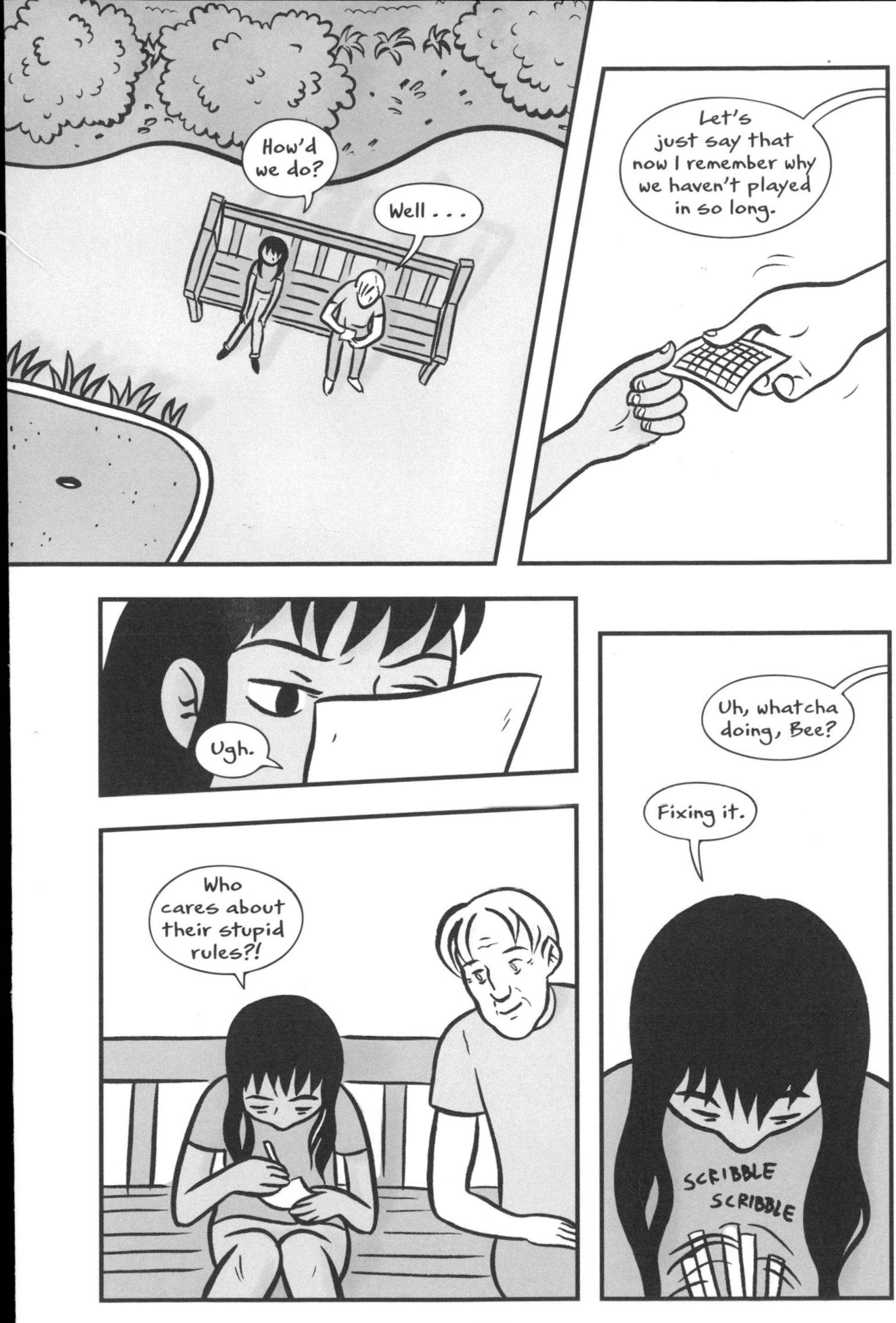
How'd we do?
Well . . .
Let's just say that now I remember why we haven't played in so long.
Ugh.
Uh, whatcha doing, Bee?
Fixing it.
Who cares about their stupid rules?!
SCRIBBLE SCRIBBLE

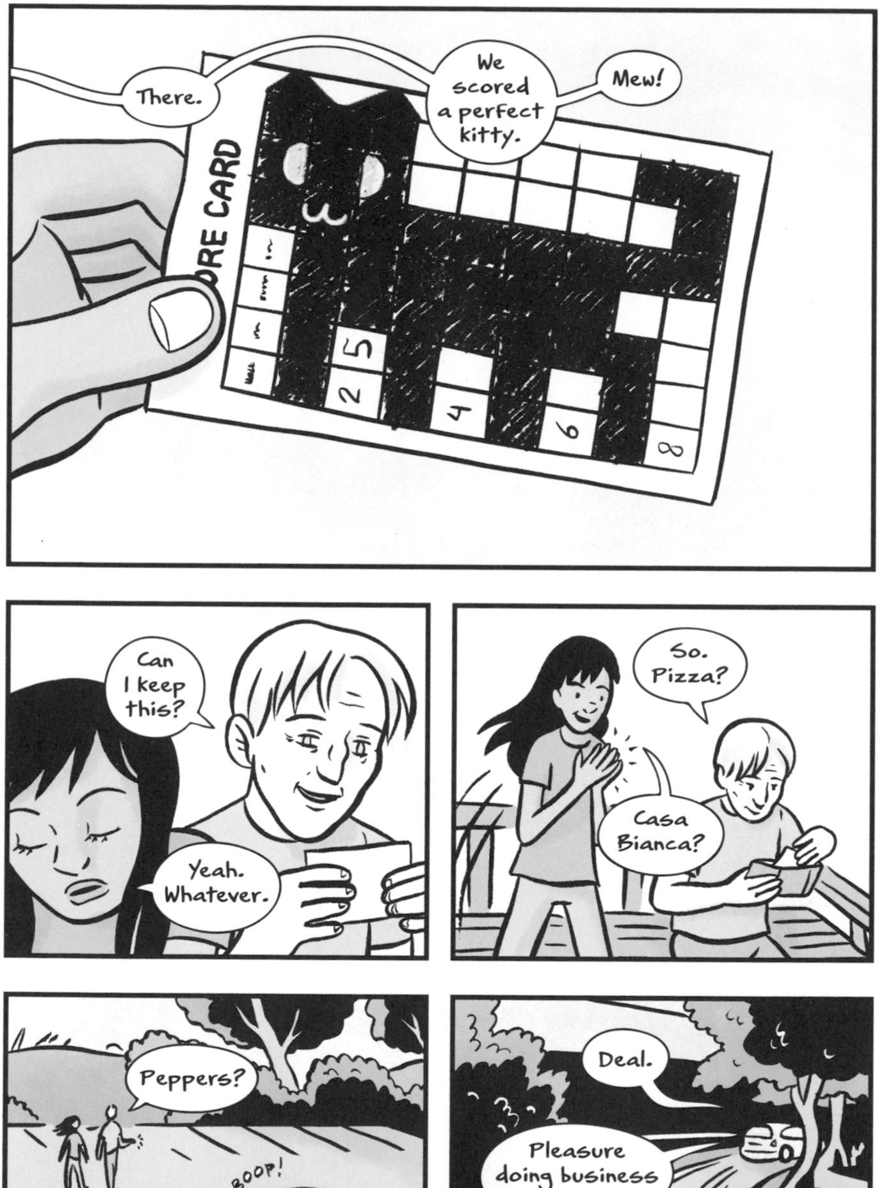
There.
We scored a perfect kitty.
Mew!
ORE CARD
Can I keep this?
Yeah. Whatever.
So. Pizza?
Casa Bianca?
Peppers?
Fine. Sausage?
BOOP!
Deal.
Pleasure doing business with ya.

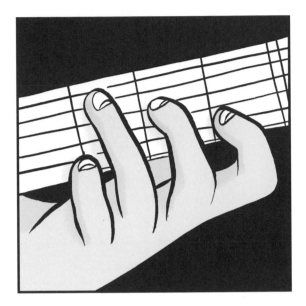

Week Five

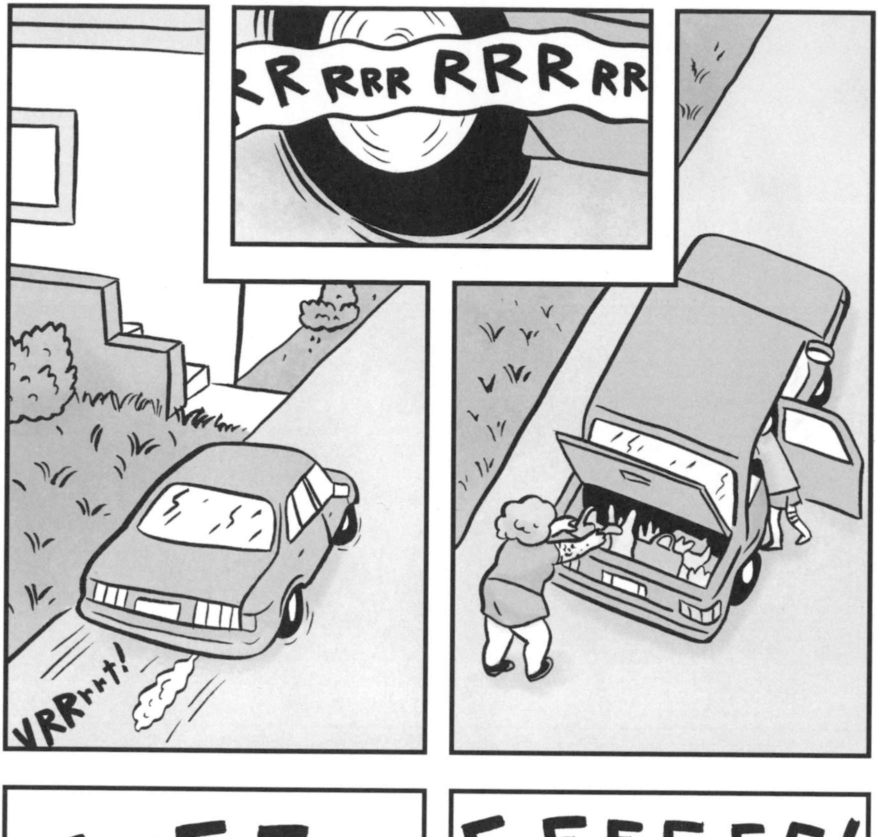
RRRR RRRRR
VRRrrrt!
EEEEE!
EEEEEE!
Aaaah! Careful!

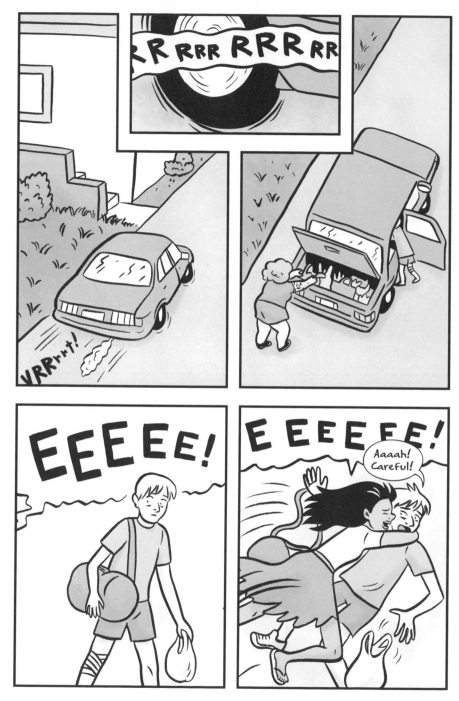

110

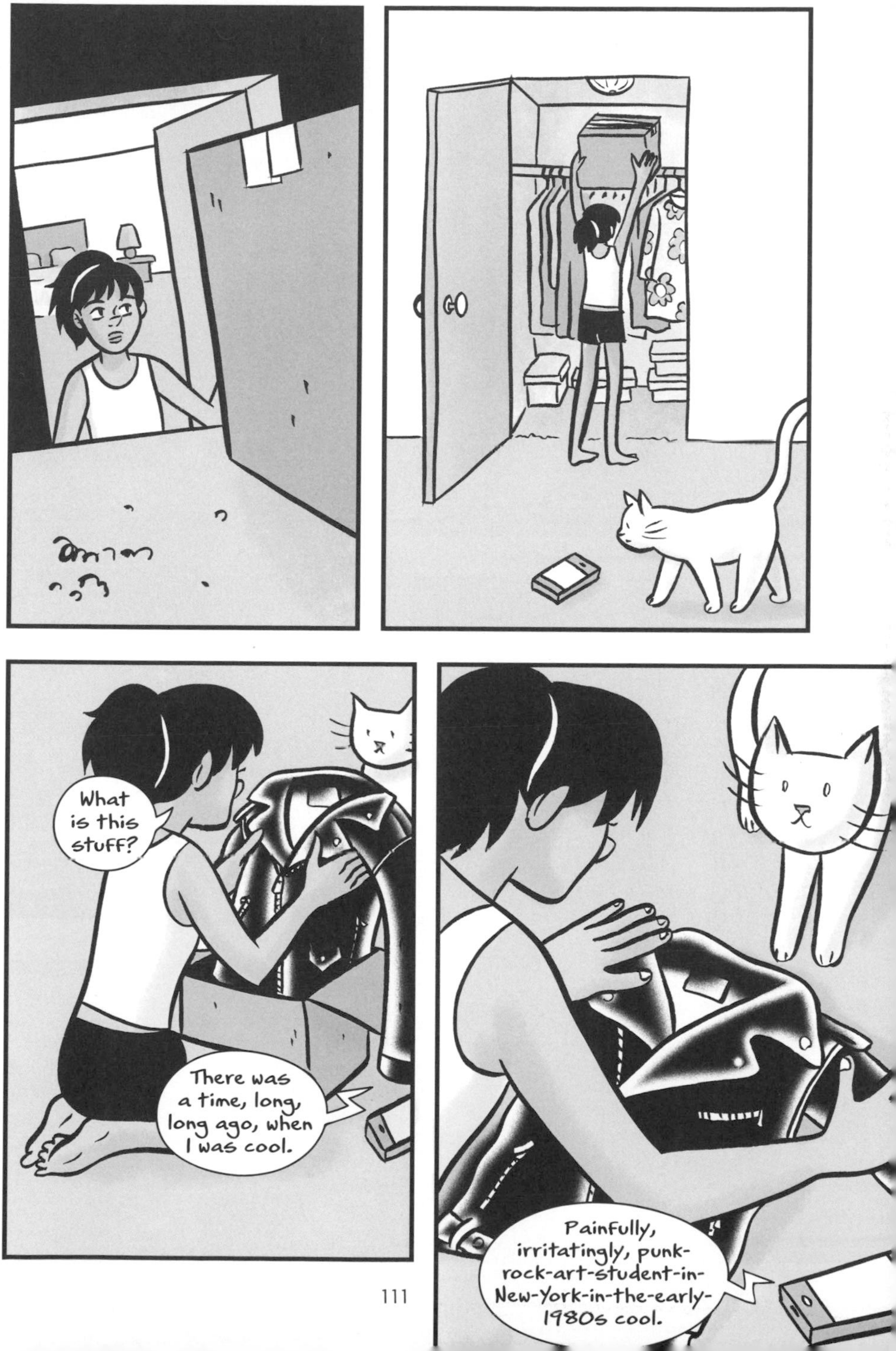
What is this stuff?
There was a time, long, long ago, when I was cool.
Painfully, irritatingly, punk-rock-art-student-in-New-York-in-the-early-1980s cool.

112

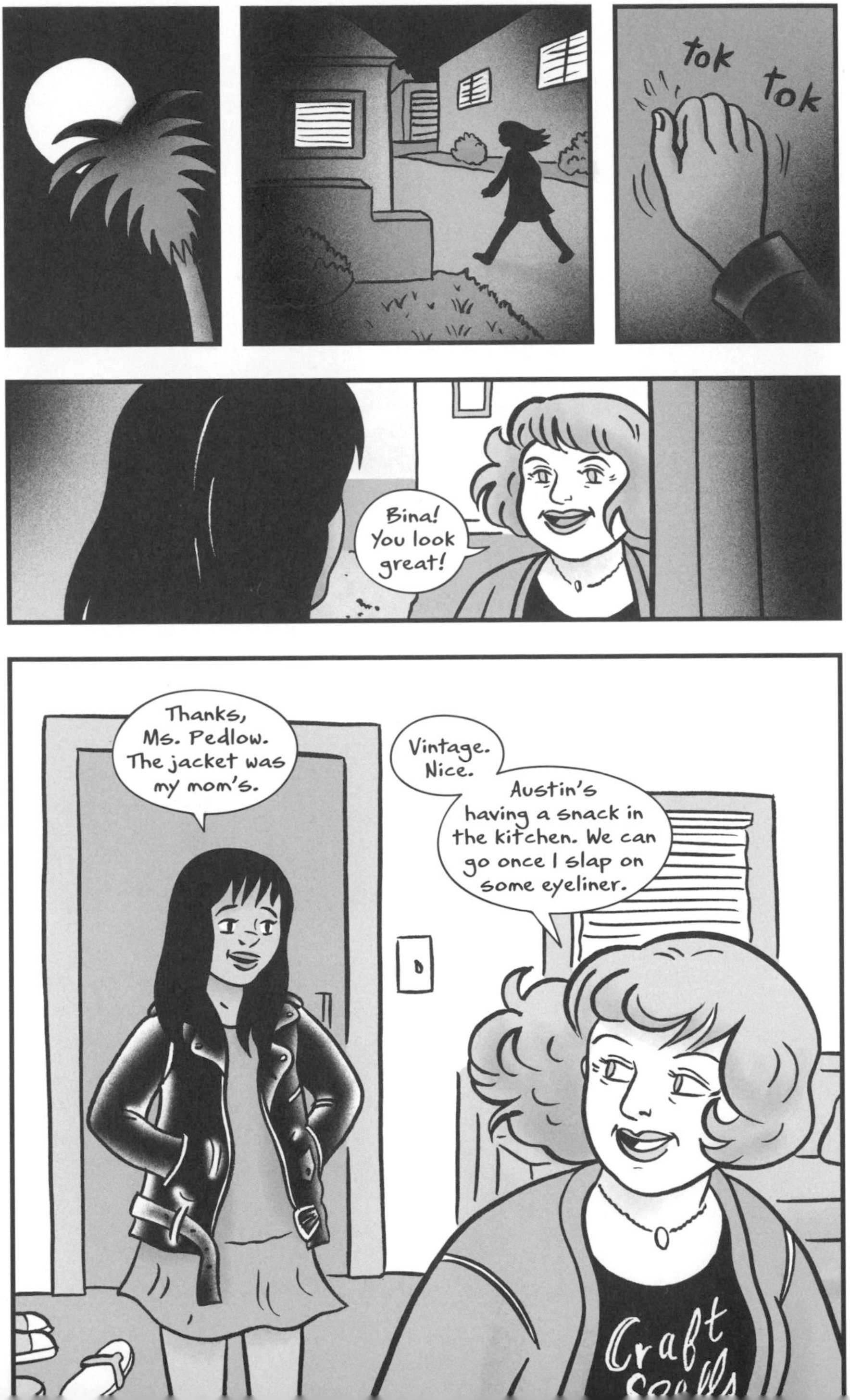
tok tok
Bina! You look great!
Thanks, Ms. Pedlow. The jacket was my mom's.
Vintage. Nice.
Austin's having a snack in the kitchen. We can go once I slap on some eyeliner.
Craft

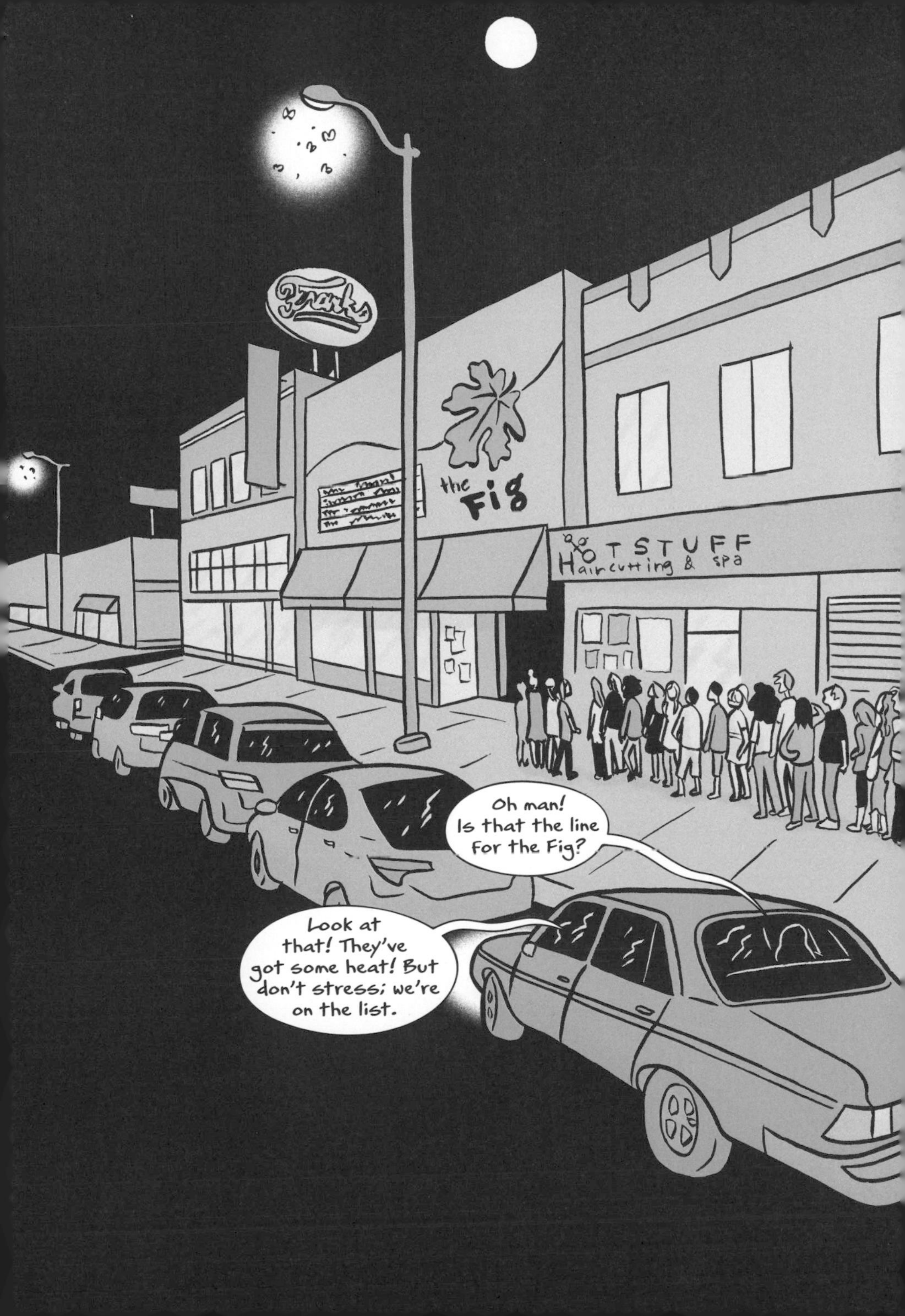
Franks
the Fig
HOTSTUFF
Haircutting & spa
Look at that! They've got some heat! But don't stress; we're on the list.
Oh man! Is that the line for the Fig?

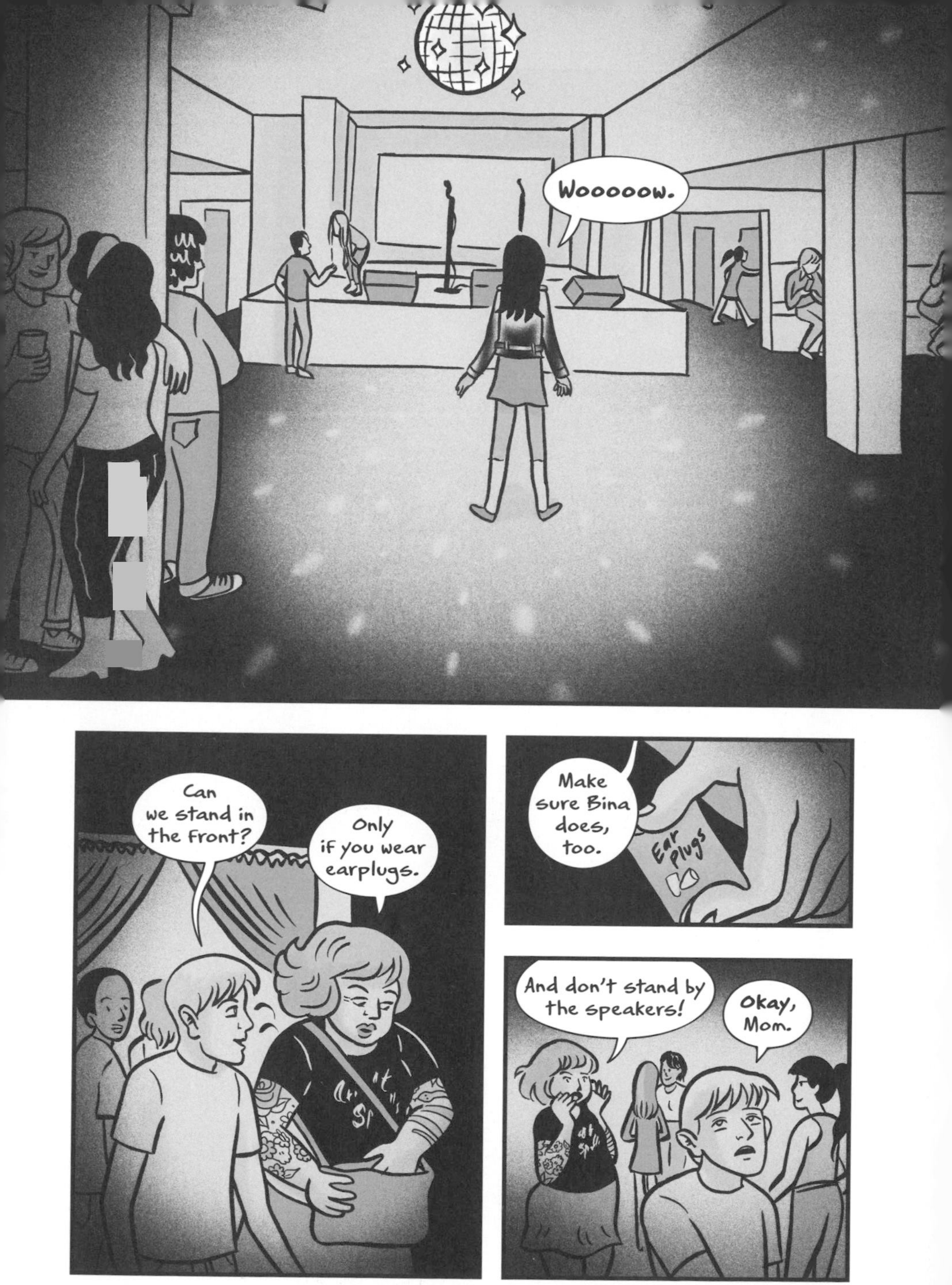
Woooooow.
Can we stand in the front?
Only if you wear earplugs.
Make sure Bina does, too.
Ear plugs
And don't stand by the speakers!
Okay, Mom.

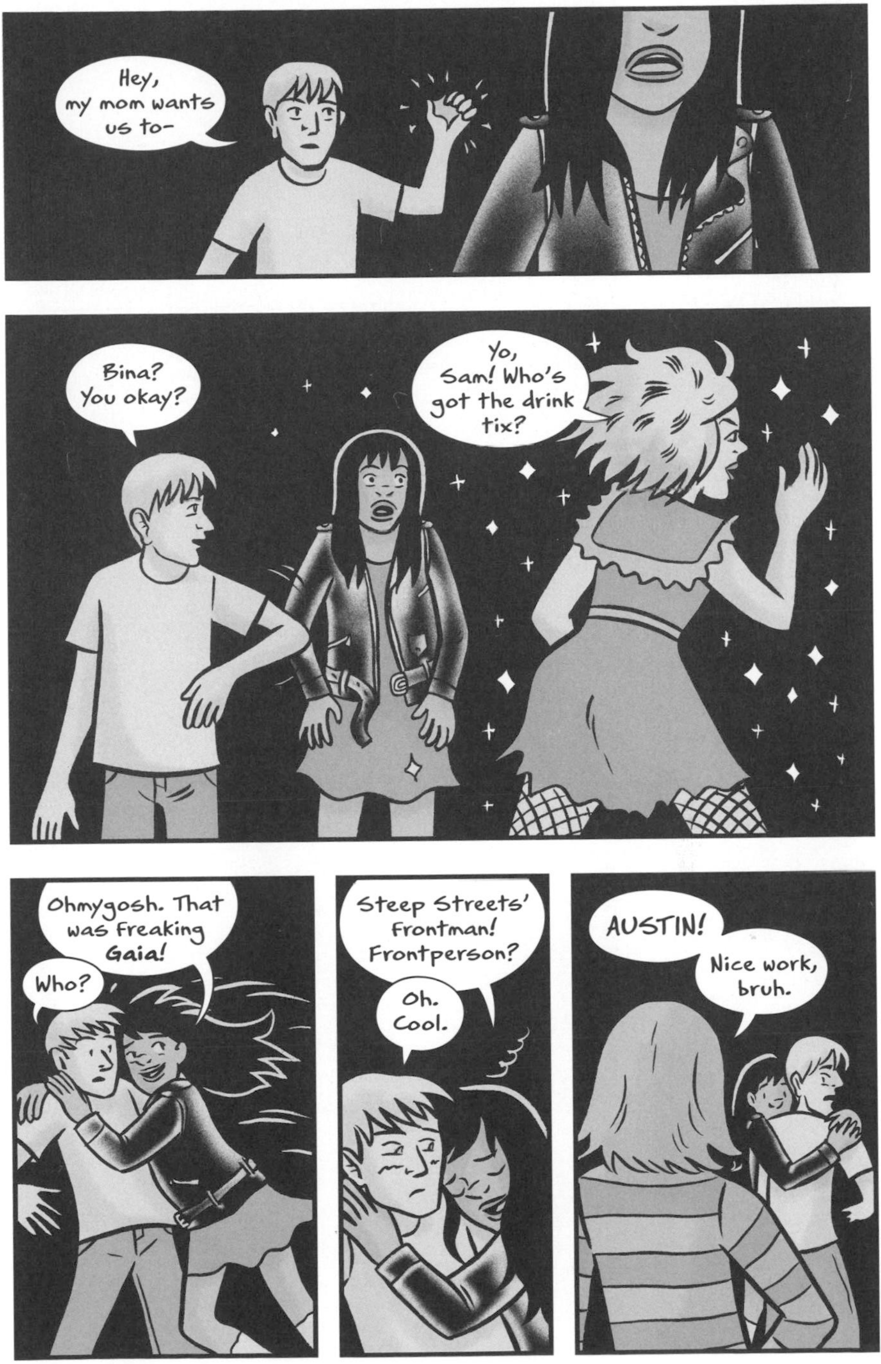
Hey, my mom wants us to-
Bina? You okay?
Yo, Sam! Who's got the drink tix?
Ohmygosh. That was Freaking Gaia!
Who?
Steep Streets' Frontman! Frontperson?
Oh. Cool.
AUSTIN!
Nice work, bruh.

120

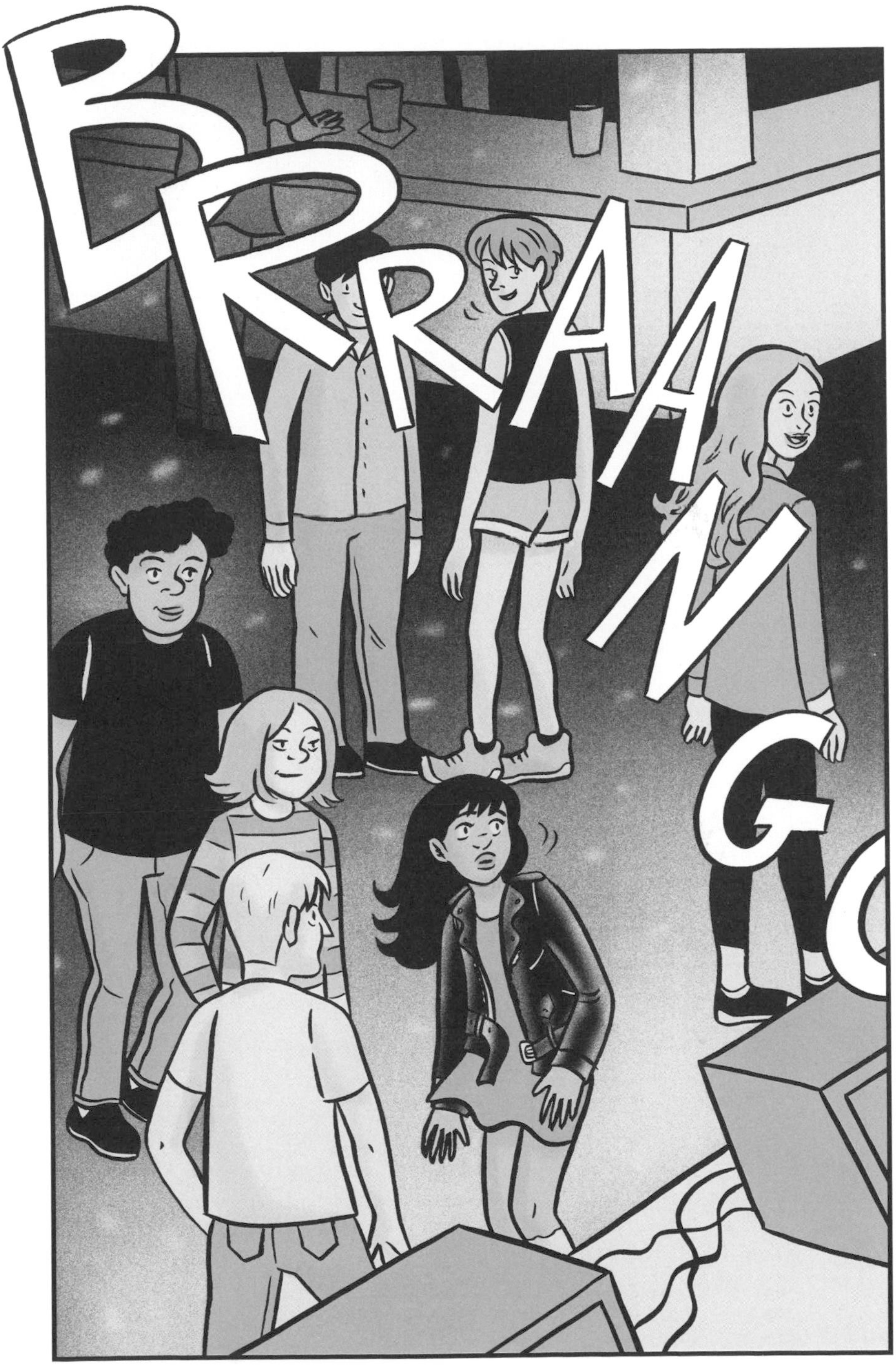
BRRAANGG

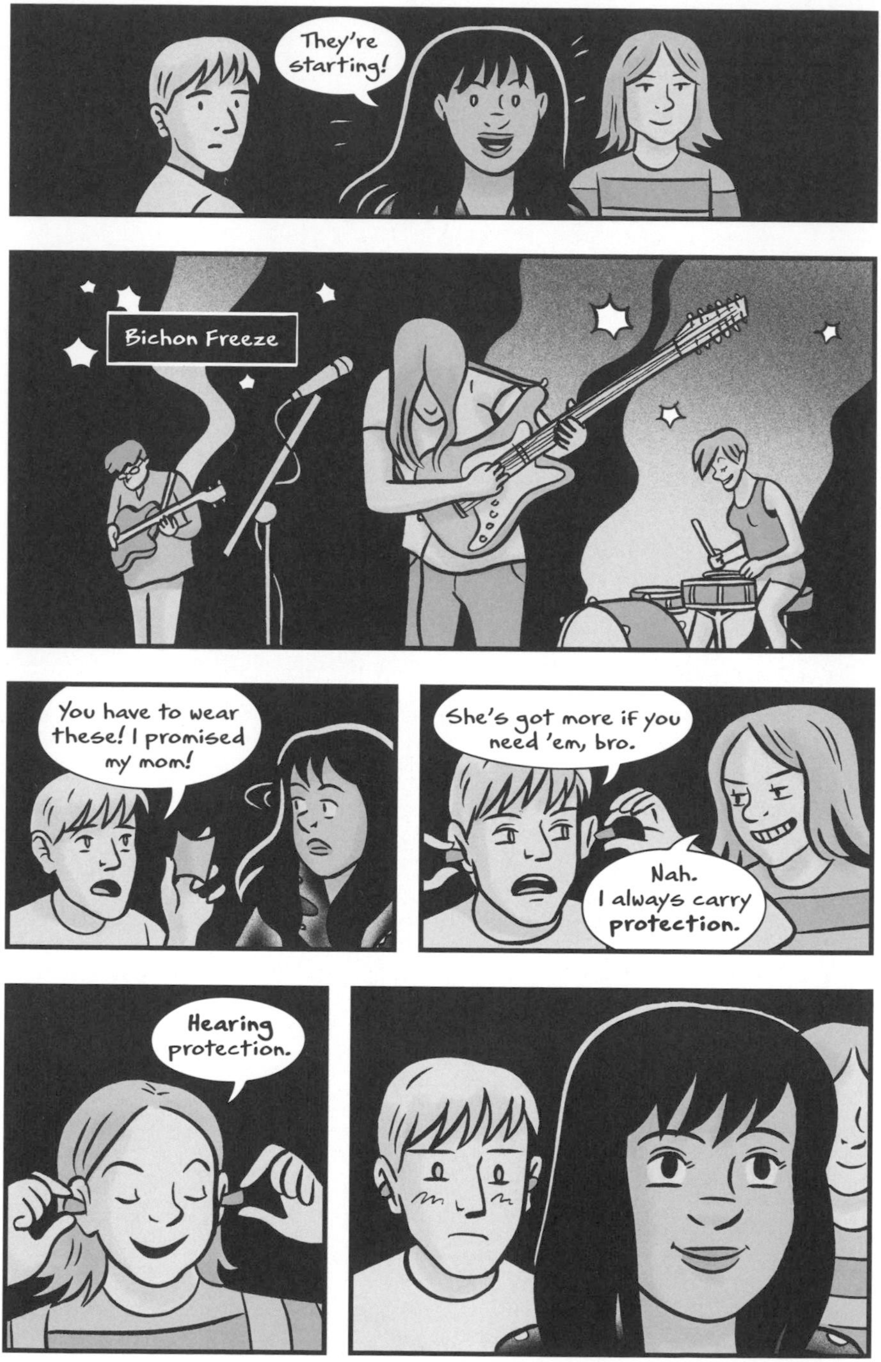
They're starting!
Bichon Freeze
You have to wear these! I promised my mom!
She's got more if you need 'em, bro.
Nah. I always carry **protection.**
Hearing protection.

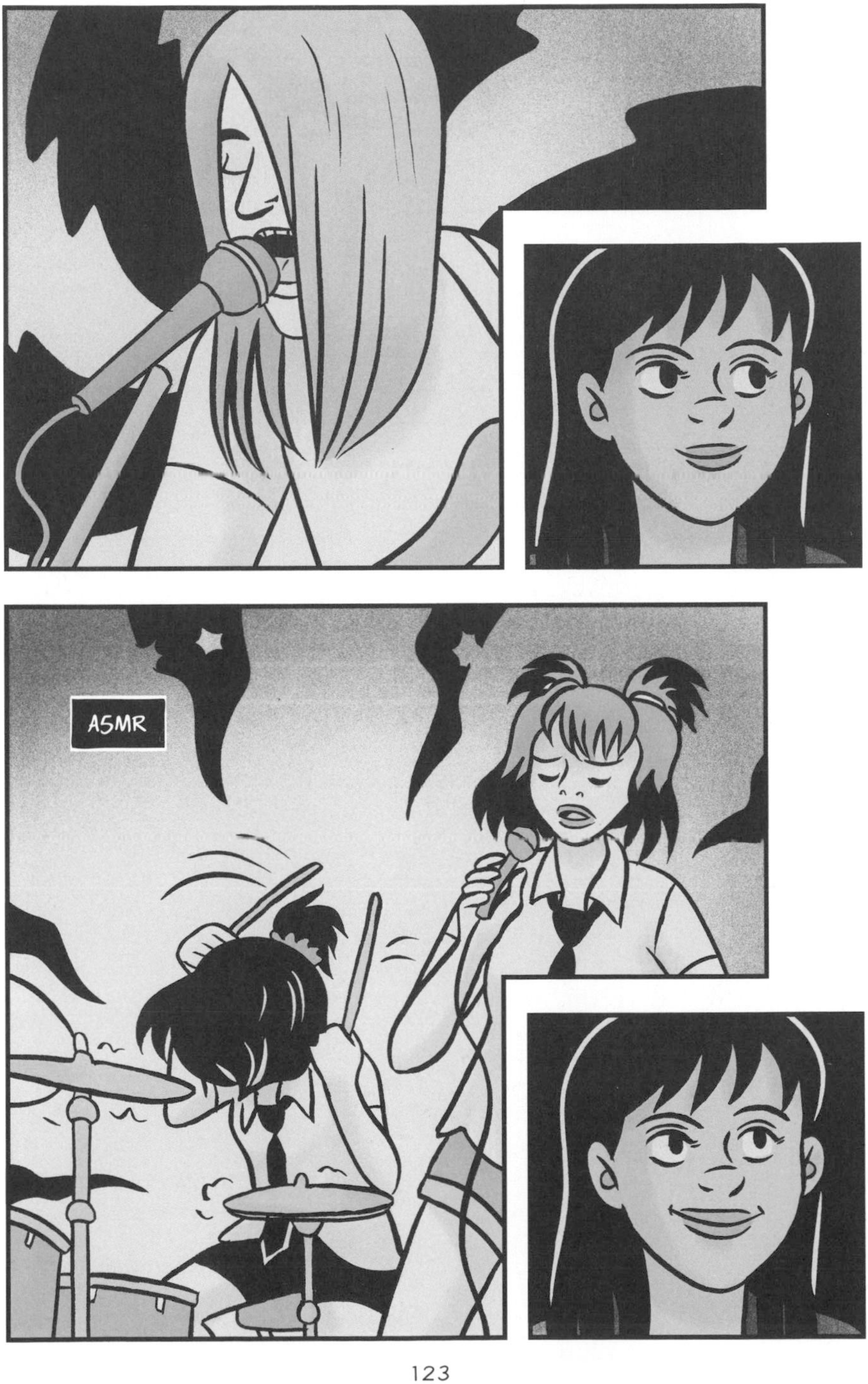
A5MR

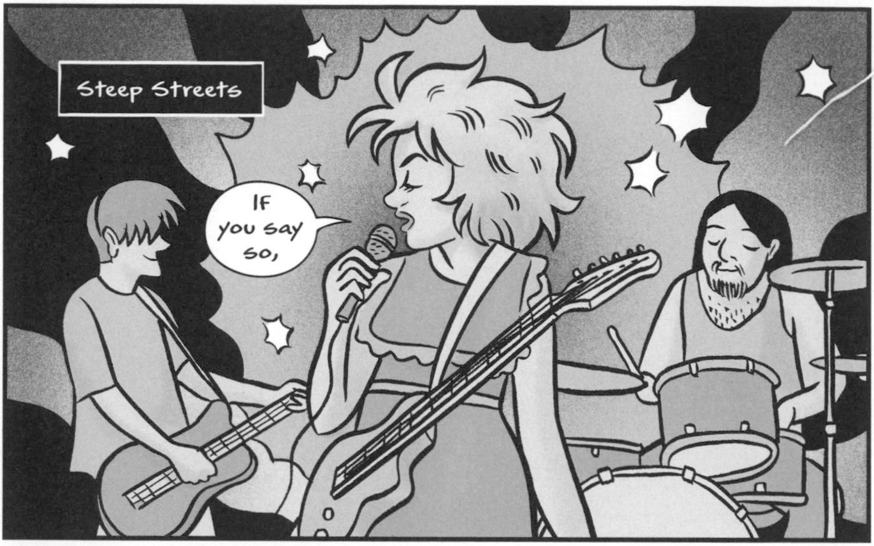
Steep Streets
If you say so,

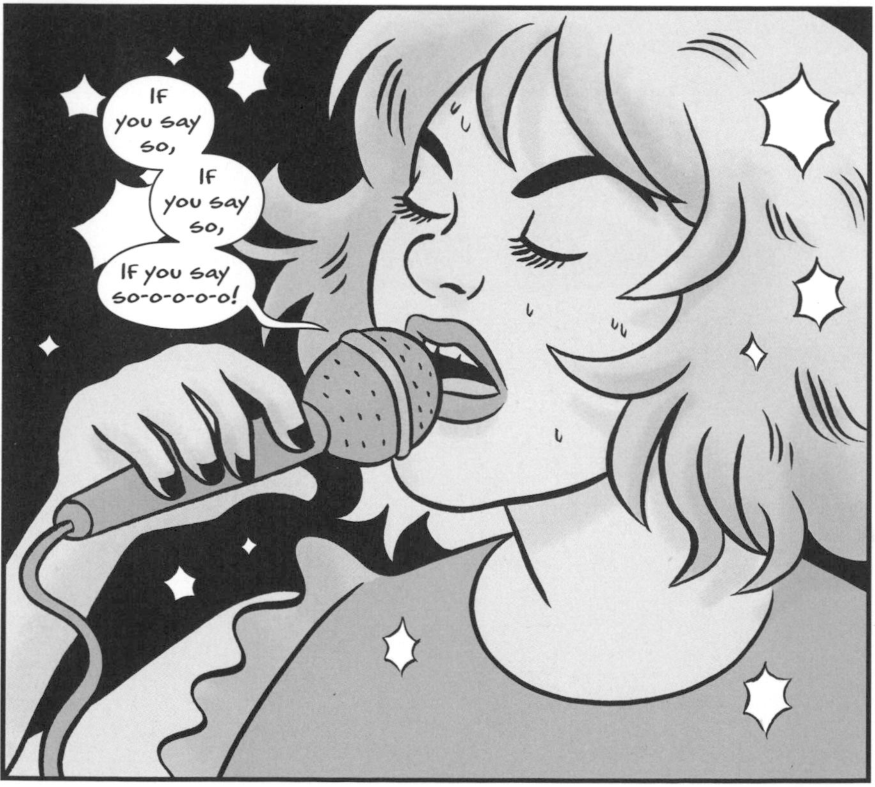
If you say so,
If you say so,
If you say so-o-o-o-o!

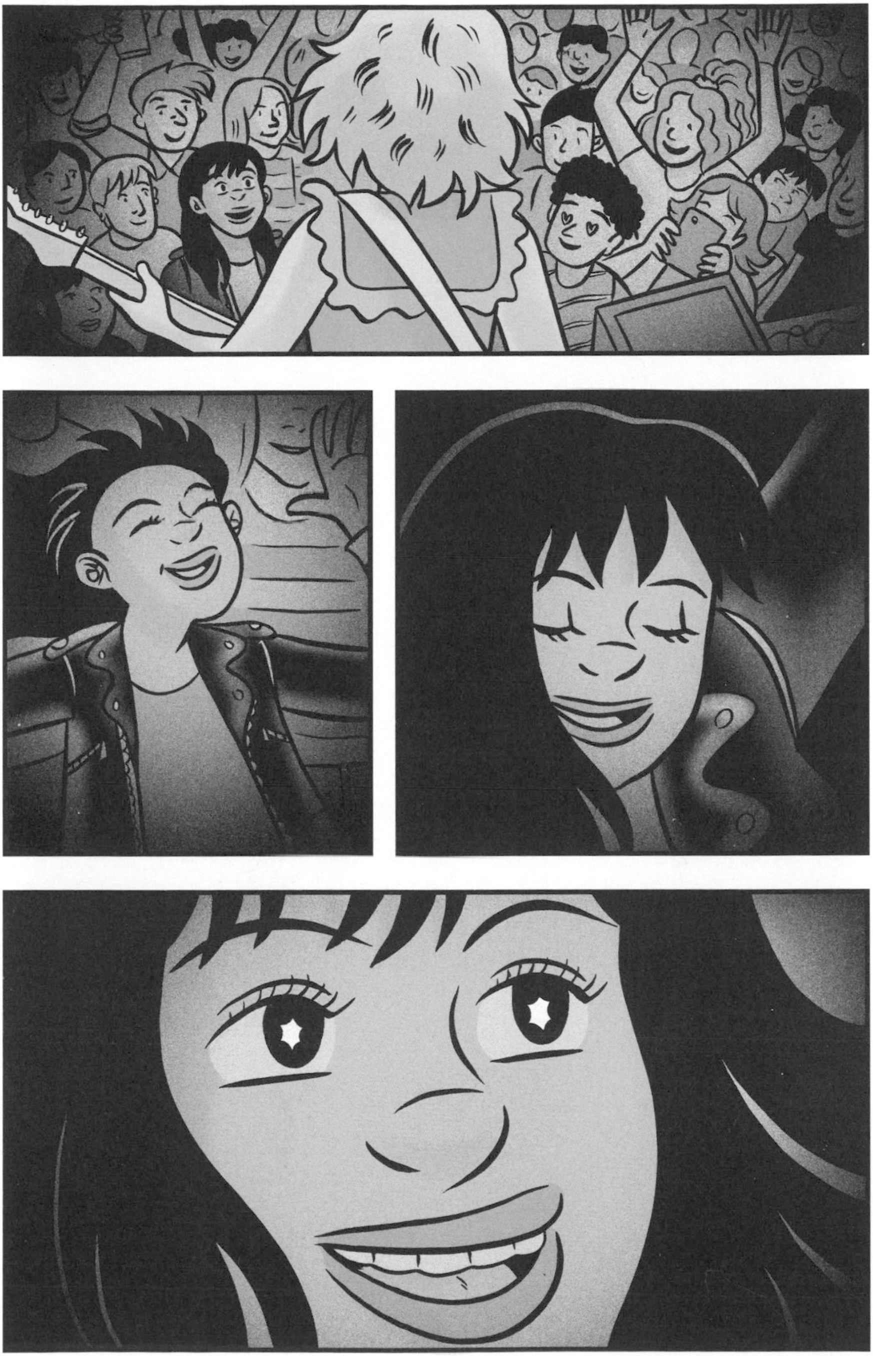

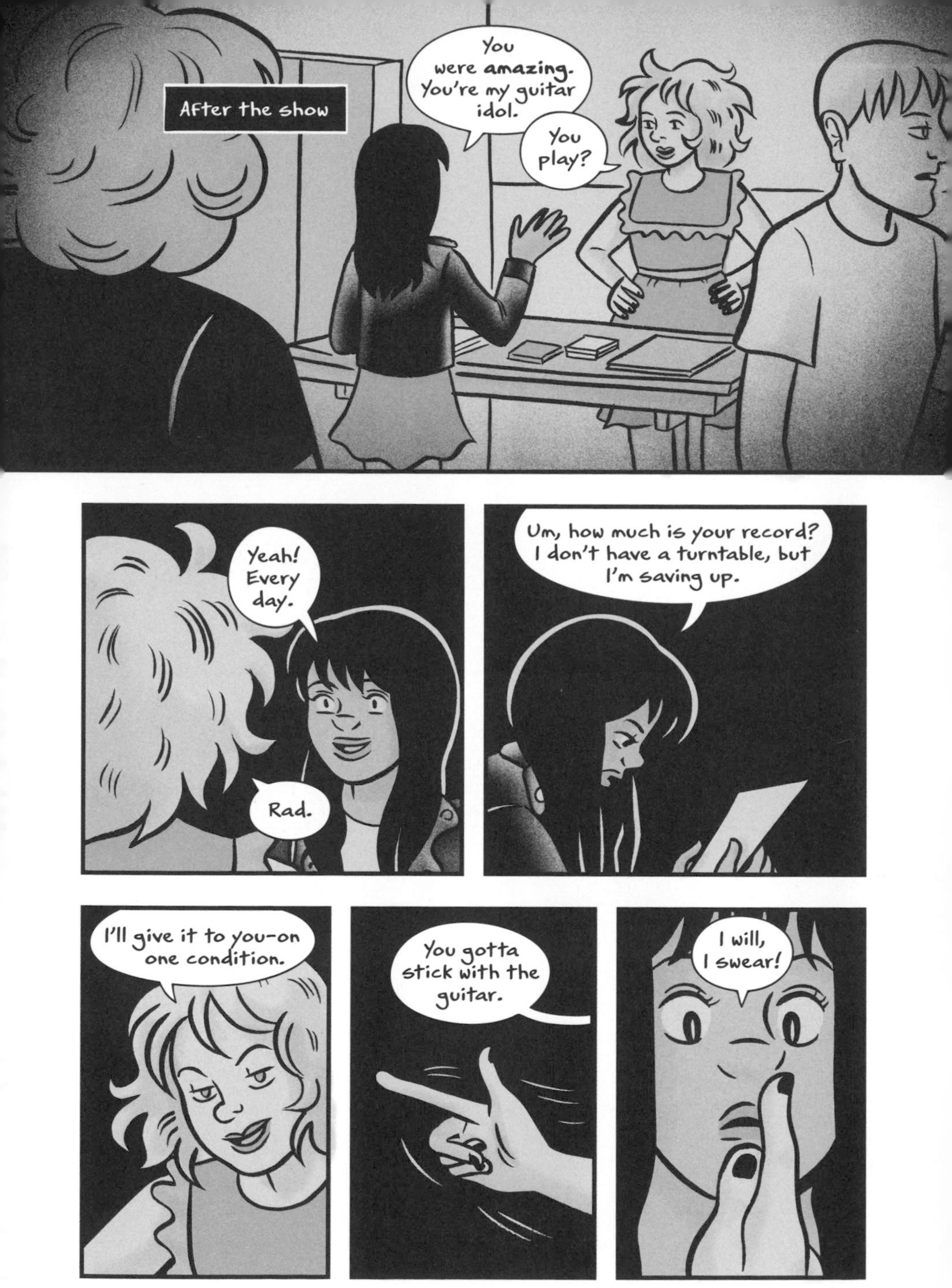
After the show
You were amazing. You're my guitar idol.
You play?
Yeah! Every day.
Rad.
Um, how much is your record? I don't have a turntable, but I'm saving up.
I'll give it to you-on one condition.
You gotta stick with the guitar.
I will, I swear!

127

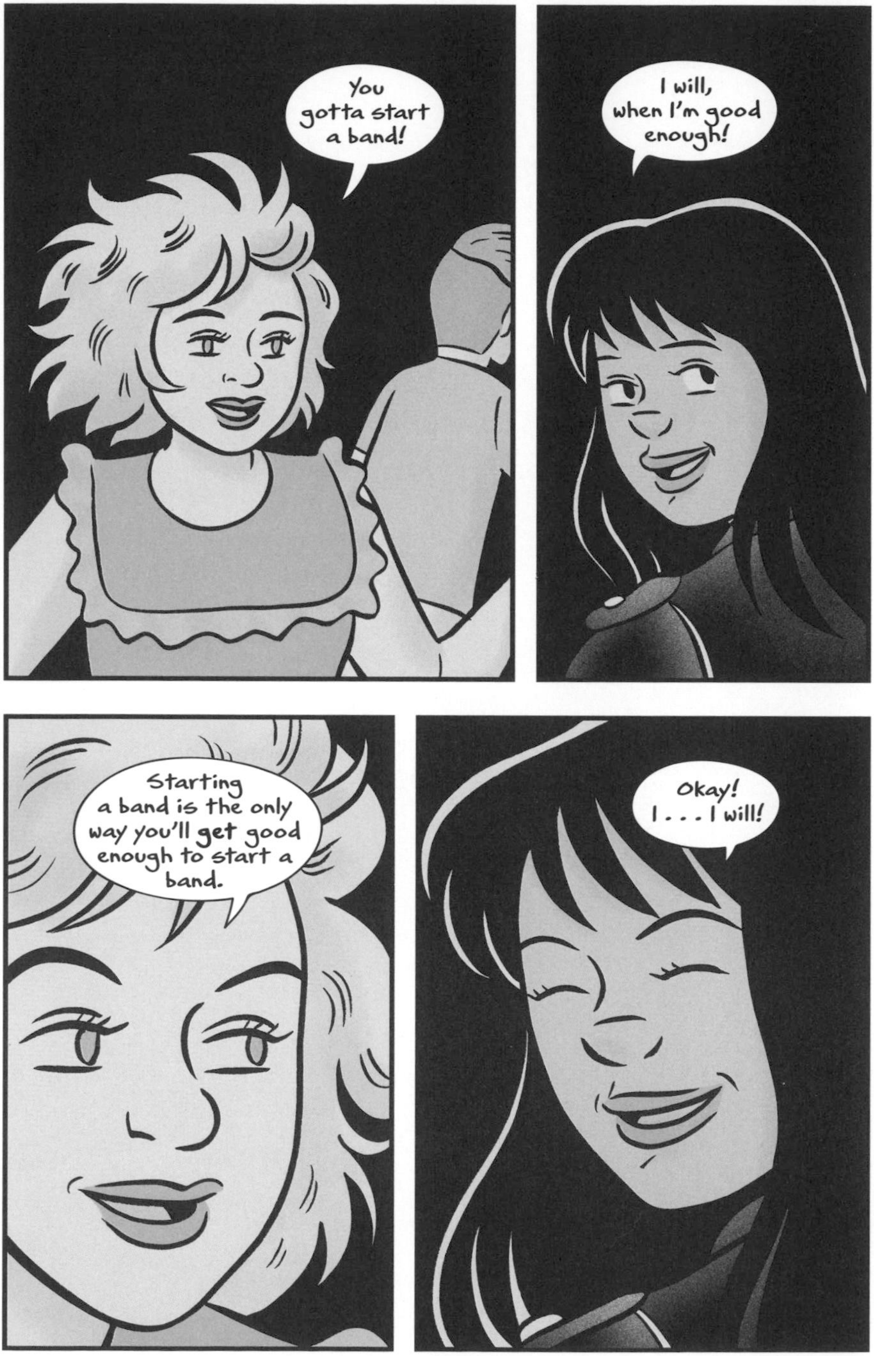
You gotta start a band!
I will, when I'm good enough!
Starting a band is the only way you'll **get** good enough to start a band.
Okay! I . . . I will!

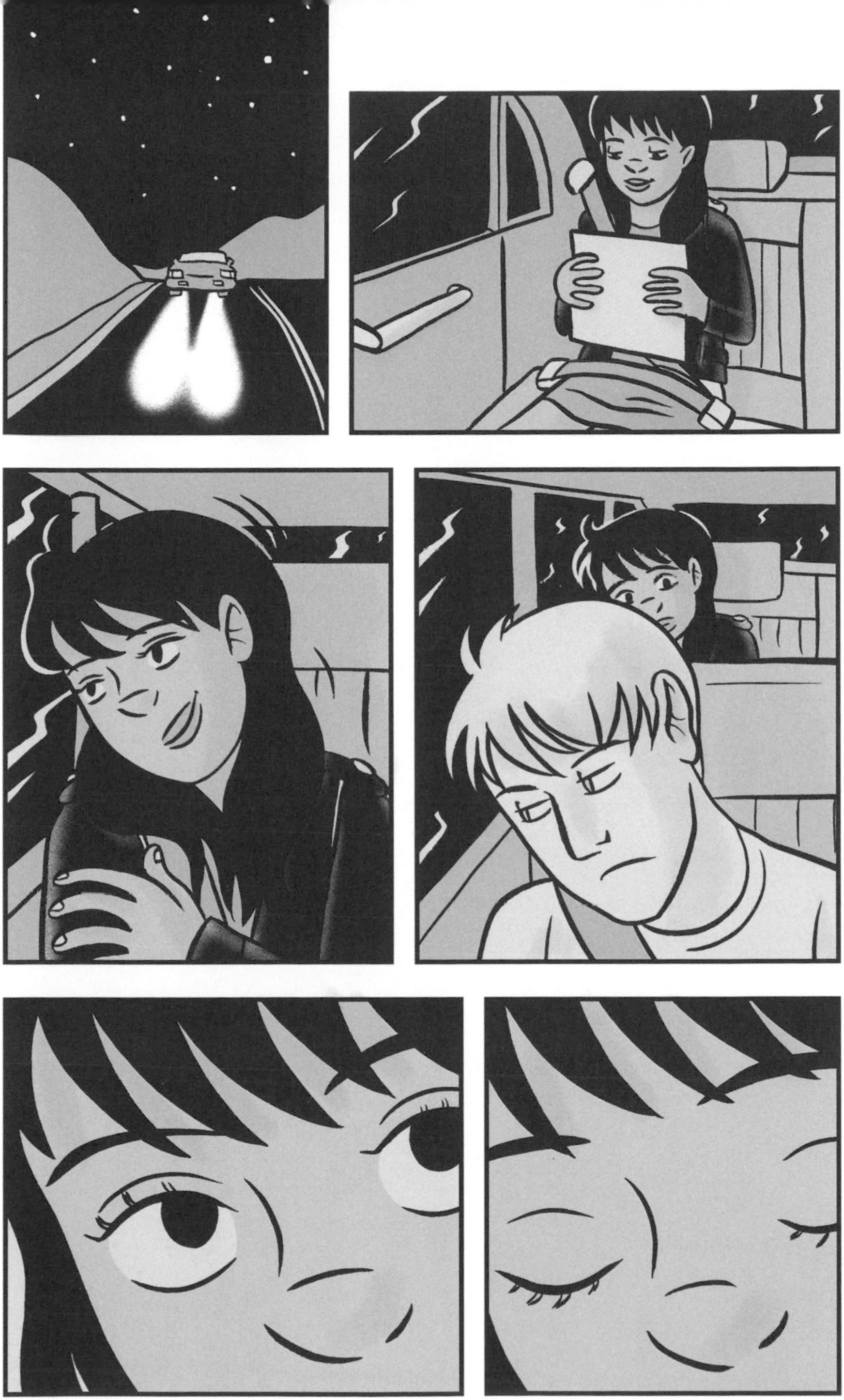

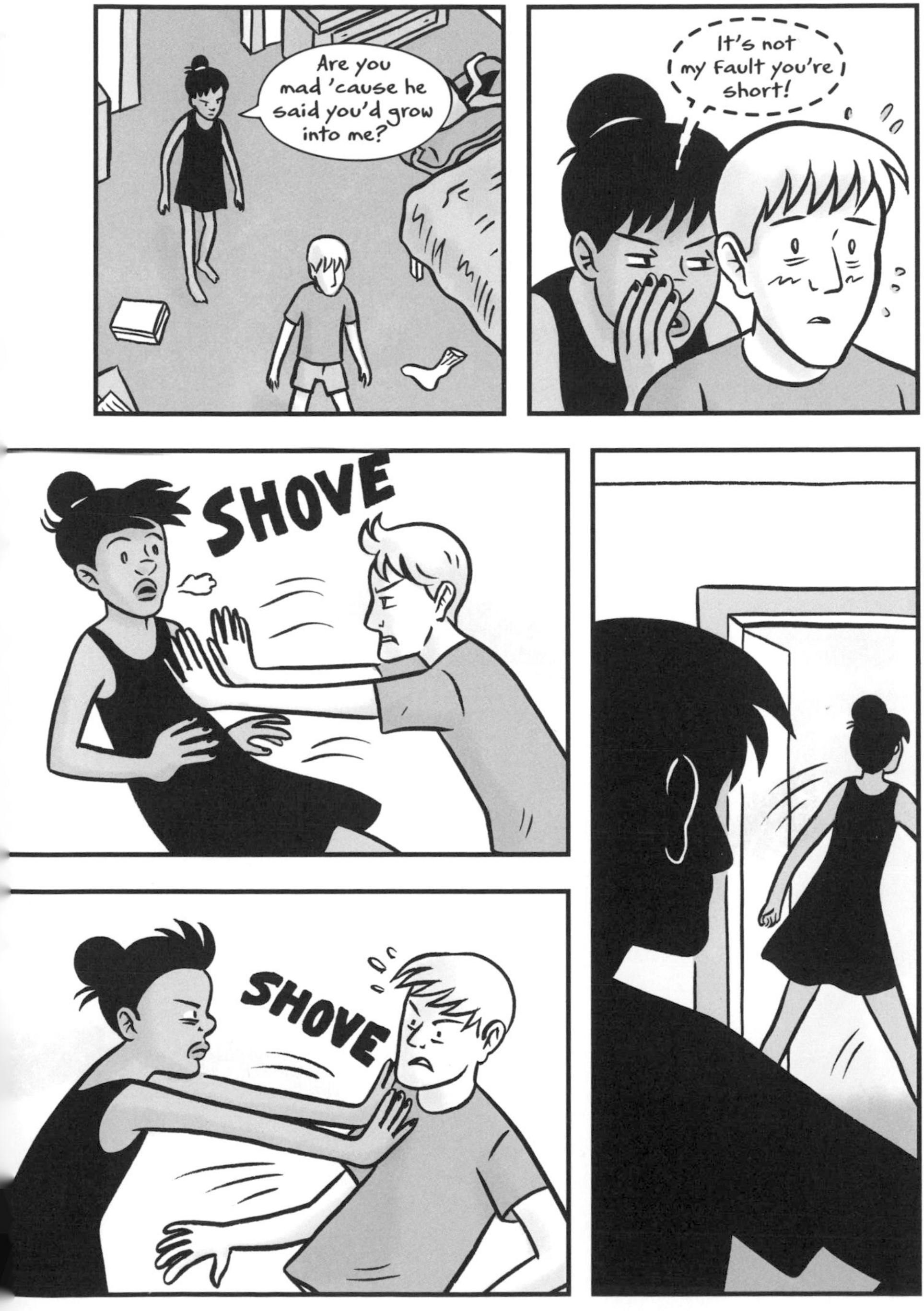
Are you mad 'cause he said you'd grow into me?
It's not my fault you're short!
SHOVE
SHOVE

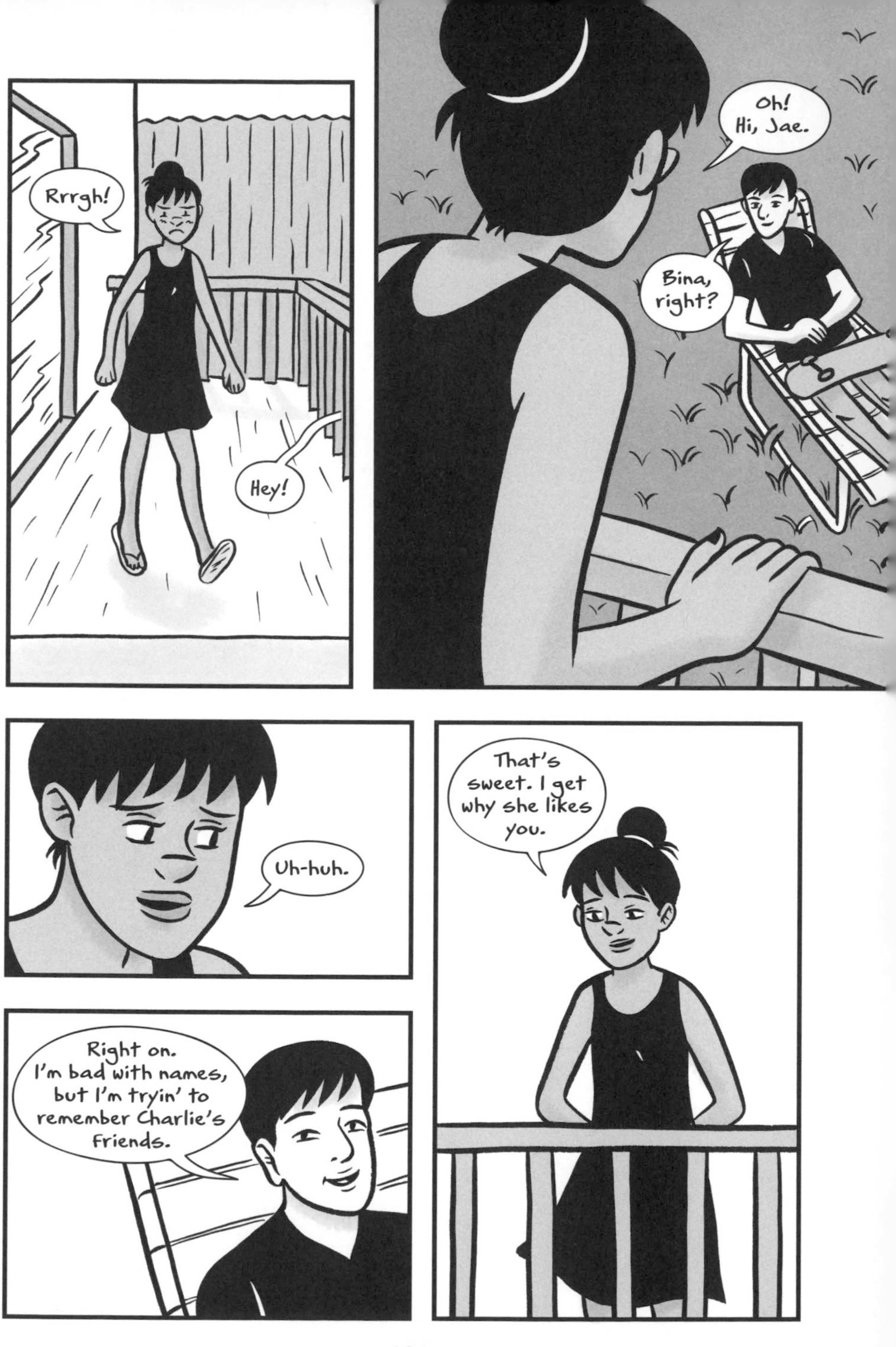
Rrrgh!
Hey!
Oh! Hi, Jae.
Bina, right?
Uh-huh.
Right on. I'm bad with names, but I'm tryin' to remember Charlie's friends.
That's sweet. I get why she likes you.

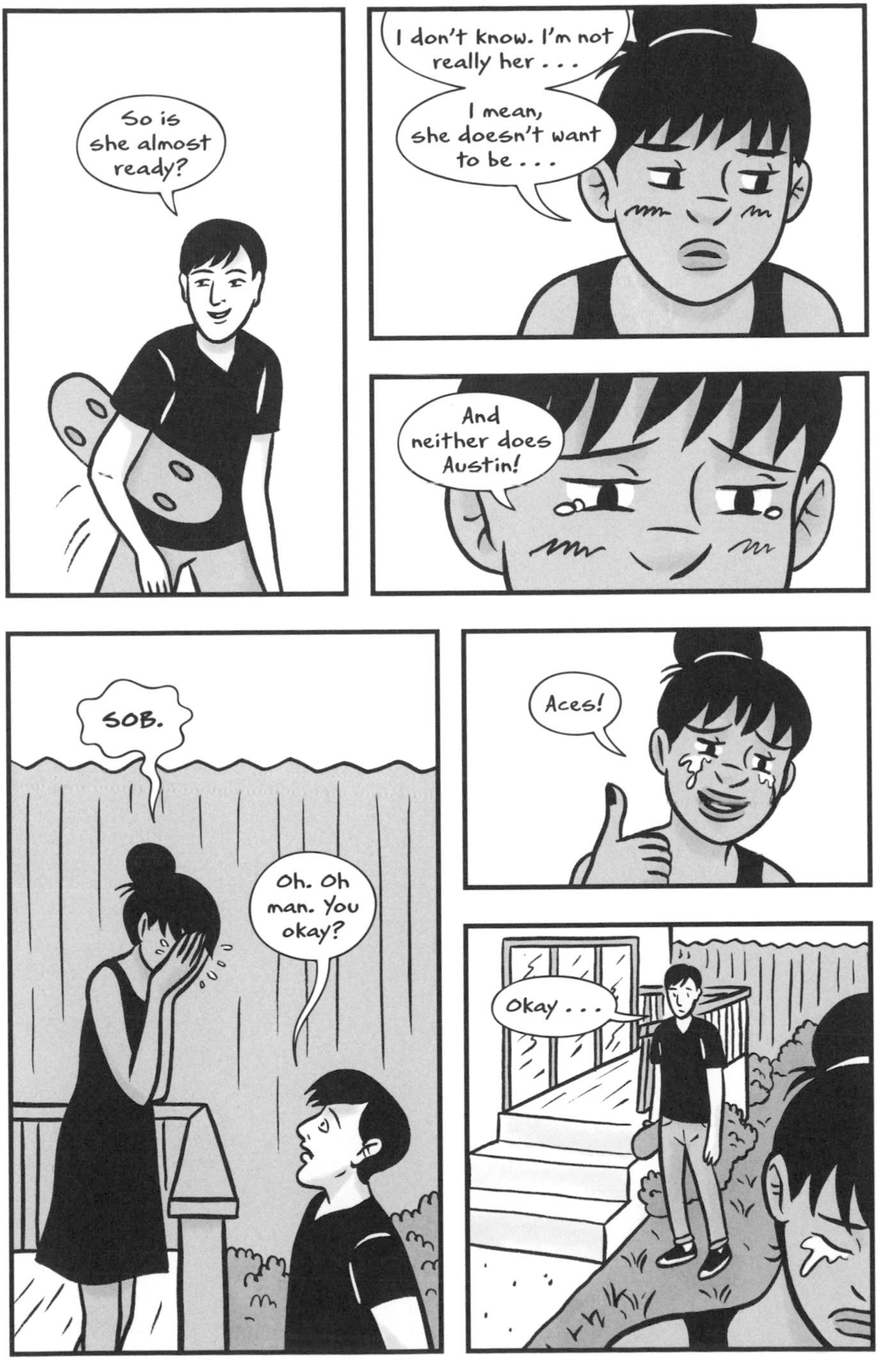
So is she almost ready?
I don't know. I'm not really her . . .
I mean, she doesn't want to be . . .
And neither does Austin!
SOB.
Oh. Oh man. You okay?
Aces!
Okay . . .

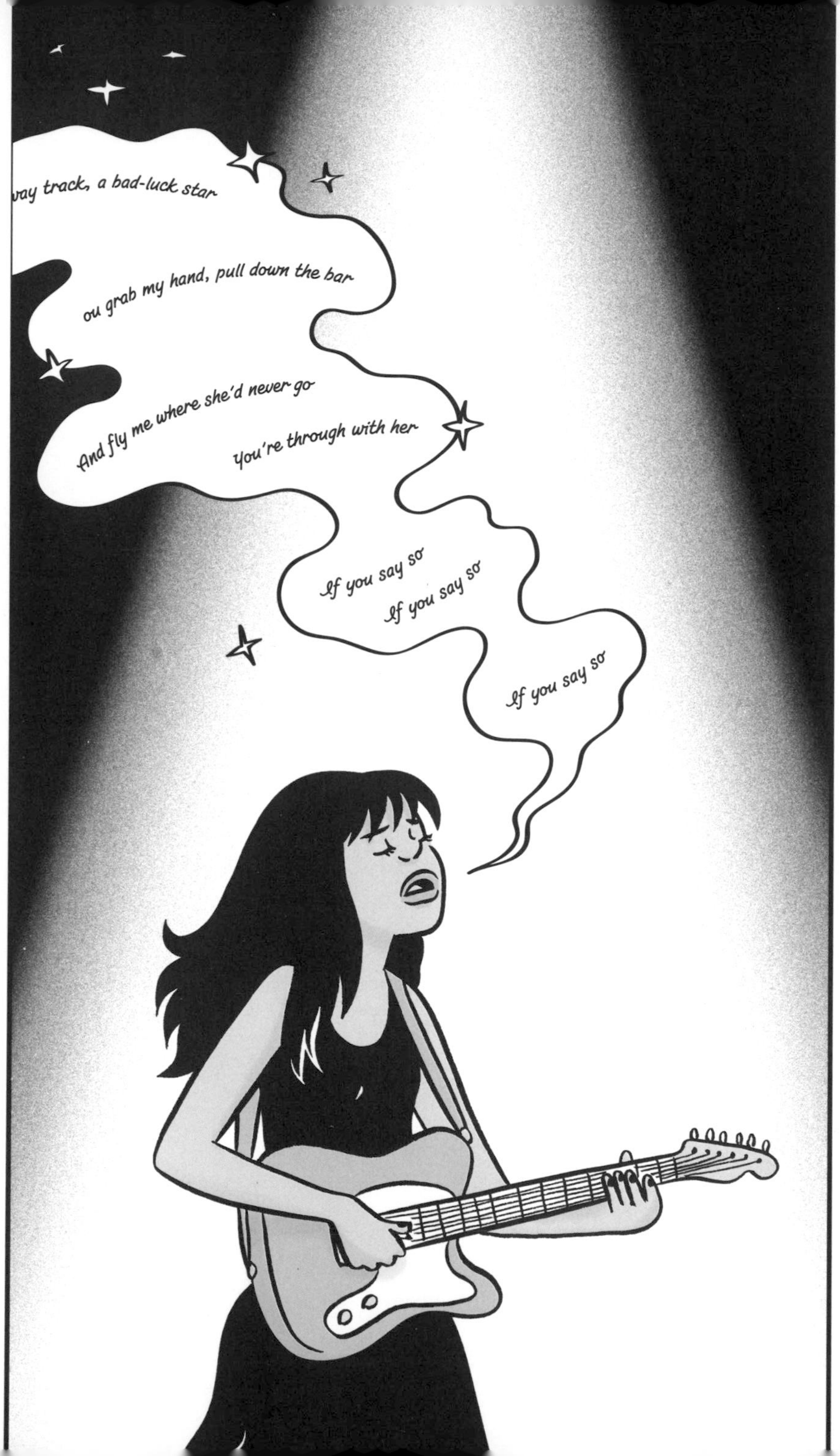

vay track, a bad-luck star
ou grab my hand, pull down the bar
And fly me where she'd never go
You're through with her
If you say so
If you say so
If you say so

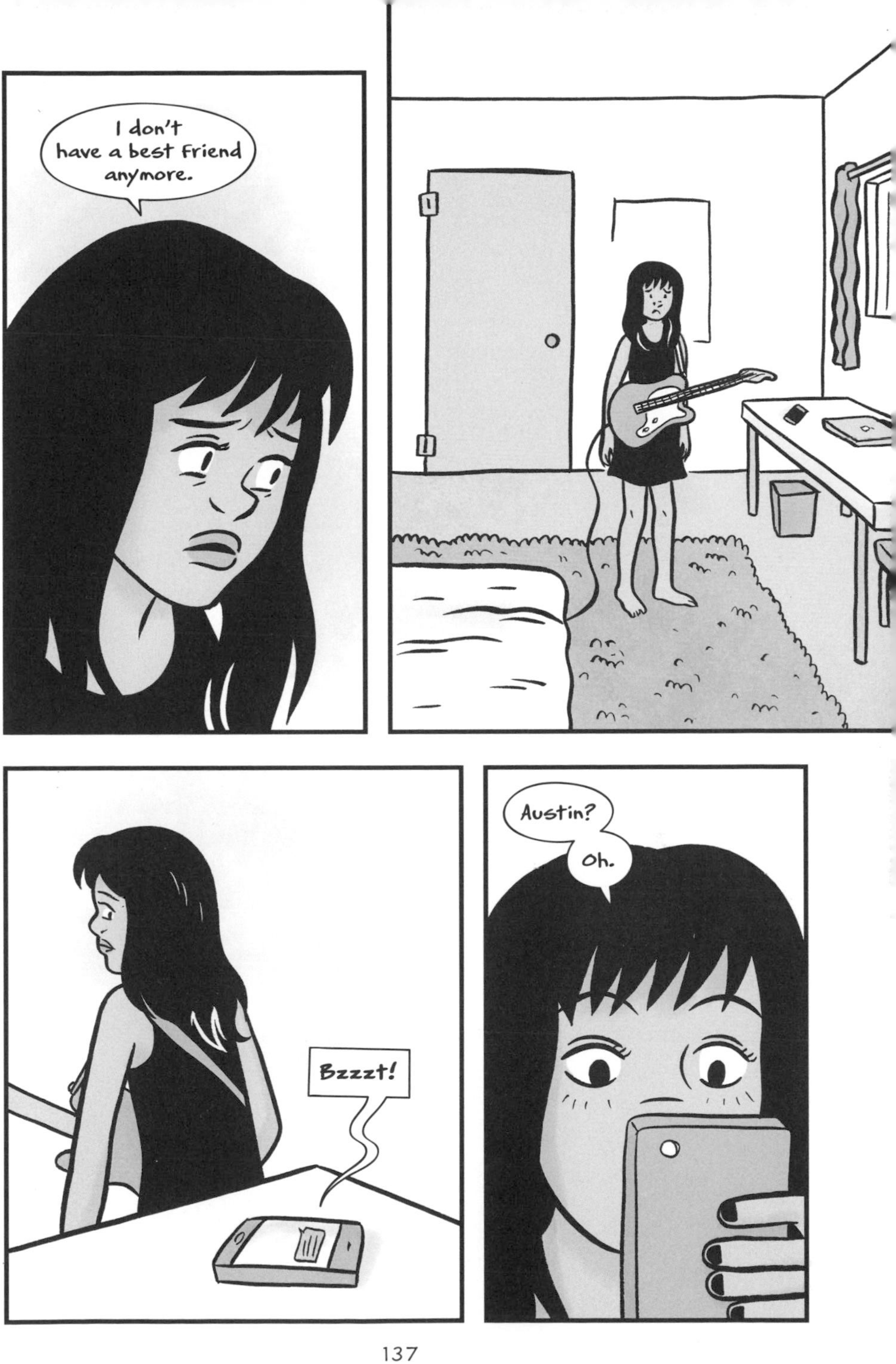
I don't have a best friend anymore.
Bzzzt!
Austin?
Oh.

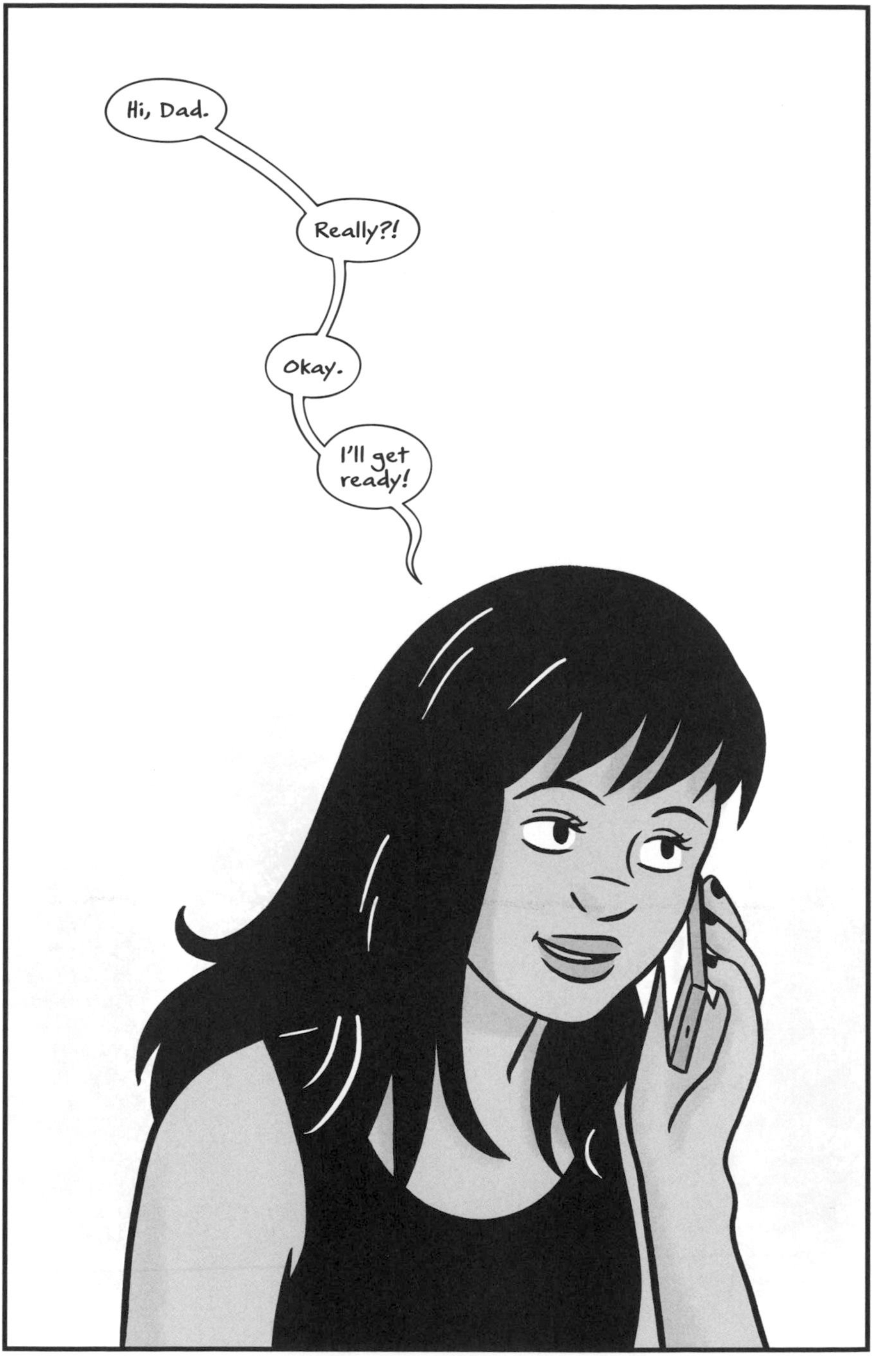
Hi, Dad.
Really?!
Okay.
I'll get ready!

CheapShuttle
to San Francisco
GATE
98
BOARD TIME
6:56AM

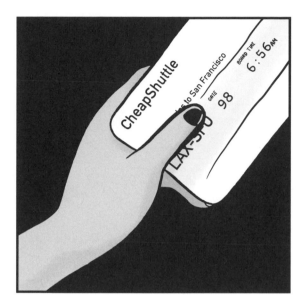

Week Six

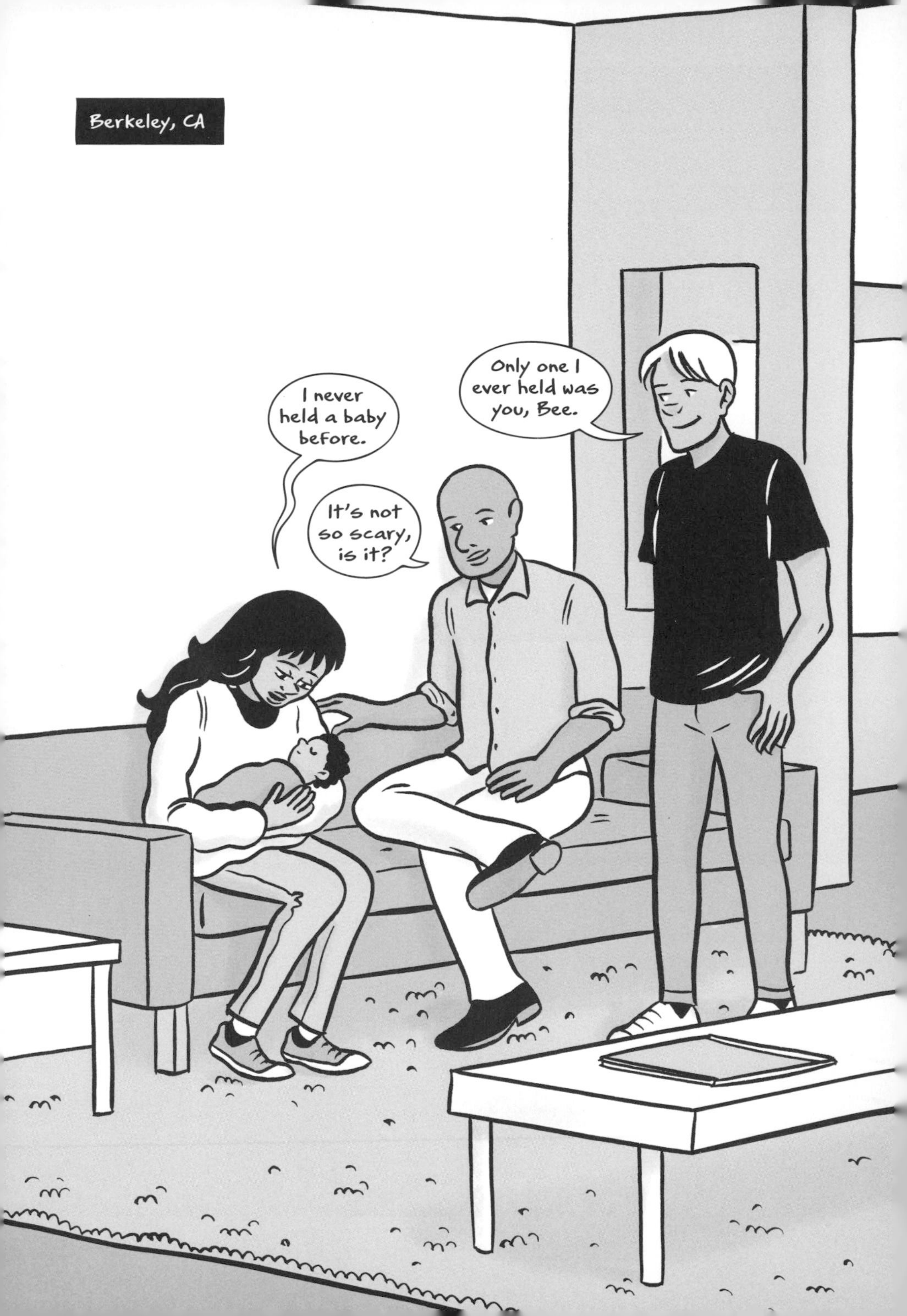
Berkeley, CA
Only one I ever held was you, Bee.
I never held a baby before.
It's not so scary, is it?

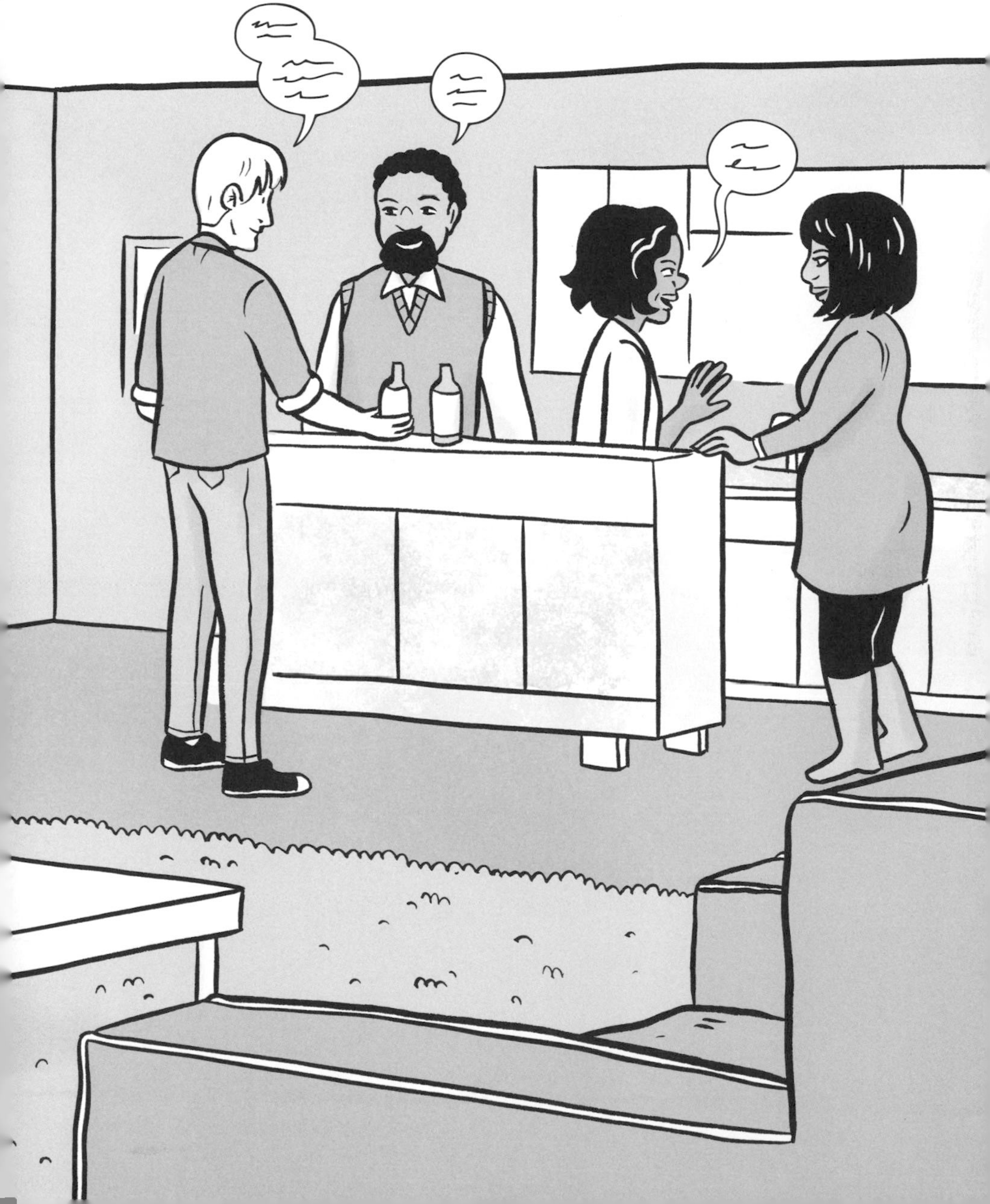

CheapShuttle
Bina Loc

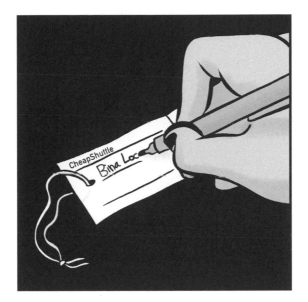

Week Seven

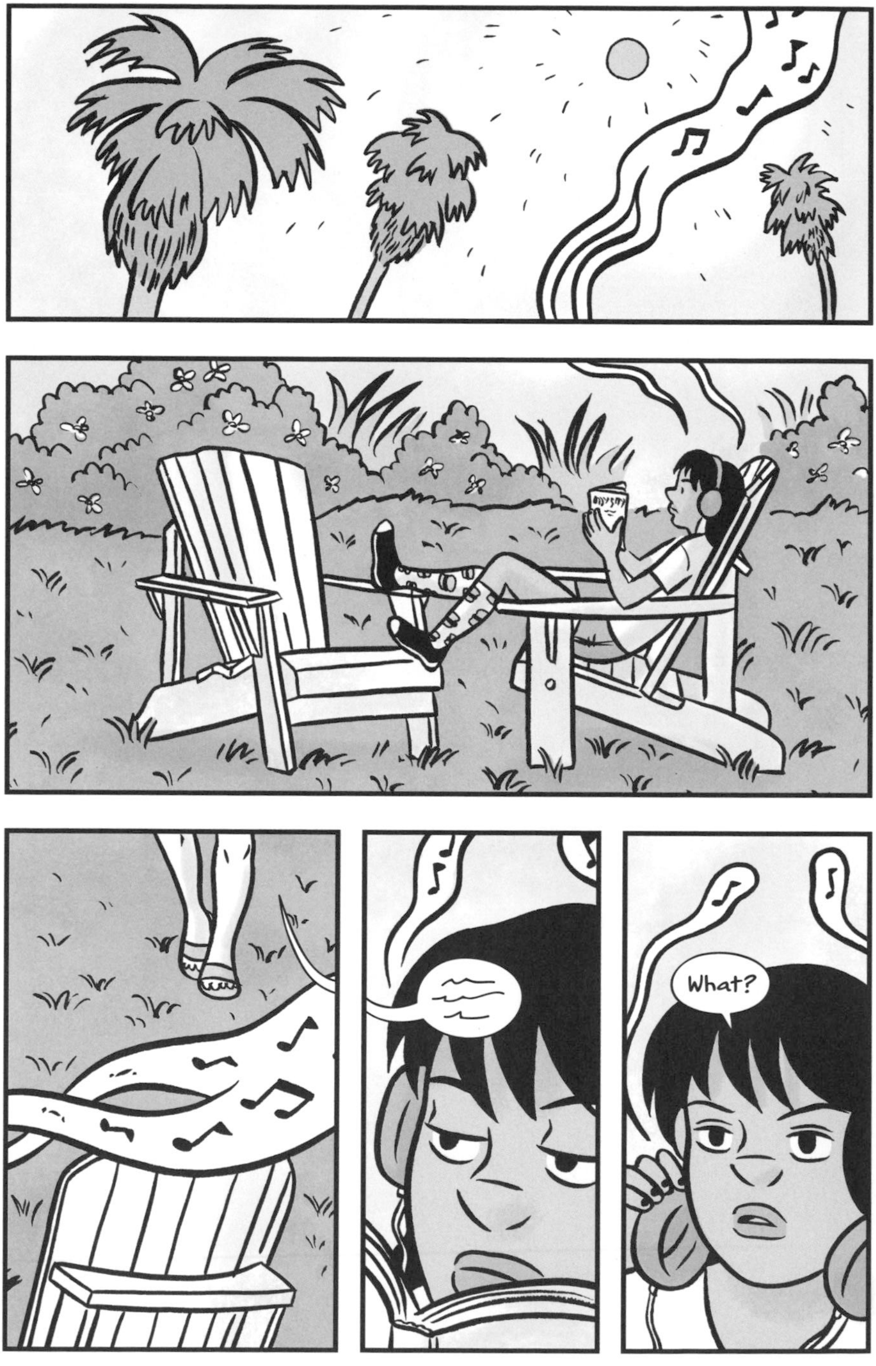
What?

147

I don't know any other guys with girl best friends.
Girlfriends- yeah. There was this one guy at camp who texted his girlfriend every night, and the whole team made fun of him.
Grant said he was whipped.

I didn't want them saying that about me.

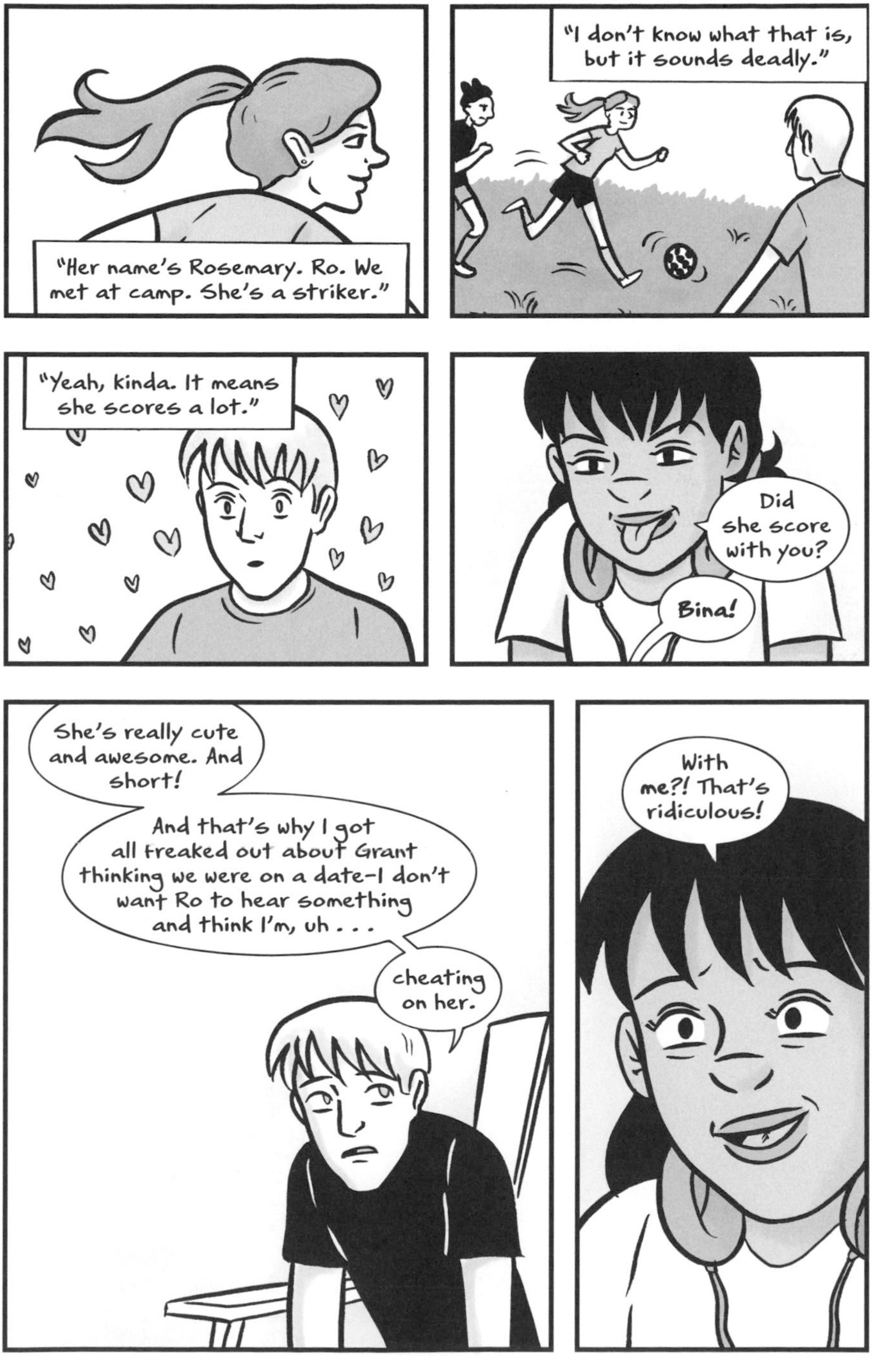
"Her name's Rosemary. Ro. We met at camp. She's a striker."
"I don't know what that is, but it sounds deadly."
"Yeah, kinda. It means she scores a lot."
Did she score with you?
Bina!
She's really cute and awesome. And short!
And that's why I got all freaked out about Grant thinking we were on a date—I don't want Ro to hear something and think I'm, uh . . .
cheating on her.
With me?! That's ridiculous!

Week Eight

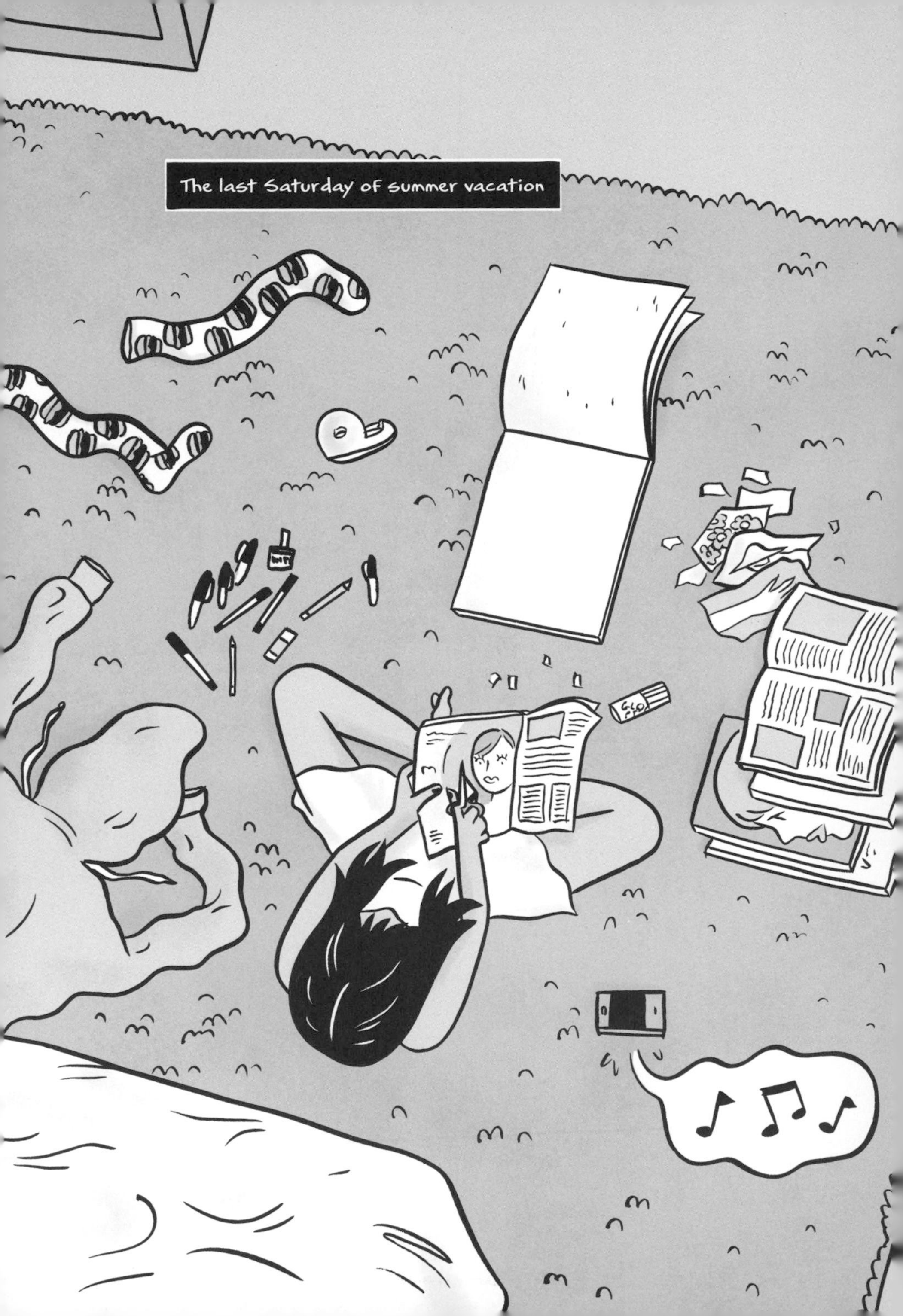
The last Saturday of summer vacation

HeY! YOU!
Join m
y

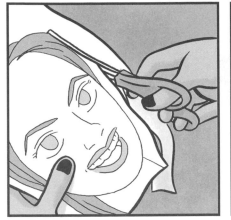

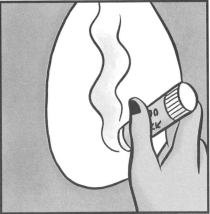

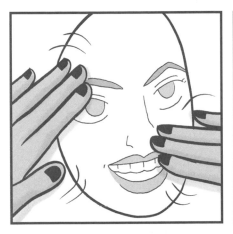

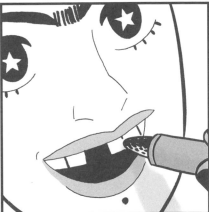

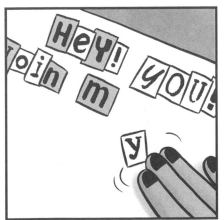

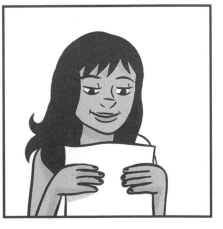

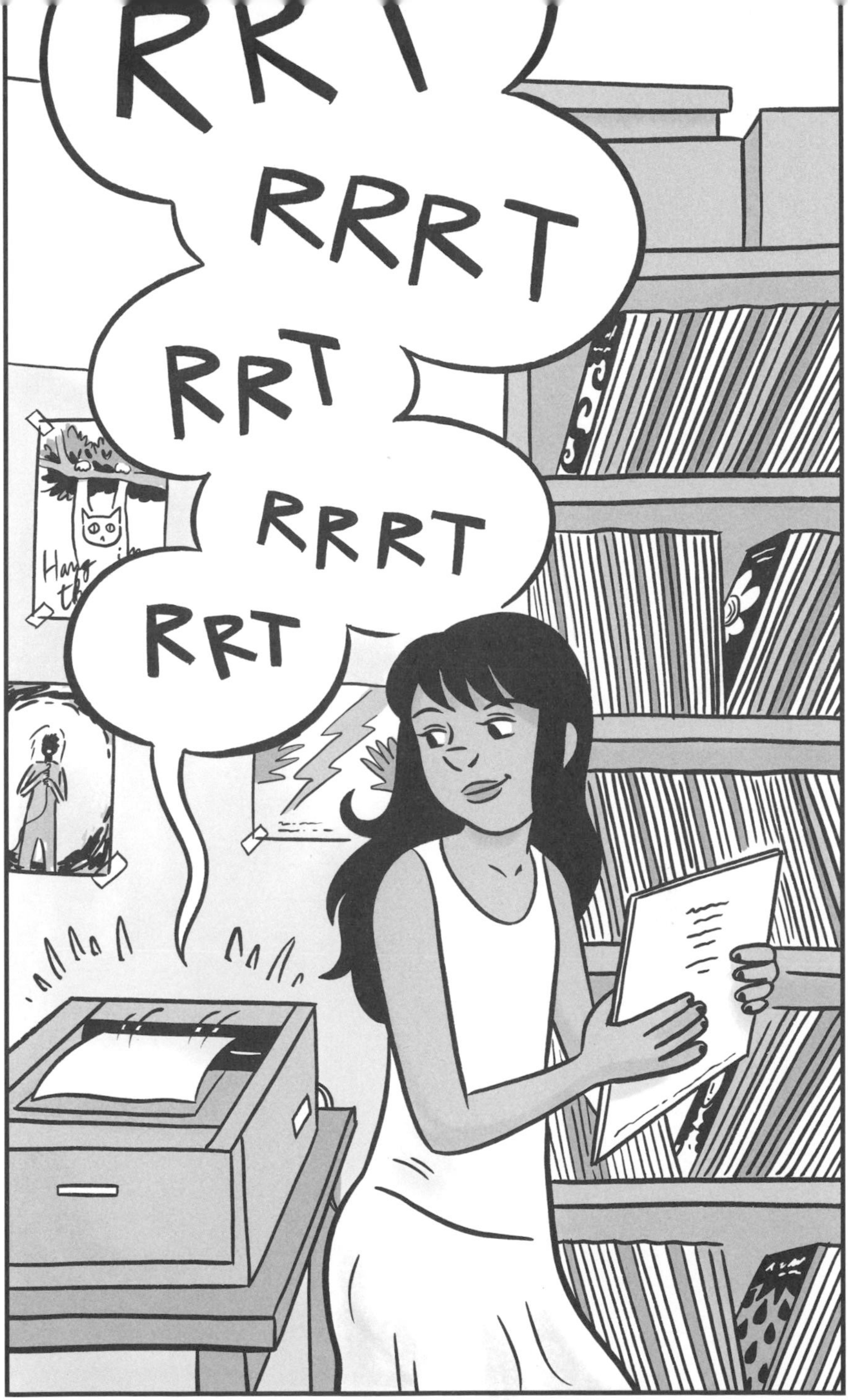
RRRT
RRT
RRRT
RRT

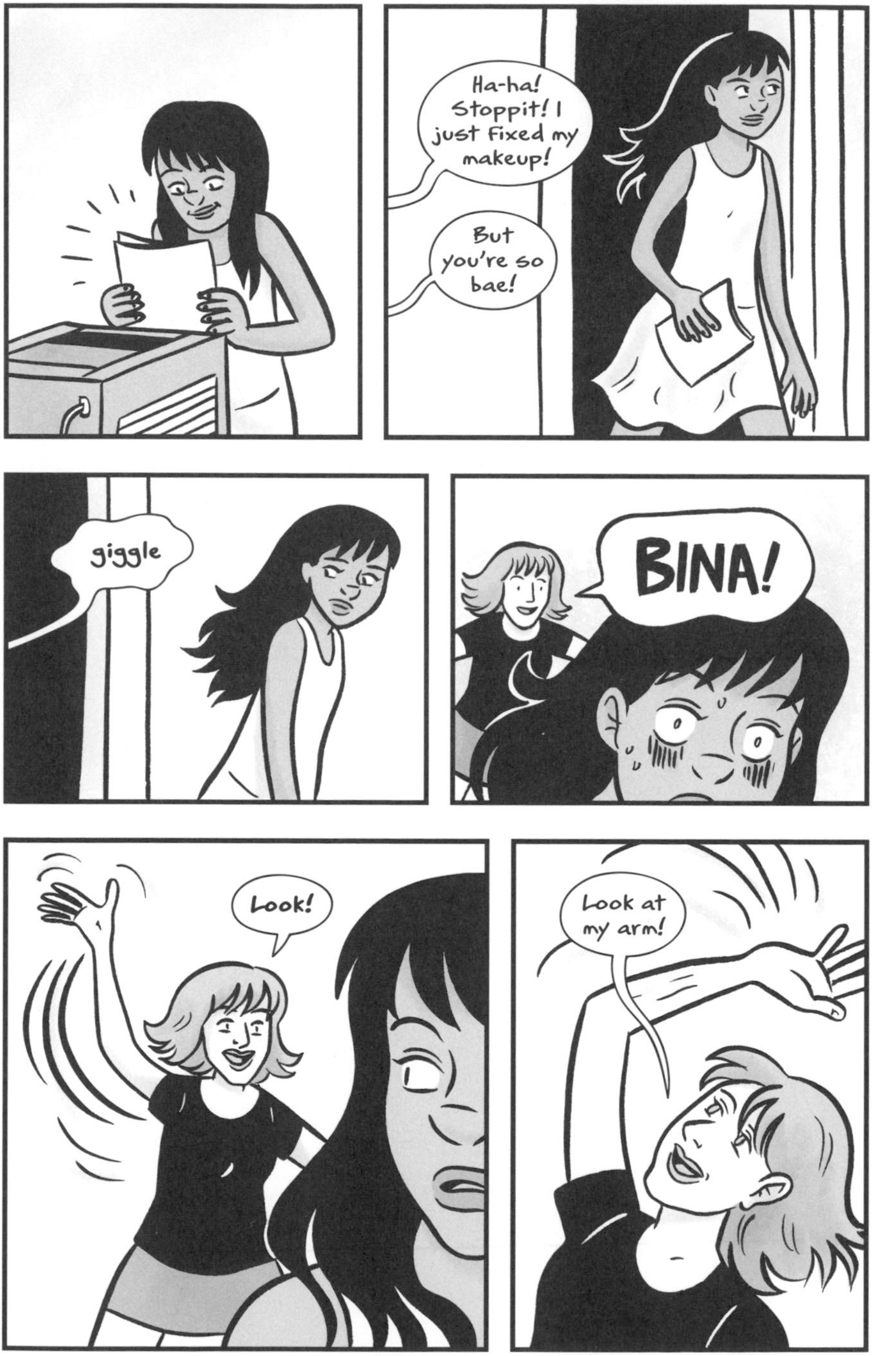

Ha-ha! Stoppit! I just fixed my makeup!
But you're so bae!
giggle
BINA!
Look!
Look at my arm!

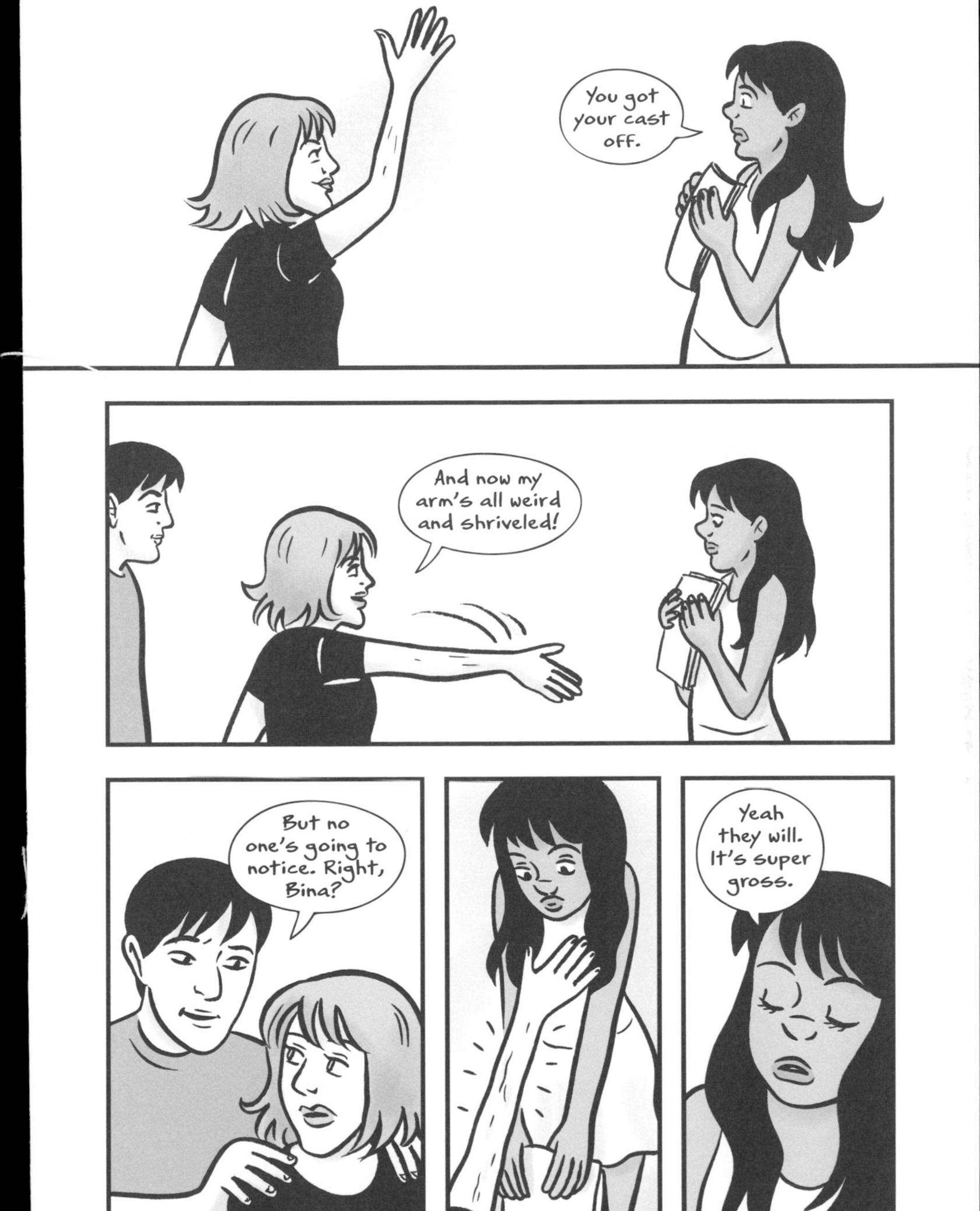
You got your cast off.
And now my arm's all weird and shriveled!
But no one's going to notice. Right, Bina?
Yeah they will. It's super gross.

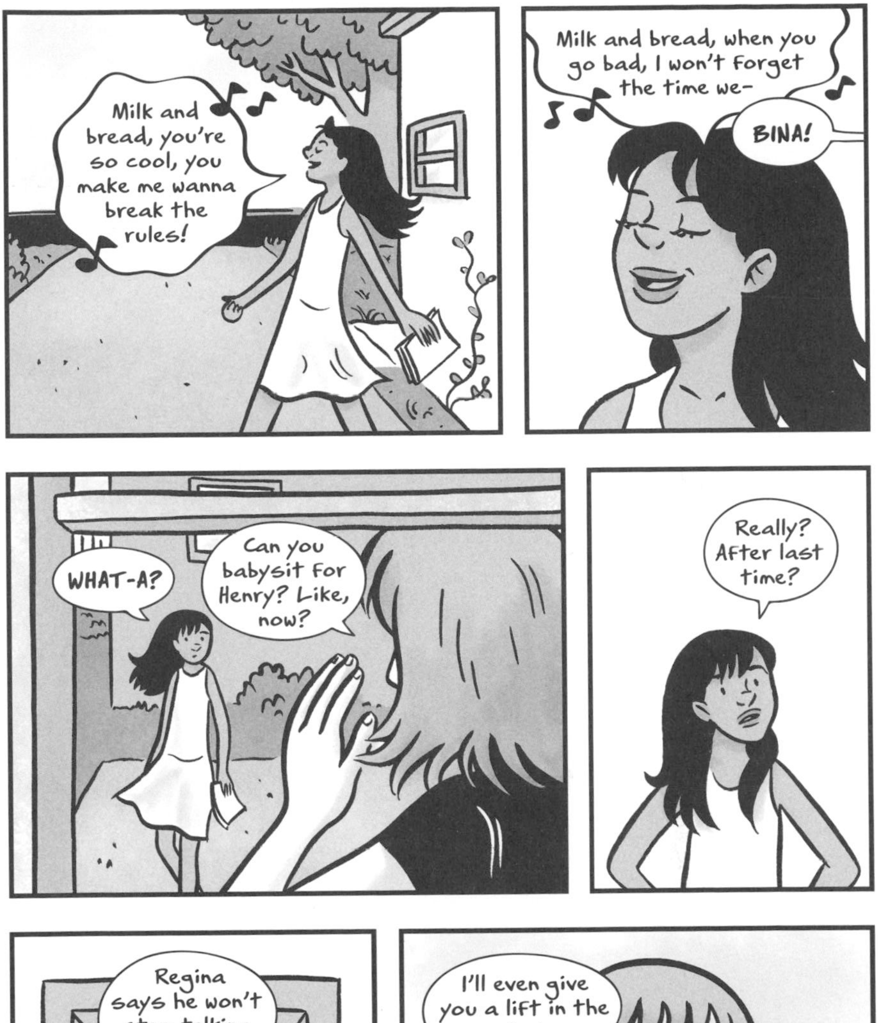
Milk and bread, you're so cool, you make me wanna break the rules!
Milk and bread, when you go bad, I won't forget the time we-
BINA!
WHAT-A?
Can you babysit for Henry? Like, now?
Really? After last time?
Regina says he won't stop talking about you.
SHRUG
I'll even give you a lift in the party bus.

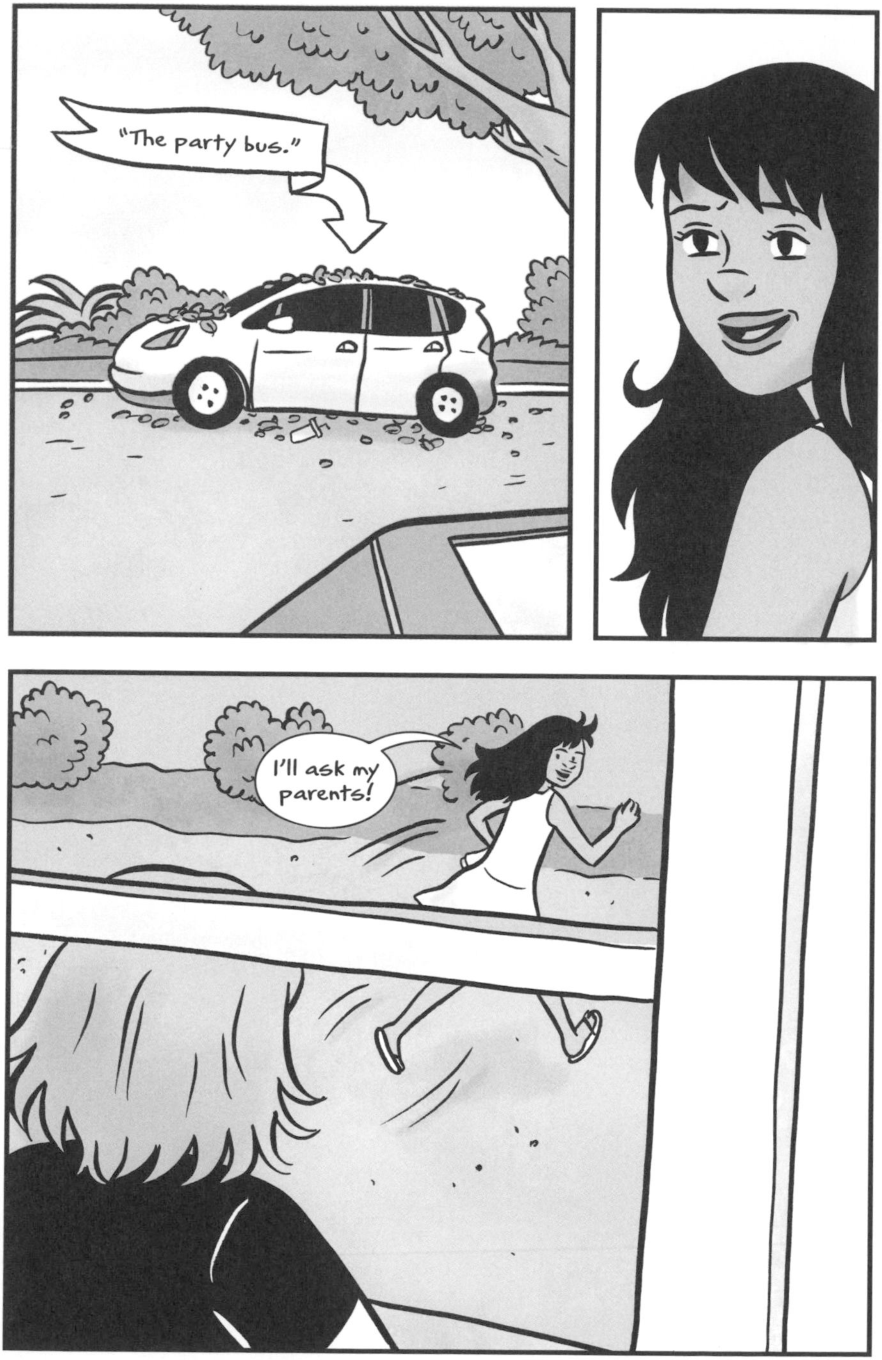
"The party bus."
I'll ask my parents!

A CD?! Is this the '90s?
It's Austin's. From your mom. I keep forgetting to give it back.
Who is it?
Steep Streets. I know they're a baby band, but you're gonna love them.
A one-way track, a bad-
You grab my hand, pull
And fly me where she'd never go
You're through with her
If you say so
If you say so
An empty flask, a Virgo moon
Her ghost is lighting up your
Unfinished
Wow.
Right?
I wish I'd gone to that show.
So do I.
Next time.
Yeah. Next time.

Week One

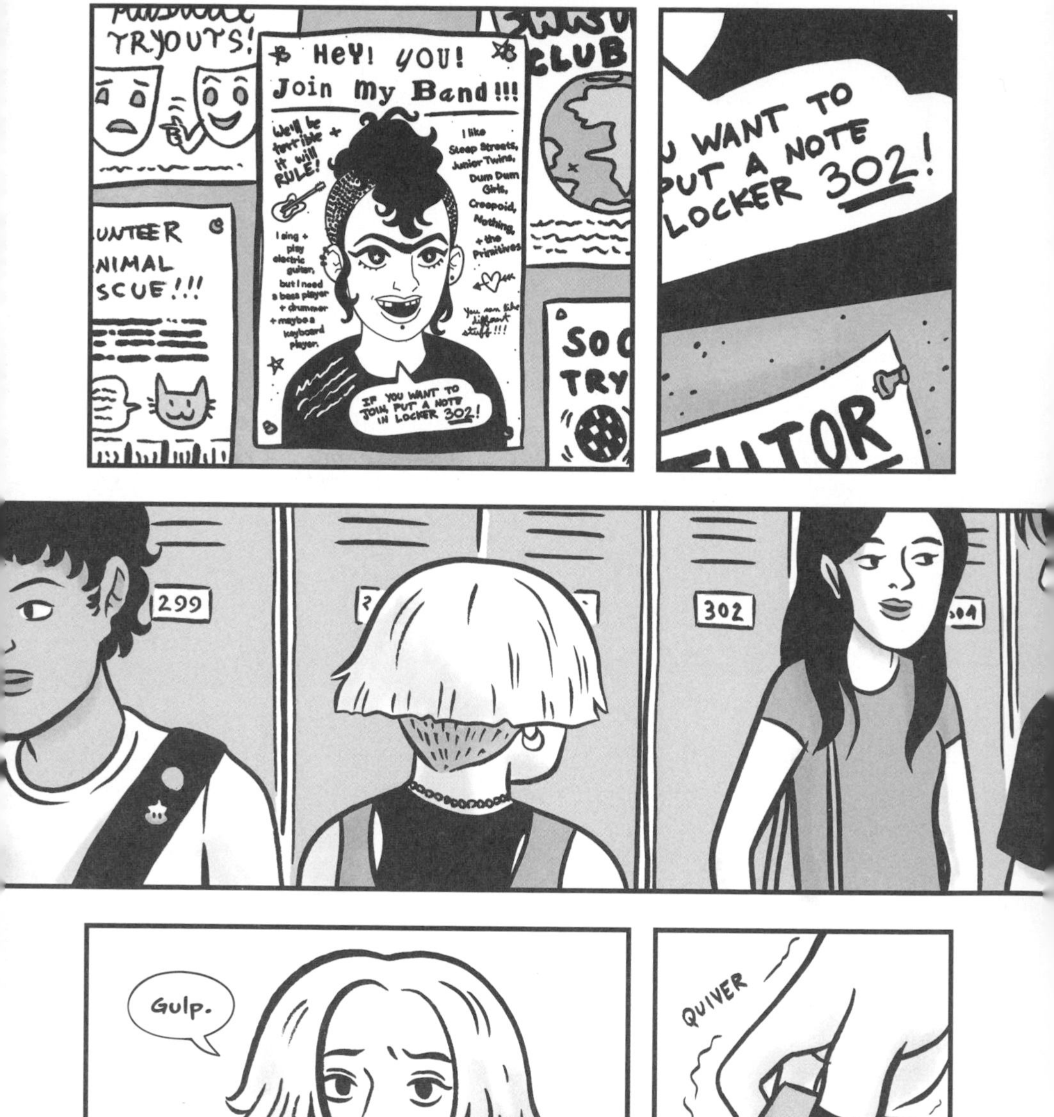
TRYOUTS!
UNTEER
NIMAL
SCUE!!!
HEY! YOU!
Join My Band!!!
We'll be terrible + it will RULE!
I sing + play electric guitar, but I need a bass player + drummer + maybe a keyboard player.
I like Steep Streets, Junior Twins, Dum Dum Girls, Creepoid, Nothing, + the Primitives
You can like different stuff!!!
IF YOU WANT TO JOIN, PUT A NOTE IN LOCKER 302!
CLUB
SOC
TRY
U WANT TO
PUT A NOTE
LOCKER 302!
TUTOR
299
302
Gulp.
QUIVER

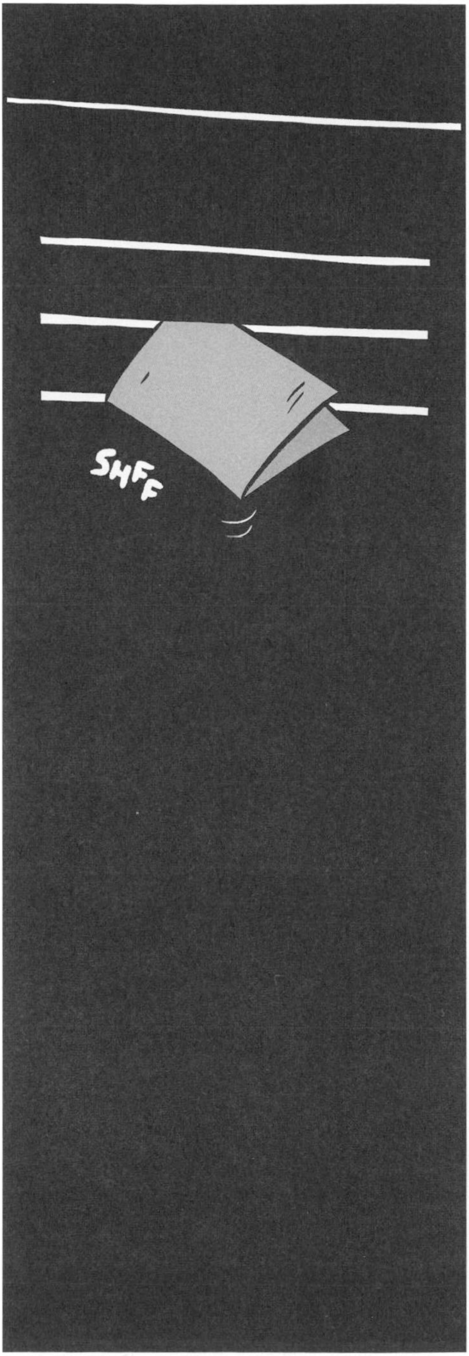
SHFF

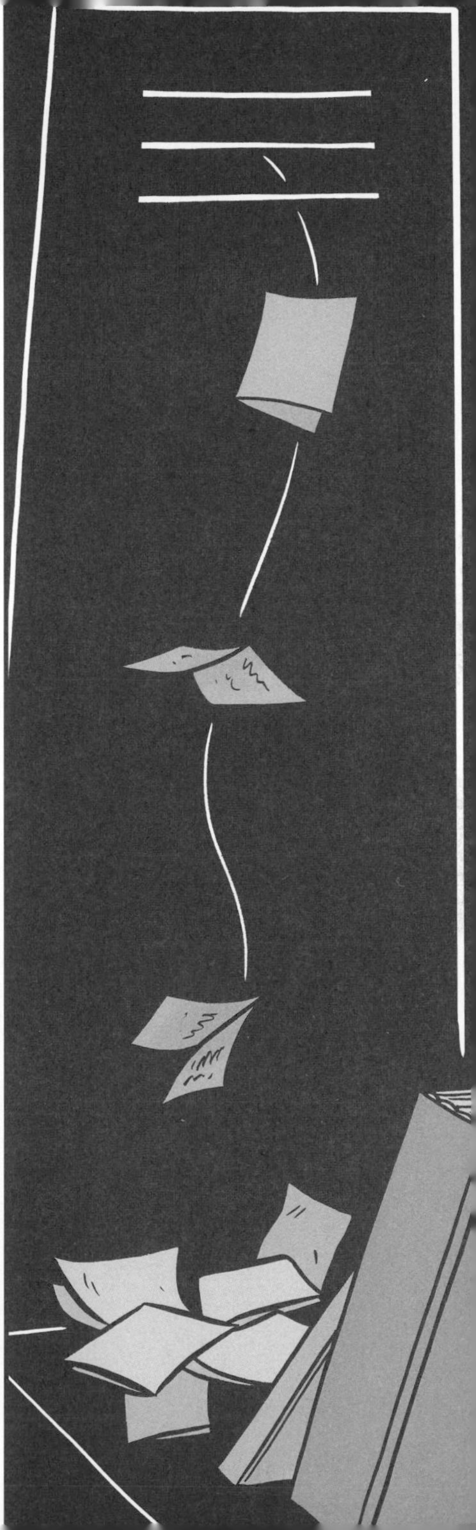

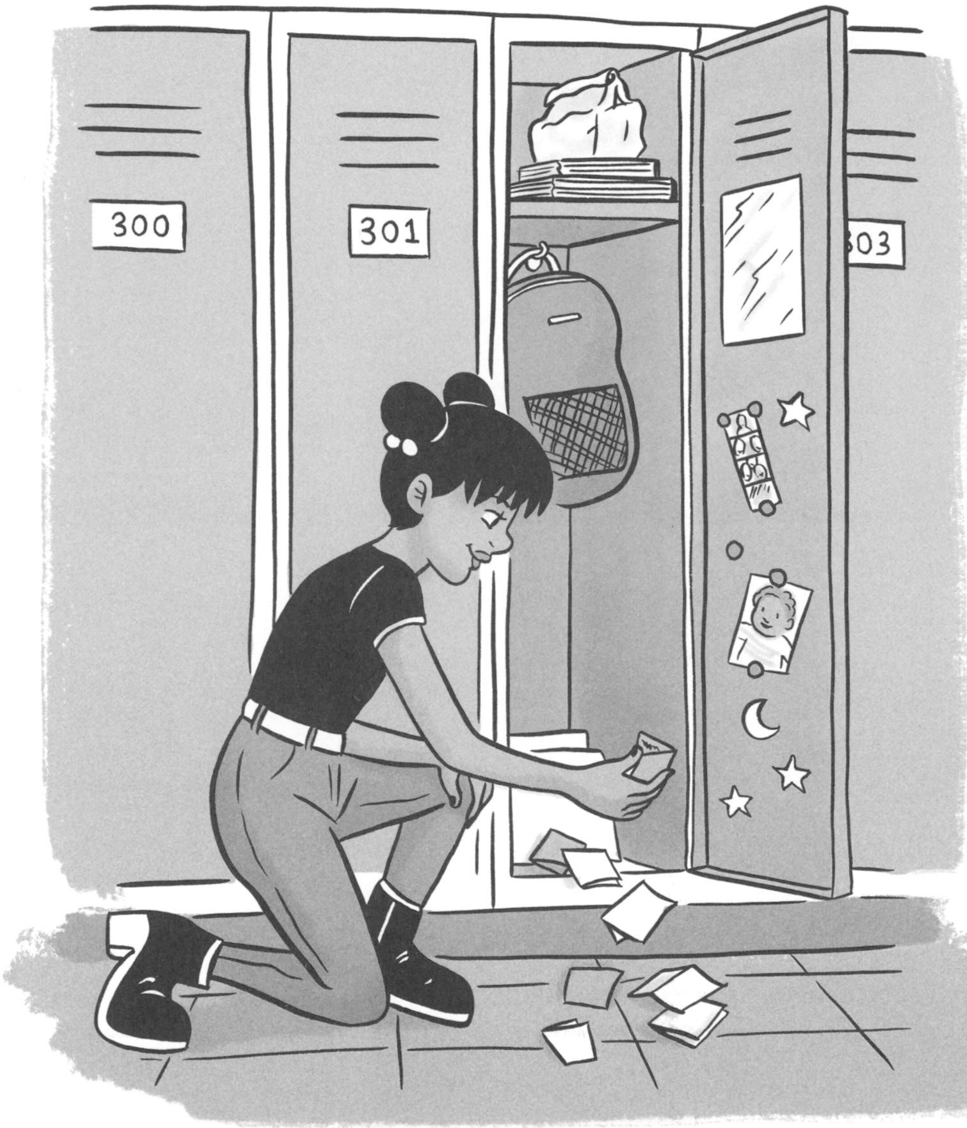
300
301
303